Karla

The Women of Valley View

Purchased through the Zip
books grant, funded by the California
State Library in partnership with Northnet
Library System & the Califa Group

SHARON SROCK

THE WOMEN OF VALLEY VIEW SERIES

Callie
Terri
Pam
Samantha
Kate
Karla

DEDICATION

It is with love and appreciation that I dedicate Karla's story to the following people:

Robin Patchen, Kaye Whiteman, Lacy Williams, Marian Merritt, Terri Weldon, Sandy Patten, Teresa Talbott, Wanda Peters, Lynn Beck, Carol Vansickle, Barbara Elis, Lisa Walker, Ann Lee, & Emily Whiteman.

This book is the final stroke in a small portion of a much bigger dream. Each of you believed in part of my vision. You read, you prayed, you supported. I've acknowledged you all along. This was the only way I could think of to make it bigger.

I can't wait to see what God has for us next!

AUTHOR'S NOTE

I'll be honest with you. Tears were shed in the production of this book.

Its hard to bid farewell to characters who have occupied space in my head for almost a decade. Our conversations and arguments have been legion. They have whispered in my sleep, pestered my waking hours, and pretty much driven me to the funny farm. They have also helped me grow in ways I would never have imagined. They've taught me wisdom, they made me think, they made me look deep inside myself for answers to questions I'd never have the nerve to ask a live friend.

So saying good bye to THE WOMEN OF VALLEY VIEW isn't easy. It's the end of a journey, and the opportunity to look forward to what God has next.

Enjoy the story!

CHAPTER ONE

A police officer pounding on your door in the middle of the night was never a good thing, even if that officer was your son. Nicolas Black stepped into the light pouring from the door, and Karla saw the glint of tears in his eyes and the tight set of his mouth. The sight threatened to buckle her knees. Her heart lodged in her throat as she grasped the door frame to steady herself. She drew in a deep breath of the cool fall air and longed to hide from whatever news her son was there to deliver.

"What...?" She lost the capacity for speech when Nicolas stepped through the door and pulled her close.

"Dad's been in an accident. You need to get dressed, so I can take you to the hospital."

She stiffened as every pore in her body soaked her nightgown in a sticky sweat. "An accident? He went fishing with Benton."

"Benton, too. I sent Tyler over to get Callie. They'll meet us at the hospital."

"But...I don't..."

Nicolas took a step away and waited for Karla's gaze to meet his. "Mom, you need to hurry. It's not good."

Karla's first ride in a police car ended before the tires ground to a halt outside the hospital's emergency room. She shoved the door open and hit the ground running with the noise of the siren still echoing in the night air. The sliding glass doors parted at her approach, admitting her to a world of bright lights and scurrying medical personnel. The scent of alcohol and antiseptics stung her nose as she paused to get her bearings. She spotted Callie sitting in a bank of chairs against the back wall, Callie's daughter Sophie on one side, and Sophie's husband Paul on the other. Nicolas's partner, Tyler, stood to the side in conversation with Terri and Steve Evans, Pam and Harrison Lake, and Karla's daughter-in-law, Kate.

How did they get here first? Their presence did nothing for the agitated state of Karla's nerves. But she ignored them and the question of their presence in favor of the admissions desk and the person sitting behind it. Dread threatened to bind the soles of her shoes to the floor, but she forced her feet to move. across the gray speckled tile.

The woman looked up at Karla's approach. "How can I help you?"

"I'm Karla Black, my husband is here—"

"Yes of course, Mrs. Black. He's in good hands." She stopped to answer the ringing phone. "ER, please hold." The woman put the phone back in the cradle and held a clipboard across the desk. "I have some paperwork that needs to be filled out."

Karla looked from the proffered papers to the clerk. "I need to see my husband."

"Of course, but—"

"I'll take care of the forms."

Karla jumped at the unexpected voice behind her. Her son's firm hands came to rest on her shoulders.

4

"Sorry, Mom. I didn't mean to startle you." Nicolas stepped around her and extended his hand. "Let me have the paperwork."

The clerk handed the clipboard to Nicolas but continued to look at Karla. "Mrs. Black, does your husband have a living will on file?"

The question drove panic a little deeper into the pit her stomach. "Yes, of course, we both do, but—"

"Good, we should be able to find a copy in our files."

"Why would you...?"

"It's a standard question, Mom. Don't assign more meaning to it than it deserves."

"Your son's right. If you'll have a seat, I'll see if I can get someone to come give you an update." She stood and shuffled away, her rubber-soled shoes silent on the polished floor.

Karla felt a hand on her back. She turned and found herself embraced in familiar arms.

"We came as soon as we heard." Terri's voice was muffled against Karla's neck.

"Is there anything we can do?" Pam asked.

"How did you—?"

"Kate called us," Terri answered.

Karla hugged Terri tight and reached out a hand, grateful when Pam took it. "I'm glad she did. Just pray. I don't understand any of this. What if...?"

"Shhh," Terri whispered. "Don't borrow trouble. Let's go sit with Callie and wait for the doctors. I know you're impatient, but they need time to get the answers you both need."

Karla allowed the younger woman to lead her deeper into the waiting area. Callie scrambled to her feet and met her halfway. Years of friendship and shared experiences bound the two women closer than most sisters. They fell into each other's arms.

"Have they told you anything?" Karla whispered.

"Not yet," Callie answered. "Come sit with me."

Their hands remained joined as they sat to wait.

Pam stepped close and motioned everyone into a circle. "You guys come close, let's say a prayer."

Karla offered her dark headed friend a nod of gratitude, watching through a film of anxious tears as Pam gathered everyone together. Pam's husband Harrison, one of Garfield, Oklahoma's, dozen practicing lawyers, hurried to her side. Day care owner Terri Evans, her shaggy brown hair more disheveled than normal, clung to the arm of her husband, Steve, as they joined the circle. Karla's daughter-in-law, Kate, held Nicolas's hand in hers as they took their places. Callie's family scooted into the circle. Karla and Callie stood, arms around each other's waists in physical and emotional support. Everyone joined hands while Pam led them in prayer. "Father, we need Your presence in this place. We bring Mitch and Benton to Your throne for healing, we don't know anything about their condition, Father, but You know, and You love them even more than we do. We surrender them into Your loving hands. Lift Karla and Callie into Your presence. Bring the comfort and the peace that only comes through Your spirit. We ask these things in Jesus name."

Amens sprinkled through the group as they dispersed to find seats. Karla sat back down, Callie's cold hand in hers once more, her head resting against the wall behind her chair. She closed her eyes. *Jesus, please, You're all we have right now. Nothing is too big for You.* Her foot bounced on the floor, evidence of nerves and impatience. She rested her free hand on her restless leg and willed it to be still. *Touch Mitch and Benton.* She squeezed Callie's hand. *Speak peace to Callie's heart and mine. We—*

"Excuse me."

Karla's eyes snapped open. It was the nurse working the admissions desk, but her attention was directed at Callie.

"Mrs. Stillman, your husband's doctor has given permission for you to go back. He's in treatment room two."

Callie scrambled to her feet and hurried down the hall.

Karla leaned forward. "When can I see Mitch?"

"It shouldn't be too much longer." She hurried away to answer the phone on her desk.

Karla settled into the hard plastic chair and tried to find a comfortable position. Footsteps on the tile floor caught her attention. She watched as a trio of people came down the hall from the treatment rooms. Two forty-something women flanked an older man with striking silver hair and sad, downcast eyes. She looked on as they took seats in a row of chairs facing the ones occupied by Karla and her friends. The women, tears streaming down their faces, leaned their heads on the man's shoulders. He held both their hands while he wept his own tears. Eavesdropping wasn't Karla's intent, but it was impossible not to hear their conversation in the hushed atmosphere of the small space.

"You girls know that your mother is in a better

place. Saying goodbye was hard, but she isn't in pain anymore." His quiet words echoed with emotion. "That means a lot."

Tears and nods were the only response he received from the women clinging to his sides.

"It's times like this when death is almost a blessing," he continued. "I loved your mother with all my heart. We did our best to make every minute count after her diagnosis. But I have to tell you, it broke my heart to watch her suffer these last few months. She's whole now, and in the arms of her Heavenly Father." He leaned, first left, then right, brushing a kiss on each of his daughters' heads. "We have to find peace in that. She wouldn't come back if she could."

Oh, bless their hearts. Father, bring comfort—

Karla's attention jerked away from the prayer as another nurse, this one dressed in green scrubs with a stethoscope around her neck, approached. "Mrs. Black, you and your son can go back now."

She scrambled to her feet, grateful when Nicolas wrapped his arm around her waist. "Is my husband going to be OK?"

The nurse's gaze shifted to the floor. "The doctor will meet you in treatment room seven. He'll answer all of your questions."

The nurse's lowered eyes raised the hair on the back of Karla's neck. *Why can't she look at me?* An invisible weight settled on Karla's chest and made it difficult to breathe. She reached out for heavenly strength. *Father...*

I'm with you.

The quiet words bolstered her courage. She gripped Nicolas's arm and allowed him to lead her away from her friends. "He has to be all right."

Her son's response came in a steady hand laid over her trembling one.

They rounded the corner, and Karla stopped when she saw Callie standing outside a closed door, her back to the hall. Karla touched her on the shoulder and saw relief in her friend's eyes when she turned.

"Did you see Benton?"

Callie nodded. "Just for a second before they chased me out so they could take an X-ray."

"How is he?"

"He has a row of stitches across the bridge of his nose, and they think his ankle is broken, but he's awake and more worried about Mitch than he is about himself. I think he's going to be OK. Mitch?"

"On my way now."

"Let us know once you've seen him."

Karla nodded and continued down the hall. It sounded like Benton would recover. Mitch would too. They were both tough old birds. She pressed a shaky hand to her chest. *I'm such a worrier.* She reached door number seven, and Nicolas stepped around her to pull it open. *I know better than to plunge off the deep end.*

Beeping machinery greeted their entry to the treatment room. She pulled away from Nicolas and hurried to Mitch's side. Her new-born hope died a cruel death. Bruises mottled his ashen face, a bandage wrapped his hairline above his closed eyes, and a foam collar encased his neck. A tube rested between his gray lips, secured to his cheek with a strip of white tape. Karla followed it with her eyes and found it connected to a machine that whooshed to the rise and fall of her husband's chest.

"Mitch?"

There was no response from the man in the bed, but the beeping and whooshing continued strong and steady.

Beeping is good, right? All the doctor shows on TV had beeping monitors. Steady beeping meant a steady heartbeat.

Didn't it?

Karla took one of his hands in hers, flinching at the cold that met her fingers. She rubbed Mitch's hand, trying to infuse some warmth into the chilled flesh. "He's freezing. Can we get some more blankets?"

A strange voice responded to her request. "Nurse, can we get a heated blanket for our patient?"

Karla looked toward the voice and saw two men standing just inside the door. The older one looked at her with compassion-filled eyes.

"Mrs. Black, I'm Dr. Reynolds." He paused and motioned to the man standing at his side. "This is Mr. Kennedy. I'm the attending physician in charge of the ER tonight. Mr. Kennedy is with the hospital's administrative staff."

She nodded but had little time for pleasantries. "Is my husband going to be OK?"

Instead of answering, the doctor motioned to the chair next to Mitch's bed. "Mrs. Black, I need you to sit down and listen to me."

Karla nudged the chair closer to the bed so she could sit without releasing Mitch's hand. She searched the doctor's face as she sank into the seat. The somberness in his expression sent her heart pounding as if she'd run a marathon.

The doctor pulled a rolling stool from under the counter, situated it in front of Karla, and sat with his clasped hands between his knees. When he finally met her gaze, the weariness in his eyes stole her breath. "Your husband's accident broke his fourth and fifth cervical vertebra."

Karla glanced back at the bed, her gasp filled the room. "Nicolas?"

Nicolas laid a hand on her shoulder. "I'm right here, Mom. Let him finish."

Dr. Reynolds continued. "As a result of this injury, his brain was deprived of oxygen for a significant period of time. The emergency crew did what they could at the scene. They opened an airway and got some forced respirations going." He paused, and his sigh filled the room before he continued. "But I'm afraid it was too late."

Karla closed her eyes against the words she was hearing and the pain that came with them. She clung to the only hope she could find. "The monitors are beeping. That means his heart's still beating." Nicolas squeezed her shoulders from behind as her voice trailed off, dragging hope behind it.

"Yes, we've maintained a heartbeat and regular respirations through mechanical intervention. But..."

She squeezed her husband's limp hand. The coolness of his skin took on a new and ominous meaning in the face of what she was hearing.

"...he can't remain this way."

Karla sucked in a ragged breath and asked a question she already knew the answer to. "What are you saying?"

"Mrs. Black, I'm sorry. Were you aware that Mitchell had a living will on file?"

She nodded, afraid to speak.

"You know what it directs you and me to do in a

case like this?"

She looked from the doctor to her husband. *So still, so pale...so cold.* She shook her head. "I can't."

"What exactly does it say?" Nicolas's voice was harsh.

"It states that if your father is incapacitated and unable to communicate his wishes, that he refuses life sustaining treatments under certain circumstances." The doctor's voice held regret. "Basically his request is that we withhold or withdraw life sustaining medical care that is serving only to prolong the process of his dying when there is no reasonable expectation of recovery or treatment."

Karla's groan of pain filled the room. *God, please don't do this to me. Don't take him from me. Please don't let it end like this.* Karla took a deep breath, struggling to find her voice. "Is Mr. Kennedy here to enforce that request?"

The other man spoke for the first time. "Of course not, Mrs. Black. No one can force you to follow the dictates of a piece of paper at a time like this. We're just making sure that you have the facts you need to make some informed decisions during a stressful time. I'm from the hospital's organ donor office. Your husband also had a signed donor card on file. I'm here to facilitate that process for you, should you choose to honor his wishes."

Karla bowed her head. Invisible bands tightened around her chest and threatened to choke her. "I...I don't know...I need a few moments alone with my son."

"Of course. We'll wait outside."

As soon as the men were gone, Nicolas walked around to stand in front of her. "Mom—"

"I can't do it, Nicolas. I know it's what we both agreed to, but I don't think I'm strong enough to let him go. What if...what if they've missed something?" She faced her son, hoping to find reassurance, looking for an ally. "I can't just let him die."

Nicolas claimed the stool that the doctor had vacated. He stared at the floor for several seconds. When he raised his head, his features were taut with grief. "Mom, you're not letting Dad die. You're putting him in to the hands of the God he served and trusted his whole life. If they unplug all of this stuff and he lives, no one will be more grateful than me. But if he's already..."

Karla closed her eyes when her son's voice broke. When he continued, his words were raspy with restrained emotion.

"If he's gone, then what's to be served by all of this? You have to let him go."

Karla leaned forward in the chair, arms wrapped around herself, while sobs tore through her body. Nicolas rubbed her back in silent comfort. Minutes...hours later she sat up and looked at her son, heartbroken anew by the tears in his eyes. She took his hand. "Would you go out and phone your brothers and sister? Tell them..." Her voice cracked under the burden settling on her shoulders. She swallowed. "Just...tell them what's happened. Tell them they need to come home. I need a few minutes to say goodbye."

Nicolas nodded, rolled the stool closer, and pulled her into a tight hug. "I love you, Mom." She felt him kiss the top of her head before he released her and stepped out of the room.

Karla sat next to the bed for several minutes, staring

into the face of the man she'd loved for almost half a century. She stood and reached out to touch his cheek. Her hand hovered over the bruises and bandages, afraid of hurting him. She finally threaded her fingers through his hair. *Was it this gray earlier?*

"Saying goodbye to you is the hardest thing I've ever had to do." Her smile was sad as tears tracked her cheeks. "I've always been a little selfish and hoped I'd go first. You're so much stronger than I am."

Karla closed her eyes. Visions of the life she'd shared with Mitch crowded her memory, vying for space. A groom standing at the altar watching his bride approach, equal portions of fear and promise in his eyes. The large, but sure hands that cradled each of their babies. Nights spent lying in bed, whispering their hopes and dreams in the dark while his strong arms held her tight. Those same arms and hands lifted in praise and surrender to the God he loved.

Karla continued to stroke his hair while her tears fell in a torrent, obscuring her view. "Oh, Mitchell, I love you. I was always proud to be your wife. It's all I ever wanted. I don't...I don't know how to be anything else." She bent and pressed her lips to his a final time, undone by the lack of warmth or response. Her goodbye turned into a prayer. "Jesus, I don't know what to do."

Let Me have him.

The words echoed through her heart, bringing fresh tears and strength. Her breath hitched in her lungs as she nodded. "Goodbye, sweetheart."

She let go of Mitch's hand long enough to step back to the door. Nicolas waited for her just outside the room. "Could you call the doctor back in for me?"

Karla sat with her head bowed and her eye's closed as the medical staff moved slowly around her. A soft snick of sound drew her attention as the respirator was turned off. Was that what life came down to at the end? The flick of a switch? She squeezed Mitch's hand. *Jesus, if there's life here, let his heart beat.*

Karla held her husband's hand as the beeping of the machinery slowed and finally sounded the single long tone that robbed her of her future.

CHAPTER TWO

Twelve months later

Karla sat on the cold, stone bench. A late-October breeze stirred her hair and rustled the leaves above her head. A few leaves, barley yellow around the edges, drifted to the ground with each gust. They swirled above the manicured grass and reminded her that fall was here. Thirty feet away a couple of squirrels chased each other from a tree, to a fountain, and back again. The whole performance emceed by a squawking blue jay as he hopped from limb to limb while keeping the racing rodents in sight.

She raised her eyes and watched the noisy bird for a few seconds. *Isn't it time for you to fly south or something?*

A leaf floated into her lap. Karla picked it up, twisting it this way and that in the sunlight, watching the colors shift from green, to yellow, to brown. "You always loved this time of the year best, didn't you, Mitch? When you could put the endless summer lawn care behind you and start looking forward to deer season and hunting with Benton." She tossed the leaf aside.

"Benton is pretty much recovered. It's been tough on him. I know he blames himself, even though you or I never would. Even when he was just barely off his crutches, he came over once a week to work in the yard. He mowed, or trimmed, or just picked up dead branches. I tried to send him home the first dozen times or so, but he just shooed me back into the house and kept at it." Her breath shuddered. "His limp is almost gone, and Callie says the nightmares are getting fewer and farther between." She stopped and closed her eyes, listening to the fountain for a few seconds.

"So much of life is getting back to normal." A stiff gust derailed her monologue and made her shiver. It wasn't cold, but she was always chilly these days. Easy to understand in a way, she'd lost fifty pounds of body insulation in the last twelve months. Her shoulders lifted in a dismissive shrug. *Grief diet. Cut someone's heart out of their chest, and eating ceased to be a priority.* She pulled her jacket close. It hung off her shoulders, almost big enough to wrap around her twice. She needed a new one before winter. The thought only made her tired. Shopping, like food...like breathing, held no appeal these days.

"Would you be proud of the new me, Mitch? Four babies, almost forty-six years of marriage. A pound here, two there, always up, never down. You never said a negative word about the way I looked. Always introduced me as your bride." *Mitch's bride, Mrs. Mitchell Black.* The tear that slid down her cheek didn't surprise her either. They were almost a daily part of the new, not so improved, Karla Black.

She lowered her eyes to the granite monument facing the bench. *Mitchell David Black. Beloved Husband.* "I miss you so much. I still wait to hear your truck in the drive. I still have dinner ready at six every evening. I made your favorite last night, shepherd's pie. There was way too much, just like always. You'd think I'd be used to cooking for one by now." Karla dug a tissue from her pocket, blew her nose, and swiped at her eyes. "Not so much." She hunched in on herself and wept.

~ * ~

Ian McAlister watched the woman's anguish from an unobtrusive distance. He had his own bench, his own marker, his own thoughts. He'd seen her here before, crying, staring into the distance, some days, like today, bent double with grief. Curiosity had driven him to her bench one day last summer. He'd waited until she'd rounded the path to her car, then waited a little longer, just in case, before he read the marker. They had a common heartache. The end dates on the monuments were identical. Today was a shared anniversary, but where she wept, Ian conversed.

The name on the granite at his feet read Alicia Beth McAlister. Ian reached into the pocket of his jacket and tossed a handful of birdseed on the ground. Alicia always loved birds, even the common types. She'd kept feeders in the yard and a picture book of Oklahoma birds on a shelf by the front door. Even when the illness reduced her to skin and bone, she still found the energy to watch the finches and chickadees and record any new species that flew its way into their yard.

Ian found a measure of joy in being able to indulge her by bringing them to her side when he came to visit. He chuckled quietly. His wife would have scolded him for the seeds in his pocket and the mess they made when he forgot to remove them before throwing the garment in the laundry. *It's my mess to deal with now.* He watched the greedy birds for a few seconds and continued his family update.

"Hillie and Michael left on their anniversary cruise a couple of days ago. They'll be back on Friday. I wish we'd found the time to do something like that. I would have enjoyed showing you the islands. No other place on earth has birds like a rainforest in the Caribbean." He scattered a bit more seed.

"Rachel brought Millicent to the house the other day. She just turned seven and talks about you all the time. I'm so glad she's old enough to remember what a wonderful grandmother you were. She left a picture stuck to the fridge. I couldn't make heads or tails of it, so I called her to ask. She told me that the stick man was me, the white thing in the corner was your cloud, and the rainbow was your smile. I think we have a budding artist on our hands..." His words trailed off as the weeping from across the way intensified. He shook his head and glanced at the date a second time. The poor woman wasn't handling this anniversary well. Maybe he should check on her.

~ * ~

"How long were you married to Mitchell?"

Karla bolted upright at the words, shying away from the stranger when he sat on the other end of the bench and offered her a bottle of water, beaded with drops of condensation.

He lifted it an inch higher. "Go ahead, it's still sealed. I've never heard anyone weep like that. Your throat must be parched."

Karla wiped her eyes, sniffed in an effort to reign in

further tears, and studied the intruder dressed in dark dress slacks and a sky blue polo shirt. He didn't look like someone she should be afraid of, and she was more than a little thirsty.

"Thanks."

"You're welcome." He held out a hand. "Ian McAlister."

Karla twisted the cap from the bottle and took a deep drink of the cool water. It felt marvelous against her burning throat. She wiped her damp hand on the leg of her pants before holding it out. "Karla Black."

"So, how long?"

"Forty-six years."

The stranger nodded his white head. "It's hard isn't it? I had Alicia for forty-five. I look back on it now, and it seems like just a moment. How did you lose Mitchell?"

Karla balanced the bottle on her knee between her clasped hands. What had she done to attract a chatty stranger, here of all places? Yes, she'd been upset, but it wasn't the first time, and it wouldn't be the last. She surveyed her surroundings. A few people meandered through the markers, so she wasn't exactly alone. She studied the man on the other end of the bench from under her lashes. His thick hair was more white than silver, his eyes crystal blue, his face relaxed and friendly. Maybe he was just lonely. *Like me.*

"Traffic accident. Your Alicia?"

"Breast cancer. We had three years after her diagnosis. Time to prepare, time to see and do some things we'd always wanted to do. I can't imagine the grief of losing someone so unexpectedly."

Karla raised her head and stared at her visitor.

Something about this stranger tickled the back of her mind. She concentrated, trying to pull in the elusive memory. "You have two daughters?"

Ian tilted his head. "Hillie and Rachel. How...?"

"You were in the emergency room the night Mitch died. You had two young women with you. I remember saying a prayer for you before..." She turned back to the marker. "Before."

"Ah." Ian tapped his pursed lips with a finger before nodding in Karla's direction. "I knew we shared this anniversary. I don't remember seeing you, but I do remember a rather large group of people huddled together along the back wall that night. Looked like they were praying."

"My friends."

Ian settled back onto the concrete bench, obviously ready for an extended visit. "Church family." He crossed his arms. "I attend Grace Community. I don't know how I would have survived this last year without their love and support. You?"

"Valley View."

"I've heard good things about Pastor Gordon and his congregation. You're very blessed."

Blessed? *Humph.* Karla fought to keep the internal sarcasm from showing on her face even as her conscience poked at her. *OK*, she conceded. *I'm blessed. I have my friends and my family, but my faith...* The faith she'd held dear her whole life seemed lessened without Mitch by her side. Abandoning her beliefs had never crossed her mind, but she couldn't quite find her balance without him. They'd been a team, even in their faith.

"Have you found your faith seesawing more than

21

normal this year? It saddens me to admit it, but mine has."

Karla gave Ian McAlister a furtive glance. *Really?* She didn't know this man. She had no intention of sharing her struggles with him. She gathered her bag and tucked the half empty water bottle inside. "Thank you for the water. It's time I was getting home."

Ian touched Karla's arm. "I'm sorry. Don't run off. I came over here to make sure you were OK. To let you know that you weren't alone in your grief." His gaze was intent on her face. "Finish your visit with Mitchell. I'll go back to Alicia. But if you ever need a willing ear..."

The suggestion earned him a disparaging look. The idea that she would share her feelings with a stranger was preposterous. She telegraphed that fact with a challenging stare.

He cleared his throat. "Yes, well, we both have friends and family, but it's hard for them to understand the little things that make our days so empty."

His comment struck a chord. "Cooking," Karla blurted out, surprised when the word left her mouth. "I was telling Mitch how hard it is for me to cook for one. He loved my cooking. I was constantly chasing him out of the kitchen and scolding him to wash his hands if he was going to poke around in the pots and pans on the stove. I end up throwing away more food than I eat." She plucked at a baggy fold in her shirt. "I don't even know why I bother."

Ian nodded and settled back in the seat, his intended departure obviously forgotten. "My biggest challenge is the laundry. Alicia never allowed me to do more than carry the baskets, even after she was sick. She said the routine chore made her feel normal." When he looked at Karla sadness marred his eyes. "How could I argue with that? I don't mind washing for myself, but I miss the smell. I never have figured out what Alicia did to make our towels and sheets smell like a garden. I miss it."

"We're a sad pair, aren't we?" Karla asked.

"Very." He studied her for a second. "I hope this suggestion doesn't send you running, but...would you like to be sad with me a little longer? I always have coffee on my way home from visiting with Alicia. I'd be happy to buy you a cup if you have time."

Karla fingered the buttons on her jacket, suddenly uncomfortable.

"Never mind," he said. "Alicia always told me I was too impulsive for my own good. I'm..." He trailed off when a ringtone sounded from the depths of Karla's bag.

Karla stared at him while she dug through receipts, church bulletins, and breath mints. *Coffee? Was he asking her out?* She rolled her eyes at the thought. Her hand brushed against the phone as the ringtone died. She pulled it out and swiped the screen to life. *Bridgett.* She could call her daughter back later, but calling her now would give the man an excuse to go back to where he came from. Karla hit redial. Her daughter answered before the completion of the first ring.

"Mom. Where are you?"

Karla looked around the cemetery, her answer evasive. "Just out getting some air."

"Will you be home soon?"

Something in her daughter's tone sent anxiety zipping across her nerve endings. "What's wrong?"

On the other end of the call, her daughter broke in to a storm of tears.

Karla leaned forward, attention focused, Ian forgotten. "Bridgett, please stop crying, I can't understand a word you're saying. Has something happened to Jeff or one of the kids?"

"No, they're all fine but...Jeff...Jeff left me...he asked me for a divorce."

"Oh, baby."

"Mom, I don't know what to do."

Bridgett's bombshell scattered Karla's thoughts. Jeff and Bridgett had been married, happily, for almost twenty-three years. "Sweetheart, I'm so sorry." Ian shifted, reminding her of his presence. She glanced in his direction. He was doing his best to look at anything besides her, but she needed to continue this conversation in private. "Let me call you when I get back to the house. Fifteen minutes, tops."

"You won't have to call me back. I'm sitting in my old room."

Her room? Karla jumped to her feet as if the concrete bench had delivered and electrical charge to her backside. "You're what?"

Ian's attention jerked back to her. "Are you OK?"

"Who is that?" Bridgett's question was a gasp of surprise. "Mom...are you with a man?"

"What?"

"I heard a man's voice. Who's there with you?"

"What? No one."

"Mom. Are you on a date?"

Karla pulled the phone from her ear and looked at it, then at Ian. She pinched the bridge of her nose with her free hand and lowered herself back to her seat.

Bridgett's question hit just a little too close to her previous musings. "A date?" Heat flooded her face at the denial Ian couldn't help but overhear. "If you must know, I was visiting your father's grave. I was upset and...a friend...stopped by to see if I needed anything."

"You have friends at the cemetery?" Sarcasm dripped from the question.

Karla slumped against the back of the bench, energy drained. "Can we get back on track here? You're waiting at the house?"

A sniff echoed through the connection. "Yes, and I need you to come home right away."

Karla blinked at the demand in her daughter's voice and the unspoken assumption that Bridgett would get what she wanted. She sounded eleven, not forty-three. *And that's petty. She's upset.* "All right. I'll be there in a few minutes." She swiped the call closed, unable to identify the emotion that made her fingers tremble.

"Trouble?"

"My daughter, Bridgett. She's had some trouble at home, and now she's here for an unannounced visit. I really do need to go."

Ian nodded. "Of course." He reached for her phone. "May I?"

Karla handed it over, watching in confusion as he punched in a number. She was more confused when ringing sounded from the pocket of his shirt. He pulled his phone free and silenced the call. "Now we have each other's numbers." He stood and put his hands in his pockets. "I've enjoyed our visit, regardless of the circumstances. I'll repeat my offer. If you ever need a willing ear, or a friendly cup of coffee, I'm just a call away." A mischievous grin lifted the corners of his mouth. "And it doesn't have to be a date."

The furious blush returned. "I'm sorry, she's—"

Ian shook his head. "No need to apologize. We aren't the only ones grieving."

He lifted his hand and strode away, leaving Karla to collect her things. She forced her feet to carry her to the car, eager to see her daughter but shrinking from the emotions that came with the visit. How could she provide the support Bridgett needed right now when her own emotional bank had been overdrawn for twelve months?

CHAPTER THREE

Ian ordered his coffee to go and carried the cup out of Ground Zero, and onto Garfield's busy sidewalk. To a newcomer passing through, the little town would be no more than an attractive wide spot in the road to bigger and better places. To his more experienced eye, the signs of continued revival were obvious in storefronts bearing fresh paint, washed brick facades, colorful awnings, and pots of flowers growing with well-tended abandon along the edges of the sidewalk's worn pavement. The summer's sweet fragranced pansies had given way to the bright orange and yellow of fall colored mums. Ian inhaled their warm and woodsy fragrance as he passed.

He sipped his drink and turned his steps toward M & M's Books and Gifts, another one of Garfield's thriving new businesses. Darkness fell early this time of year, and something new to read would make the solitary evenings pass a little quicker. *I've read all of your mysteries, Alicia, and then some. I need something fresh.*

Ian window shopped while he walked. He stopped at the large plate glass windows of the gym to watch much younger men pump iron. The next shop was in the process of renovation. Gossip was rife as to its future purpose. He tarried for a moment in front of

Sweet Moments Bakery, where he talked himself out of the tempting display of cookies. *I still have half a box from a few days ago.* A young couple stood, hand-in-hand, outside of Bing's Jewelry store, giggling and pointing from one engagement set to another. Young love radiated around them in a tangible haze.

Ian stepped around them and reached for the door to the bookstore, holding it wide for a young woman with a loaded shopping bag in one hand. The other hand firmly gripped the shoulder of a young boy.

The youngster giggled as he stepped past Ian. "Mama, he whistles just like me." He puckered his lips and filled the air with an off-tune melody that faded away as the boy and his mother moved down the sidewalk.

Ian's steps faltered to a stop at the child's comment. He closed the door and leaned against it. *Was I whistling?* He thought back over his meandering path down Garfield's four- block main street and felt the corners of his mouth lift. *I do believe I recall whistling.* A full blown grin bloomed across his face at the realization.

Ian James McAlister, I can always tell when your soul is happy. That horrible noise you call whistling is a dead giveaway.

The memory of Alicia's words gave him pause. *Happy?* Maybe content, maybe comfortable, but happy? He searched his heart and found the dark corners where grief reigned just a little lighter than he remembered. *So what has you whistling today, Ian McAlister?*

Ian shook his head as he moved toward the rack of new fiction. He couldn't explain it, but he'd take it. He picked up a newly released science fiction novel and read the back cover while he sipped his coffee.

"Ian McAlister!"

He flinched, fumbled the book, and turned to face the glowering co-owner of the store. "Morning, Maggie."

"Don't you good morning me. What have I told you about bringing drinks in here?"

Ian held the coffee up in one hand and the book in the other. "I was doing fine until you startled me."

Maggie Raynes regarded him with a frown.

"Have I ever spilled a single drop while I browsed?"

She planted her fists on her hips. "No, but I can't allow every handsome man that comes into the store to break the rules. You're a bad influence on my other customers."

Ian ducked his head in exaggerated shame and studied the slight figure of Maggie Raynes from under his lashes. A beautiful slip of a girl...woman he corrected...since he knew she was at least forty with teenagers and a husband at home.

Maggie owned the store with her twin brother Micha. The siblings both sported the red hair, fair skin, and freckles that spoke of Irish in their family tree, but where Micha was bookish and quiet, Maggie tended to be outgoing and flirtatious.

As fellow members of Grace Community Church, they'd had a nodding acquaintance but no real reason to take it deeper. That changed on Ian's first visit to the store, shortly after Alicia's death. Maggie had decided that the grieving old man needed a friend. She'd been flirting with him ever since, using her lighthearted banter to chip away at the wall of grief encrusting his heart. This morning her compliment echoed in his ears.

Handsome? He knew her flirting to be harmless, but for some reason it pleased him today, a little more than normal.

The sound of Maggie clearing her throat pulled him out of his woolgathering. He looked up and found her eyes locked on the cup in his hands. Ian turned in a slow circle and took in the empty store. "Are they hiding?"

"Who?"

"The other customers you speak of."

Maggie stomped her foot. "You are an impossible man. I stand by my original warning. You drip a drop of that brew on one of my books, it's yours. I don't care if it's the mushiest romance in the place."

"You're a cold woman, Maggie Raynes."

She jerked her chin in a sharp nod. "Don't you ever forget it."

The swinging doors that led to the storeroom opened, and Micha entered, his arms full of books, his glasses crooked across the bridge of his nose, and his shirt dusty from heaven knew what chore. He frowned at his sister. "Maggie, leave the man alone." And grinned at Ian. "What is she harping about today?"

Ian raised his cup.

Micha nodded. "When it comes to these books, she's worse than a she-bear with her cubs. You'd think she'd written them all."

"I'm protecting our investment, thank you very much. Speaking of"—she waved her arm to an empty shelf on the other side of the store—"Those go over there, please, and thank you, and mind your own business."

Micha's muttered "Women!" earned him a heated

glare before he turned to do her bidding.

Sibling confrontation complete and customer scolding delivered, Maggie moved to Ian's side, slipped an arm around his shoulders, and plucked the book from his hands. "Sci fi? That's not your general fare."

Ian took in the array of new mysteries and courtroom dramas, and some that Alicia would have termed *shoot'em ups*. They just seemed too dark for his mood. "I've a taste for something different."

"Do tell?"

"Something's...shifting. It's nothing I can explain, but today just feels different, in a good way."

Maggie studied him. "Well, there's a smile on your face, and that's a plus."

Micha edged into the conversation, peering over Maggie's shoulder at the book. "That's a great choice, but it's number four in a series."

"Do you have the first three?"

"I think so." Maggie turned to her brother, her expression saccharine sweet. "Micha's all dusty anyway. I'm sure he wouldn't mind digging them out for you."

Ian gave Micha an apologetic look. "Sorry to be a bother, but if you can find them, I'll take the set."

"Oh, I like it when you're happy," Maggie said.

"No bother," Micha assured him as he turned back to the storeroom. "It's our...*my*...job."

Maggie opened her mouth, but the bell over the door cut her retort short as a new customer entered the store. She patted Ian's arm. "Micha shouldn't be long."

Once Maggie left, Ian browsed the racks while he waited. A colorful cover caught his eye. The Art of Cooking for One. "The perfect book for my new friend." He picked it up, and the image of Karla's face flooded his memory. *A fine looking woman despite the sadness in her green eyes.* The heaviness of his grief lightened a few shades at the thought. "Hmm..."

Micha came around the corner. "Here you go. The complete set."

Ian laid the cookbook aside, accepted the books, and studied the covers. "Have you read these?"

Micha shook his head. "I'm not much of a sci fi fan, but the reviews are good." He tapped the newest release. "Garfield's resident author, Steve Evans, was on our doorstep bright and early Friday morning to get his copy."

"Bag them up then. You haven't steered me wrong yet."

The younger man leaned back against the counter. "Even about the kitten?"

Ian nodded. "Even about that. Polly has turned out to be a great companion."

Micha straightened. "I'd never say I told you so, but I told you so. I still have a couple left if you decide she needs a playmate."

"No thanks, one is plenty. But if you're having trouble finding good homes, have you thought about tacking a card to the bulletin board at church? I'm sure there's someone at Grace Community who'd take them off your hands."

"That's not a bad idea. And if anyone needs a recommendation about their temperament, I'll send them to your pew." Micha moved behind the counter and scanned the books. "Anything else?"

"Yes, actually." Ian handed Micha the cookbook. "I want this one as well." He'd keep it in the car. They were bound to run into each other again. Ian remembered the new number in his phone. *Or maybe I won't wait for happenstance.*

~ * ~

Karla hit the remote fastened to the dash and raised the garage door. The sight of Mitch's truck brought fresh longing to her heart as she parked her car next to it. *Is it selfish of me to wish you were here to deal with Bridgett?* Karla pushed the thought aside, climbed out of her car, and checked the deep freeze on the way to the kitchen door. At least there was ice cream. She grabbed a quart-sized carton of double chocolate surprise, snagged two spoons on her way through the kitchen, shrugged out of her jacket, and went in search of her daughter. Muffled sobbing led her up the stairs and straight to Bridgett's childhood room. The fall sun shining through the windows of the pink and yellow room would have made for a cheerful haven except for the luggage dumped on the floor next to the closet and the weeping woman lying face down on the bed. How many times had she seen this exact scene during Bridgett's high school years? *Too many to count. I thought we'd outgrown them.* Karla put the ice cream on the bedside table, sat on the edge of the mattress, and stroked her daughter's chestnut colored hair.

"Baby, I'm so sorry. Why don't you sit up and scoot over. Let's talk."

"There's nothing to talk about."

"Sweetheart, we've been talking your problems out in this room for as long as I can remember."

Bridgett's response was muffled by the blankets. "This is bigger than being stood up for the prom." She rolled over with a dramatic sigh and pushed herself up against the stack of pillows arranged at the headboard. Her eyes locked onto the carton of ice cream. "But for ice cream in bed, I could pretend to be in high school again."

Karla patted her daughter's leg. "Some memories never go away, huh?"

Bridgett took a spoon while Karla pried the lid from the container. "Twelfth grade. Micha Raynes. He stood me up for the senior prom." She dipped her spoon in the frozen treat and managed to scrape a decent sized bite off the unyielding top. "I haven't thought of Micha in ages, but I'll never forget how mad Daddy was that night."

Karla nodded. "You were his princess. The only boys allowed to put tears in your eyes were your brothers, and they were mostly old enough to know better. While your father paced off his mad, I brought up ice cream and two spoons. We had a feast and a talk."

Bridgett scooped up another bite with a nod. "And we decided that boys were scum." She licked her spoon while a tear slid down her face. "They only get scummier with age."

Karla let the comment stand. Pushing her daughter for explanations was counterproductive. They'd get there when they got there. This afternoon it took a third of the carton to arrive at the anticipated destination.

Bridgett shoved her spoon into the carton and rolled from the bed. "Jeff asked me for a divorce last night."

Karla waited.

Her daughter crossed the room to the window,

moved the curtain aside, and stared down into the back yard. "Things have been really weird since Daddy died. As hard as it hit me, I think it messed with Jeff's head worse than mine." She turned, and Karla ached at the despair in Bridgett's eyes. "He was quiet and withdrawn for a while, then he threw himself into his job like never before. He's always been a bit of a workaholic, but nothing like the last few months. Out early, home late, gone most weekends. When I tried to talk to him about it, he told me not worry, that everything was fine. He said Dad's death just shook him up and made him realize how uncertain life is. He had some extra things going on at work to make sure that we were provided for if anything unexpected ever happened to him." She circled the room. "I didn't like it, but it sounded reasonable. The last couple of weeks were actually better, he seemed...happier. I thought we were finally getting over the hump. I thought we were finally going to have a life."

"A life?"

Bridgett came back to the side of the bed and dug out another bite. "Edie just headed back to college for her junior year, and despite my objections to his choice, we packed David off to boot camp last week. I enjoyed being a stay-at-home mom, but I've looked forward to this time in our lives. No more kids in the house. No more frantic evenings juggling school activities, vehicles, and jobs. No more nightly boyfriend, girlfriend drama. Just me and my husband. I thought we might do some traveling, get reacquainted—"

"Umm..." Karla interrupted. "Workaholic husband?"

Bridgett sat back down. "Yeah. But that was necessary if I was going to stay home with the kids, and that's what Jeff and I both wanted. I always figured that would change once it was just us. I even talked to a travel agent last week, brought home some brochures so we could start planning." She dropped her head into her hands. "Jeff came home early last night. After dinner, I spread the flyers out on the table. Sandy beaches, turquoise water, snow topped mountains, a smorgasbord of gorgeous destinations. He got all quiet. And me? I'm just jabbering on, thinking he's so enthralled with my idea he's speechless." She jerked back to her feet and returned to the window.

"Appalled is more like it." She turned her back on the sunny day, her normally pretty face marred by puffy eyes and a red nose.

Karla flinched as the pain of her daughter's hurt seeped to her already raw heart. Her own eyes filled with tears. *Jesus, this is my baby. Show me how to help her. Give me the strength to hold her up right now.*

"Mom, how could I not know? I love this man. I've given him almost twenty-three years. We've raised a family together. We've built a life." Bridgett shook her head. "When I handed him the resort guides and told him to pick our first destination, he laid them aside and calmly asked me for a divorce. I thought it was some warped joke at first. Like he was saying he didn't know how to live with me without all the busyness we're used to. I actually laughed until I got a good look at his face. He was dead serious. No hint at what was coming, no anger in the delivery, no opportunity for discussion. Just a deadpan announcement. He told me that he'd leased an apartment in the city, and that I'd hear from his lawyer. Then he got up and walked out the door."

"Oh, honey."

"Yeah, I don't even have an address, and he isn't answering his phone." Her face crumpled, and she climbed back onto the bed and into her mother's arms. "I didn't know what to do. I just knew I had to come home."

Karla held her close. "Of course you did." Karla rubbed Bridgett's back while she cried out some more of the hurt. When Bridgett finally sat up, makeup was smeared across her face, and Karla figured her blouse was trash. She brushed hair out of Bridgett's eyes and cupped her chin.

"I know there's nothing I can say right now to make things better."

"I don't think better is an option." Bridgett's chin quivered. "I just needed a place to think."

"Well, you have that for as long as you need." Karla looked at the remains of the ice cream, frozen no longer. "Why don't you get settled, and I'll take this down and see if I can find something in the kitchen—" Her cell phone signaled an incoming text. Karla pulled it from her pocket and read it with a frown.

"What?" Bridgett asked.

"Oh nothing. It's Bible study night at Callie's. She wanted me to pick up some napkins on the way. I'll let her know that I'm not coming tonight."

"Don't do that."

"But—"

"No buts," Bridgett told her. "I really do just need some time to think, and there's no reason for you to disrupt your schedule. Go and have a good time. I'll manage."

"Are you sure?"

"Yes, go. Tell Callie you'll bring the napkins."

"You can come along if you want."

"So you and your friends can dissect my problems over coffee and cheesecake?" Bridgett shook her head. "Thanks, I'll pass."

~ * ~

While Maggie readied their night drop deposit, Micha made a final pass up and down the aisles of the store. *Thank you, Jesus, for another successful business day.* He straightened books, swiped dust from shelves, and considered himself a very blessed individual.

He looked up when Maggie muttered at the computer screen. The frown between her eyes made him smile. People who discounted the bond shared by twins needed to spend a week with him and his sister. He could almost read her mind. "Problem?"

She waved him back to his cleaning without looking up. "Nothing I can't handle. Nothing that's going to get you out of the housekeeping chores this evening."

Micha snorted and moved to the next row. They alternated the work between them, each taking a week of cleaning then a week of end of day computing. He'd take dusting over a spreadsheet any day.

He finished the final shelf and turned to look across the store. Pride in what he and Maggie had accomplished in the last two years and gratitude to the God who made it possible swelled his chest. Owning a bookstore was a long held dream for both of them. When the automotive plant closed, leaving Maggie's husband Greg without a job, the time for a change seemed perfect. Where better to start fresh than the thriving little town they'd grown up in?

There'd been opposition to their plan to return to Garfield. Maggie's husband felt his chances for employment were better in a more metropolitan area. Their parents couldn't understand why it was necessary to move their grandchildren three states away. Maggie's kids didn't want to leave their friends. Micha and Maggie launched an all-out prayer campaign. Their plan received the green light when Greg landed a job at the Air Force base forty-five miles west of town. The employment package included a hefty increase over his previous salary. Parents, kids, and husband found themselves silenced at the display of God's provision.

While Maggie prepared to move her family, Micha had come ahead to scout out the land. The rest, as they say, is history. Or backstory, as his writer friend Steve Evans would put it. Micha adjusted a final book and grinned at Steve's name on the spine.

He stuffed the rag in his back pocket. "All done."

Maggie sat up at his words, and Micha heard her back pop from across the room. "Good grief, Sis, if you don't learn to sit up straight, you're gonna have a permanent hump in your back before our forty-fifth birthday."

"Oh, nag...nag." She pushed away from the counter and stood, and another pop filled the air. Micha shook his head but let the moment go, caught off guard when she tossed the money bag to him without warning. He managed to snatch it from the air before it smacked him in the face.

"Hey!"

"Good catch." She powered down the computer. "Everything's done, but I need you to drop it by the bank for me. Russell has a meeting with the career counselor at school and wants Greg and me there. I'm cutting the time short as it is."

"And what if I had plans?"

Maggie grabbed her jacket. "I'd faint in surprise or sing for joy, but we both know that the only thing waiting on you are your cats." She pulled the zipper up, her mood changing with her heartbeat. "Why don't you let me set you up with a nice woman?"

"Don't start."

Maggie ignored him. "It's been six years since Janice cheated on you. Don't you think you've paid enough tribute to your busted marriage?"

He looked away. "I'm praying about it. I'm happy—"

"Malarkey."

She knew him too well. "OK, maybe content is a better word. I know God has a plan for my life. I'm content to wait on it."

Maggie crossed the room. "Sometimes you're such a girl." She placed a hand on his shoulder and used it to boost herself up to kiss his cheek. "I love you, little brother."

"You're older than me by three minutes."

"Still makes you the baby. I'll see you tomorrow."

Micha watched her leave and busied himself with the final chores of lights, alarm, and locks, ignoring the small seed of restlessness that thoughts of Janice's betrayal always stirred in him.

With nothing but the security lights burning, he returned to the stool behind the counter. He'd never say a word to Maggie, but her words pricked at the unrest building inside him day by day.

Two years of dating, ten years of marriage, six years

of brooding recovery, and at the end, no wife, no family. Just eighteen wasted years. Not what he'd hoped his forty-four-year-old existence would be. He rested his head on his crossed arms.

"So how about that plan, God? I'm not getting any younger. I thought by now..."

What? What had he thought? Where had he imagined his life going? And how could he petition God for more when he didn't know what more he wanted? He raised his head and surveyed the store in the gloom.

"We have our store. I'm back in Garfield. I'm blessed." His muttered words didn't scratch the surface of his discontent.

Somewhere a memory stirred. Sapphire blue eyes surrounded by delicate features floated across his mind. Eyes gone ice water cold with hurt as a class ring barely missed his head. *Don't ever speak to me again!* "Seriously...?" He shoved the image aside. He hadn't seen the girl attached to those eyes in more than two decades. *So why is she on my mind tonight?* Some things couldn't be made right no matter how many do overs you prayed for. And when it came to Bridgett Black...not only had the ship sailed, it had sunk a long time ago.

CHAPTER FOUR

Karla hurried though the market Monday evening. She filled her basket with more than just the napkins Callie requested. Bridgett needed to eat while she stayed at the house, and Karla's cupboards leaned toward bare these days. Bread, sandwich meat and cheese, eggs and bacon, assorted other ingredients that would become some of her daughter's childhood favorites. *You're coddling.* She pushed the thought away. This was more than a flare up of the *Bridgett drama* they'd lived with during high school. This was pain, legitimate and deep. There wasn't a lot Karla could do to make it better, but comfort food was a good first step.

She glanced at her watch and increased her pace. Where had the day gone? A quick review of her hastily prepared list showed most of what she needed checked off. One final item had her dashing to the other side of the cavernous store. Karla paused in front of rows and rows of laundry products. She reached for the brand she normally bought, hesitating before she dropped it into the cart. *I never did figure out what Alicia did to make our towels and sheets smell like a garden.*

"And this smells like..." Karla unscrewed the stopper and took a deep sniff of the contents of the bottle. The scent of an ocean breeze filled her nostrils. "Nice, I guess I never really paid a lot of attention." *Did Mitch ever notice those tiny details of our lives?* She replaced the cap, added the bottle to her cart, and studied the other available selections. Clean Linen, Brown Sugar, Citrus Fresh, Lilac, and something called Summer Rain. Karla moved down the aisle searching for anything with garden in the name. She'd almost given up when she spied a bottle on the far end of the bottom shelf with the words *Country Flowers* emblazoned on the label. When she opened the lid, the soft floral fragrance that wafted out of the bottle made her smile. *Very nice.* Nice enough that she picked up a second bottle for herself before heading to the check out. It might not be exactly what her new friend was looking for, but it couldn't hurt to offer it to him.

New friend? The words arrested her steps. Since when did a single conversation equal a friendship? Since when did she have friendships with men? Karla fixed an image of Ian McAlister in her mind. A pleasant enough face with eyes that held his own grief but still contained enough empathy to let her know he had room to share hers. He'd been easy to talk to, and since there weren't any mind readers in the vicinity, she could admit to herself that his attention had soothed something inside of her. Something she hadn't known needed soothing. She shook her head as her feet carried her forward. *You're a sad, pitiful old woman.*

Two hours later, their weekly Bible study complete, Karla sat at Callie's table with half a piece of peanut butter cheesecake on the plate in front of her. Samantha Wheeler, her granddaughter by love and marriage, sat next to her, rubbing circles around her pregnant belly, her eyes fixed on Karla's remaining dessert.

"Grams, are you going to eat that?"

Karla laughed at the title bestowed on her since Kate married Karla's son Nicolas, and Kate's son, Patrick married Samantha. How could she have known that Nicolas would give her grandchildren and great-grandchildren with a single *I do*? God must have had a plan when He'd brought Samantha and Iris into their lives six years ago.

I still do.

The words caught Karla by surprise and brought her upright even as she pushed her plate over to Samantha. She tried to focus on that still, small voice, but Callie chose that moment to come through the door from the kitchen to the dining room. She stopped, hands fisted on her hips, a blue-eyed frown directed at Sam.

"Samantha, you already had two pieces."

Karla ducked her head and hid a snicker. Sometimes having the admin to your OB doctor as a close personal friend was *not* a good thing.

Samantha groaned and pushed her long dark hair out of her face. "Oh, Callie, I know, but I'm so hungry all the time. I swear this baby is going to grow up to be the gourmet chef Daddy teased me about becoming. He just never gets full."

Terri Evans shook her head and dunked a carrot stick in low-fat ranch dressing. She stared at it despondently and dropped it back onto her plate. "Leave her be, Callie. Let her enjoy that twenty something metabolism while it lasts." She looked down at the growing evidence of her third pregnancy. "I'd trade her this whole plate of rabbit food for one bite of cheesecake."

Pam Lake sat forward and rubbed Terri's arm. "You wanted babies."

Terri let her head fall back on her shoulders. "I know...I do. I'm just so sick of this diet. Gestational diabetes, why me? I'd give...well I don't know what I'd give, but I'd give a lot for a slice of that cake."

Kate popped the tab on a can of decaffeinated diet soda and slid it across the table. "Drink this. It's fizzy, it's sweet. You only have three months to go." Karla's blonde daughter-in-law slipped a bite of dessert into her mouth and chewed in exaggerated satisfaction. "It'll go fast."

Terri straightened in her seat. "I think I hate you."

Kate took a second bite of the creamy cake. "Absolutely wonderful."

Terri stuck out her tongue.

Karla's shoulders shook with waves of genuine amusement. "You girls sound like teenaged sisters."

Callie took her seat next to her oldest and dearest friend and rested a hand on Karla's arm. "They're pretty silly. But, whatever the reason, it's good to see a real smile on your face tonight. Today had to be tough. We've all been praying extra hard for you."

Karla patted Callie's hand. "And I felt those prayers. It's been a...weird day—"

"Of course it has." Terri leaned forward, pregnancy angst obviously forgotten. "We all miss Mitch."

Karla shook her head. "Weird," she repeated. "But not for the reasons you guys might think."

Pam pushed her plate aside. "You know we're here for you if you want to talk. We just didn't want to force a conversation on you if you needed your space."

Karla looked around the table. Her friends waited

for her to take the lead, their expressions filled with compassion and understanding. This was her circle. The people she ran to for support. There was wisdom and love gathered at this table. She decided to start at the tail end of her day. "Bridgett came home for a visit."

"That's wonderful," Kate said. "I know it meant a lot to have her with you today. How long are they planning to stay? Nicolas will want to spend some time with her and Jeff before they go home." A moment of confusion flickered across her features. "I'm surprised you didn't bring her with you this evening."

Karla toyed with the edge of her napkin. "Jeff didn't come with her. Bridgett came home because he's asked her for a divorce."

"What?" The same word from five mouths echoed from around the table.

Karla nodded and shared the story Bridgett had related a few hours earlier. "She says she was completely blindsided by Jeff's demands." She rolled her head on her shoulders. The stress of the day was catching up with her. "I know that's the truth as she sees it, but I think once she gets some distance from the shock, she'll see some warning signs she missed. How can you live with a man every day and not know he's unhappy?"

"Agreed," Callie said, "but, bless her heart, she has to be devastated. Let her know that we'll keep her in our prayers."

"I'll do that." Karla twisted her coffee cup in her hands. "Pray for more than just her marriage. Her faith has really taken a beating this last year. Losing Mitch is part of the problem, but there's more going on than that." She caught her lip between her teeth. "I wouldn't mind a few extra prayers too. I was at the cemetery when she called to tell me she was waiting at the house. I'm ashamed to admit it, but I almost dreaded going home. She's always been a bit of a drama queen, and well...I just wasn't sure I was up to the challenge. I'm still such an emotional wreck. I have a hard time facing my own problems in the mirror. I'm not sure how much help I can offer to Bridgett."

Pam frowned at the mention of the cemetery. "I told you to call me if you went out there today. I mean, I know you go there a lot, but today...today was special. It was my day off. I would have gone with you." Her brown eyes brightened with moisture. "We could have cried together."

Karla reached out and patted Pam's hand. "I almost called you, but I needed to go alone." She hesitated, not sure if she should mention her encounter with Ian McAlister. *Maybe they can help me sift through this hodgepodge of feelings.* If nothing else, they'd give her the chance to talk it out for herself. "Besides, I wasn't alone for long. That's the other thing that made the day weird. I met a man—"

Benton stuck his head through the door. "Hey, ladies, sorry to interrupt, but I'll be out of your hair in a sec." He focused his attention on Karla. "Karla, the weather's supposed to be nice this weekend. I'll come over and mow for a final time and weed eat for you. Get everything squared away for winter."

"You don't have to do that."

Benton ignored her objections and stepped into the room long enough to steal a bite of Callie's cheesecake. "Hey, that's pretty good. Did you save me a piece?"

Callie nodded and pointed to the kitchen. "On the counter."

He dropped a kiss on her head. "You're a good woman." He headed for the other room and his waiting dessert. "Y'all get back to your hen party. Karla, I'll be over about nine on Saturday morning."

Karla watched him leave. "Callie, keep that man at home this weekend. I have a grown son who can take care of the yard, and even if I didn't, I can hire someone to do it."

Callie shook her head. "You know better than that."

Karla leaned her head in her hands. "It's not his fault."

"He was driving that night. No one could have stopped those deer from bolting across the road when they did, but he feels responsible. If doing your yard work makes him feel less guilty, do me a favor, say thanks and let him do it. Better he be busy at your house than moping around ours."

Karla shook her head but allowed the subject to drop. When she looked up, Kate's gaze was fixed on her face. "I say we let Benton do what Benton does best. Can we get back to the part where you met a man?"

"Kate..."

Kate shook her head at her mother-in-law. "Oh no, no, no." She jabbed a finger in Karla's direction. "You brought it up. We need to hear this story. Because sad day or not, there was a definite gleam in your eyes just then. Let me stop long enough to say praise God and hallelujah, but if you think you're leaving this room before you dish the whole story..." Her daughter-in-law sat back and crossed her arms, "Think again."

A gleam in my eye? They were already taking the story the wrong way, and she hadn't even told it yet. She lifted her cup. *Maybe they'll let me off the hook.* The cup returned to its place, contents untouched. "There's nothing to tell."

"Tell it anyway," Kate insisted.

Karla frowned at Kate. *I should have known better.* She shrugged in an effort to minimize the story. "I went to the cemetery right after lunch." She looked at Pam. "And yes, while I was there, I broke down. I just..." Her voice hitched. "I still miss him so much. Anyway..." She gave her friends an abbreviated version of her meeting with Ian McAlister. "We talked for a few minutes, then Bridgett called and I left, end of story."

"But you liked him," Kate persisted. "I can tell."

Karla dismissed Kate with a wave of her hand. "We had a nice conversation." *You have laundry soap for him in your car.* She ignored the thought. "If you really want the truth, it was a little creepy. I mean, what sort of man strikes up a friendship in the cemetery?"

Terri tapped her nails on the table. "Ian McAlister...Tall, white-haired gentleman, handsome smile, sad eyes?"

Karla tilted her head. "You know him?"

"Not really, but I have his granddaughter, Millicent, after school at the day care. He's picked her up a couple of times. Seems like a nice guy. I'm glad he was able to offer you some comfort."

"Wait a minute," Callie said. "I know him too."

"Does everyone know him except me?"

"It's Garfield, Karla."

Karla stared at her friend and waited for her to explain.

"His wife, Alicia, was one of our breast cancer patients, at least she was until the clinic transferred her care to a cancer center. I heard that she died, but between losing Mitch and taking care of Benton, I never gave it a lot of thought. I can tell you he was devoted to Alicia though, never missed an appointment and took an active part in her care."

Callie patted Karla's arm. "At least you know he isn't an axe murderer. Maybe you'll see him again, under less 'creepy' circumstances."

"He invited me for a cup of coffee," Karla mumbled.

Pam pounced on the admission. "Wait a minute. Repeat what you just said."

Karla rubbed the bridge of her nose, silently chastising herself for speaking her thoughts aloud. *Too late to take it back.* "I said, he offered to buy me a cup of coffee. He even gave me his phone number." This time, when she lifted her cup, the coffee made it to her mouth. "He's probably as lonely as I am."

Samantha spoke up for the first time. "I think you should go."

"Me too," Callie agreed.

Terri raised a hand. "I'll third that."

Pam nodded her approval.

Kate grinned at her mother-in-law. "I'm good with it. Nicolas will be thrilled."

I always have a plan.

You too, God? Karla sent the thought heavenward and looked from one woman to the other. "It's so nice to know I have everyone's permission, but I don't think so."

Callie frowned at her. "Why not?"

Karla sat back in her chair and crossed her arms. "Mitch is the only man I ever cared about, and the only one I want." *Oh, sweetheart, you've been gone a year, but my heart is still married to you.* She held up her hand to stave off the objections she saw brewing around the table.

"I'll admit I was a little flattered by the attention this afternoon. His smile melted a little of the ice around my heart, but I've no desire to take it one step beyond a casual conversation should our paths cross again." She shrugged. "Ian McAlister might be the most terrific man in the world, but I'm sixty-five years old. That part of my life is over."

CHAPTER FIVE

Bridgett unpacked her bags in the solitude of the empty house Monday night. Mom was off with her friends. Bridgett had no illusions about her return to Garfield and the reason behind it remaining a secret. *My problems will be dissected and served up just like tonight's cheesecake.* She carried another armful of clothing to the chest of drawers in the corner of the room. She didn't really have an issue with that. She'd known Callie her whole life, grew up with Pam, and babysat Terri more than once. Mom's friends were her friends too, and despite her snarky response to her mother's invitation to tag along this evening, Bridgett looked forward to seeing them...just not while Jeff's hurt lay across her heart like an open wound.

She'd find an excuse to avoid Valley View's mid-week service as well. *Why not? You've avoided services in your home church plenty lately.* She pushed the thought aside along with the tug on her conscience that came with it. God seemed to have deserted her lately, why not return the favor? *But, I'll go to Sunday service with Mom. I've got enough on my plate. I don't need any lectures about the condition of my heart.*

Bridget focused on refolding a shirt. Anyway, by the time Sunday came around, the reason for her return home would be old news. Her hands stilled. *To everyone but me.* She swallowed back the raw emotions and looked up as thunder from an approaching storm rumbled in the distance. A sudden gust of wind kicked up from the south and slammed into the house. The shutters and the windows rattled, followed by creaking and popping as the structure settled around her. Far from being alarmed, Bridgett found a measure of comfort in the familiar noises. They spoke stability to her troubled heart. Mom and Dad had purchased this house when she was ten-years-old, so it had plenty of experience when it came to weathering storms. *If only my heart were half as sturdy.*

"Let it rain," she spoke aloud, indulging a sudden need to fill the silence. "Wind and thunder and lightning." She closed the last suitcase and carried it to the closet. "I'm in the mood for a good storm, maybe some hail. Golf-ball-sized would be good. Not here, but just in a ten-foot square where ever Jeff's car is parked." She looked at the ceiling, addressing the God who seemed to have forgotten her existence over the last year. "Can you at least do that much for me? I may not know where he is, but You do. I don't want him hurt. I just want him to suffer." She stopped, forced to swallow around a lump in her throat the size of the hail she was requesting. "Just a little bit. I think I'd feel better if I knew that he was as miserable as I am." She didn't get an answer, didn't really expect one. Her sigh filled the room. She'd looked forward to this season in her life. Never in her wildest dreams had she imagined spending it alone.

Is this how Mom feels? She rolled that around for a bit and came up with a better than likely probability. Well, they had each other now, and they were going to make it just fine on their own. *Men be hanged.*

~ * ~

Five pair of eyes gawked at Karla, five expressions held disbelief at her flat statement.

Karla's gaze tracked around the table, meeting each stare with her own level glare. Circuit complete she lowered her eyes. These women loved her. They shared a bond closer than blood sisters in a lot of ways. She knew they had her best interest at heart. She fully expected disagreement about where that best interest lay.

Callie's was the first voice to challenge. She sat back and crossed her arms. "OK, but I think you're going to have to explain that."

Karla mirrored her pose. "I just did."

Callie's voice was thoughtful. "No, you said that Mitch was the only man you ever cared about. I get that, I think we all do. Forty-six years is a long time. You guys had something very special, and it's hard to see beyond losing that. What I don't get"—she motioned to the other women at the table—"what we can't fathom is why you feel like any part of your life should be over."

Karla rested her hands on the table and picked at a roughened cuticle. *Is there any way to make them see?* She focused on her hands. "I know you guys have tried to understand where I've been the last year, but I don't think any of you can."

She glanced at Kate. "I know you buried two husbands before marrying my Nicolas, but each of those marriages lasted months, not years. I'm not negating the love you felt for them or your grief at their passing, but neither of those relationships come close to the life-long bond I shared with Mitch." Karla watched her daughter-in-law shift in her chair, Kate's mouth opened and closed as if sifting through possible answers. She finally nodded. "I'll accept your point for the sake of this argument. Grief comes in all shapes and sizes, but I'm still waiting for you to answer Callie's question."

Karla shook her head and let her gaze slide passed each of theirs. She drew in a deep breath and took the plunge into honesty. "My identity is gone."

Her confession hung in the air. Her friends remained silent. The only reaction—Callie's hand on hers. Karla closed her eyes and absorbed the truth she'd been unable to utter until now. She forced the rest of the words out into the open.

"I went straight from Mom and Dad's home to the one Mitch and I made. I was their daughter and then his wife. When the kids came along, I was always somebody's mother, but beyond that I was Mitch's wife. Being Mrs. Mitchell Black was the only identity I ever really wanted. When he died, he took that with him." She opened her eyes but kept them focused on the table. "I'll be the first to admit that there were times I didn't like the man, but I always loved him. Every morning I woke up next to him, proud to be his wife, content in the knowledge that he felt the same about me." She battled tears, refusing to let them fall. Her friends had seen enough of them from her to last everyone's lifetime.

"Mitch was the best part of me, the thing that made

me whole. Now that he's gone..." she searched to find the right words, cringing at how contrived her attempted explanation sounded. "I'm just half a person. Each day is a struggle. Maintaining my faith is almost more than I can do sometimes." She stopped, surprised to have said so much. A shrug accented her words. "I don't know how to be whole without him. I'm used up." She shook her head. "Even if another man wanted to be a part of my life, I have no life left to give."

Callie held an imaginary violin to her neck and mimed pulling the bow across the strings. Samantha's gasp was audible as she sat back and looked from one woman to another.

"Are you done?" Callie asked.

Karla stiffened in her chair. "Excuse me?"

"I asked if you were done, because, I've got to tell you, that was the most ridiculous thing I ever heard in my life."

Karla locked eyes with her dearest friend. Her mind struggled to process the unexpected response even while her stomach threatened to return the little bit of cheesecake she'd eaten. "I...you...I..."

"Oh, calm down. I'm not negating your grief," Callie said, tossing Karla's words right back to her. "We know how much you loved Mitch. But you're a half person? Really?"

Heat crept up Karla's neck. "I just spilled my guts on your table."

"You certainly did. And then you wallowed in it. You want to know what I think?"

Karla looked at the other women around the table. Sam's expression held wide-eyed surprise, but Pam, Terri, and Kate seemed to be waiting in expectation and agreement.

I didn't come here for this. Karla reached for her bag and pushed back from the table. "I don't think so."

Callie grabbed Karla's arm. "Sit still, because I'm going to tell you anyway." She leaned back and studied Karla with shrewd eyes. "You're terrified. There was a little part of you that liked this guy, and now you're running scared."

Kate drew a line in the air. "Score!"

"Got it in one," Pam nodded.

"Nailed it," Terri agreed.

Callie continued. "It scared you because you loved Mitch so much that the idea of another man paying attention to you feels disloyal. That you actually liked it? Well, that's just got to be wrong. You'd rather be 'half a person' than be unfaithful to the man you loved."

"Love."

Callie nodded. "OK, love." She stood and retrieved an envelope from the china cabinet. "I saw this card at the store the other day. It made me think of you. I wasn't sure if the time was right, but I think it is." She held it out.

Karla took the pale yellow envelope. Her hand shook, evidence of betrayal. *These are my friends.* Statement or question? She broke the seal and removed the card. Her voice was unsteady as she read the words aloud. "Grief never ends, but it changes. It's a passage, not a place to dwell. Grief is not a sign of weakness, nor a lack of faith. It is the price we pay to love."

She swallowed hard and looked at her Callie. "That's beautiful."

Callie leaned forward. "Karla, Mitch isn't coming

back. It's been a year. It's perfectly normal for you to start coming out of your grief at some point. It's nothing to feel guilty about. Maybe you've reached that point. Don't you think?"

Karla clutched the card and shook her head.

"So you plan to live the rest of your life alone?"

She met Callie's stare and lifted her chin. "Yes."

Callie studied her. "What do you think Mitch would say about that? If the situation were reversed, what would you say to him?"

Karla looked away. "It's different for a man. They need a woman from the day they're born."

"Women have needs too."

Karla cut her eyes back to her friend in surprise. She didn't need a mirror to know that her face flushed at Callie's words.

"I'm not talking about intimacy...well not entirely. But we never outgrow the need for companionship and conversation." She stopped and tilted her head. "Have you asked God about His plan for your future?"

Karla crossed her arms. "I don't think God is going to force me into a relationship I'm not interested in having."

"You're right, He'll let you live in that black hole of self-pity until He calls you home if that's your choice, but Jeremiah 29:11 says—"

"Oh, I know this one!" Sam leaned forward. "'For I know the thoughts that I think toward you, saith the LORD, thoughts of peace, and not of evil, to give you an expected end.'"

"Good job, sweetheart." Callie faced Karla. "Thoughts of peace, Karla. Good thoughts. You're my oldest friend, I love you like a sister. I'm sorry if my honesty hurt your feelings. That wasn't my intention. But think about this. Which is the better thought? Living the half-life you just described, or taking a chance on restoring some of what you lost?"

~ * ~

Bridgett prowled the house, waiting for her mother's return. The storm fizzled, dying without a sprinkle. The lack of the anticipated thunder and lightning left her in an odd mood, disquieted and twitchy with pent up nervous energy.

Her stomach growled, reminding her that all she'd had since lunch on the road was the ice cream she'd shared with Mom. She opened the fridge and frowned at the contents. A quart of milk, half a dozen containers of yogurt, some eggs, and, she raised the tin foil on a dish, left over shepherd's pie. She counted take-out containers from five different restaurants. She closed the door. *No thanks.*

Mom had promised fresh groceries when she returned, but this was ridiculous. *Is this how she's been living for the last year?* Bridgett continued to explore the kitchen, muttering as she found the cabinets and pantry nearly as bare as the fridge. She'd expected Nicolas to do a better job of looking after their mother. But then, Nicolas and Kate were still newlyweds, still working to get Kate's foundation launched. Maybe she expected too much. Maybe it's a good thing she was home for a while. Mom obviously needed someone to look after her.

Bridgett snagged an apple from the basket on the dining room table. This would do until Mom got home, and then they could sit down and have a conversation about getting both of their lives back into some sort of routine.

She wandered into her parents' room. *Mom's* room, she corrected. The reminder tugged at her already aching heart. Bridgett missed her father, and that was mildly put. She stopped just inside the door, swamped with a sense of déjà vu. How many times had she stood in this very spot, asking for permission, awaiting a decision, saying good night? At first glance the space was Karla-Black neat. The solid navy comforter smooth and wrinkle free, the room absent of any real clutter. Bottles of cologne, four of hers, one of his, lined up on the top of the tall chest of drawers.

Bridgett crossed the room and picked up a half used bottle of British Sterling. The stuff was ancient. How had Mom managed to keep Daddy supplied all these years? She wiped dust on the seat of her jeans, frowned, and took a closer look at the bottle and the top of the piece of furniture. Mom's half was as clean as Bridgett would have expected, Dad's portion lay under a thick film of dust. *Oh, Mom.*

Bridgett lifted the cap from the bottle and inhaled deeply. The familiar fragrance filled her eyes with tears. Heartbreak forced her whispered words into the empty room. "Daddy, you would have known what to do right now. I need one of your hugs. I miss your wise words and steady faith. I miss you so much."

The cell phone on her mother's nightstand came to life, and Bridgett turned to it. *Well that's great.* Mom would be up a creek if she had car trouble or something on the way home. *She really should keep this with her.* It was just one more indication that Mom needed a watchful eye. The ringtone sounded again and Bridgett hurried to pick it up. She glanced at the screen but didn't recognize the number.

"Hello."

"Hello, may I speak to Karla please."

The deep male voice on the other end of the connection took Bridgett by surprise. "I'm sorry. She isn't here right now. This is her daughter. May I take a message?"

"Would you let her know that Ian McAlister called?"

Something about the voice danced on the fringes of Bridgett's memory. "I'm sorry, do I know you?"

"We've never met, but I was visiting with your mother when you talked to her earlier in the day. I have a small gift for her and wanted to see when I might get it to her."

Bridgett's fingers tightened around the bottle of her father's cologne. So this was the *friend* Mother had been talking to. *Over Daddy's grave, no less.* And now he was buying her presents? *I guess I'll just have to start putting a few things right a bit sooner than I expected.*

"Look, Mr. McAlister, Mom's been going through a bit of a rough time lately. I'm not sure what she told you or what she might have led you to believe, but she's pretty unstable right now. I don't want to hurt your feelings, but could you not call her anymore? I mean, she still needs some space. I think giving that to her is the best thing for everyone."

She disconnected the call before the man had a chance to answer. A few swipes of her fingers gained her entry into the call log, and she deleted both the recent call and the number saved to the phone. A few seconds in the settings function had incoming calls from Mr. McAlister's number blocked. A trick she'd learned from her teenagers. Conscience tugged at her but she ignored it.

Bridgett looked around the empty room, taking in other subtle signs of neglect. She remembered the empty fridge while she bounced the phone in her hand. She'd spoken the truth to Ian McAlister. Mom was in a bad place. *I can identify.* Maybe they could help each other, but whatever they managed to work out between them, this was no time for Mom to involve herself with a man. *Looks like I came home just in time.*

~ * ~

"That was...odd." Ian bounced the dead phone in his hand. "The girl hung up on me." The curled kitten in his lap lifted her head. Both green eyes blinked up at him in question.

His finger hovered over redial for a second. "No." He lowered his hand and laid the phone on the table next to his recliner. The kitten tilted her head. Her solid white fur, marred by a single black patch over one eye, never failed to amuse him, tonight was no exception.

Ian stroked the silky fur. "Polly, maybe I really am just a foolish old man who doesn't know when to leave well enough alone." The cat began to vibrate under his hand. The sound of her purring filled the too quiet room.

He looked at the array of entertainment options scattered across the end table. A cross word puzzle, the TV remote, a tablet that would take him into cyberspace, and the stack of books he'd purchased earlier. Nothing appealed. "I'm restless," he admitted to the cat, finally isolating the thing that twitched at his nerve endings. "No offense, but I need conversation, I need companionship." His glance fell on the phone again. "I need someone to share my days with."

The truth of the words took him by surprise. *Where did that come from?* Karla Black's face floated into his memory. He didn't have to try too hard to picture the sadness in her lovely green eyes replaced with laughter, even if he'd never seen it. The image lifted the lingering weight of Alicia's death a little further from his shoulders.

Was it time? He cocked his head, stared across the room, and dropped into a memory.

Alicia looked up from her book and peered at him over the top of her reading glasses. "I need you to make me a promise."

Ian turned the TV down and gave his wife his full attention. "If I can."

She shook her head. "None of that hedging nonsense, Ian McAlister. This is important, and I'll settle for nothing but a yes from you."

He looked at her. Thinner than he'd ever seen her, the veins on the back of her hand a mottled purple and black from recent blood work, a colorful scarf wrapped around her head left bald from chemo and radiation. The report from the doctors today hadn't been what they'd hoped for.

His heart ached. He'd take this illness on himself if God would allow it, but that prayer had gone unanswered... He guessed that meant the answer was no. "How can I agree to something when I haven't heard it yet?"

Her reading light was bright enough to see the tears that brightened her eyes. "Please just say yes. It's important."

Ian crossed the room, sat on the sofa next to her, and took her hand in his own. He caressed the bruises with a light touch, careful not to inflict further damage to the paper thin skin. "You've had my heart for nearly forty-five years Alicia. If a promise makes you happy, I can give you that as well. Now, what have I agreed to?"

Alicia smiled the same smile he'd fallen in love with all those years ago. She lifted her free hand to his cheek, resting it against the stubble of his late day whiskers. "That you won't grieve for too long."

"Alicia—"

"Hear me out. We're doing everything we can to fight this thing, but I don't think...I'm not giving up, just being realistic. I don't think it's doing any good, and I'm so very tired. I know that, when the time comes, you have to grieve, but listen to God while you do. You have so much life left ahead of you, I want you to live it, and I don't think God ever intended you to live it alone."

"Sweetheart, I can't think about this right now."

She pulled him close, frail arms wrapped around his neck, her words a weary whisper. "I know, but when the time is right, I want you to remember that you have my blessing to love again."

Ian closed his eyes and savored the memory of Alicia's selfless love. He'd made her a promise, one they never spoke of again, one he never considered. But now...

Is it time? The thought reverberated. He could almost hear Alicia's beloved voice in his ear.

Yes.

"God?"

"It is not good that man should be alone."

"Father, I can quote that Scripture too, but it's only been a year." Polly nudged his hand for attention. She looked at him, her head tilted, ears pricked forward in anticipation. He chuckled and scratched under the cat's chin. "It seems I'm out voted."

Ian lifted his eyes to the ceiling and huffed out a breath. "I can tell when I'm being ganged up on. I'll do what I can to get to know the lovely Widow Black. But..." His eyes went back to the phone. "You are going to have to figure out a way to get me past the sentry."

CHAPTER SIX

Wednesday morning, Karla eased her car into a parking spot in front of Sweet Moments Bakery. Bridgett continued to brood, silent and miserable. Maybe some fresh blueberry muffins for breakfast would put a smile on her face, if not her heart. *If I ever get my hands around Jeff's neck, I'll squeeze the very life out of him. He could at least have the decency to return her calls.* She climbed out of her car, her own thoughts gloomy, her words muttered for no one's benefit but her own. "I don't know why men have to be so obstinate!"

"Oh, I doubt we all fit into that category."

Karla jumped and whirled to look behind her. Ian McAlister stood in the spot next to her on the other side of a small blue car. She wasn't sure of the make or model, but she thought of them as clown cars. The sort they drive into a circus tent carrying a dozen men in fuzzy wigs and red noses. No matter how she tried, she had trouble imagining Ian's six-foot-plus frame fitting inside it.

Karla slumped against the side of her own car, one hand over her pounding heart. "You just took ten years off my life."

Ian leaned on the roof of the small car. "I certainly hope not." He raised an eyebrow. "I will say that I prefer the temper over the tears, though. Tell me, Miss Karla, what's put all of mankind on your bad side this morning?"

Karla crossed her arms. "Inconsiderate son-in-laws and men who sneak up on me when I'm not looking."

Ian straightened. The wind was doing a job on his hair, tossing it over his forehead and into his eyes. He raised his hands. "I wasn't sneaking, just getting ready to get my morning coffee and go for a little stroll." He smoothed the hair from his face. "Speaking of coffee. I can forego the stroll if today is a better day."

"For...?"

"For getting better acquainted. My invitation still stands. I'd love to buy you a cup of something warm and visit for a bit, if you have the time."

Karla shook her head. "I really can't, but I'm glad we ran into each other. I bought you something."

His blue eyes lit with unmistakable anticipation. "You bought me a gift?"

Why did the man have to look like an eager puppy? "Not really a gift...just..." She stuttered to a stop, her feet shuffled in place, and she hoped she wasn't blushing despite the warmth spreading up her neck. "I mean..."

Amusement spread across his face.

She motioned with a hand. "Just stand there for a second." She ducked into her car, and came back with a bottle of laundry detergent. "I saw this at the store when I was shopping Monday night and I thought of you." When her eyes met his over the top of his car, she noticed something in his hands as well.

He held the object out to her. "I found this at the bookstore the other day and thought you might like..."

They stared at each other's offerings in silence for a

few seconds before mutual laughter sprang up to ring through the chilly morning air.

"You bought me a cookbook?"

Ian nodded. "You said you were having issues scaling down your meals."

Karla circled his car and held out the bottle of soap. "And you said you missed your garden. I hope this helps a little." They exchanged their gifts. Her heart stuttered a bit when their hands brushed, and she jerked hers away. *What...?*

For I know the plans I have for you. Callie's words rang in her ears. She stared at Ian, not sure where to go from here. Surely his gift deserved a bit of her time. "Maybe I can stay, for just a minute. A cup of coffee with a new friend sounds pretty nice."

Ian swept a hand toward the sidewalk. "Then allow me."

Ian ordered them both a large cup of coffee. He took his to the table while Karla lingered over the selection of creamers. She glanced at her new friend from beneath her lashes as she stirred hazelnut flavored liquid into her cup. *Mitch always used plenty of milk and sugar in...* She shook herself back to reality. *What am I doing?* Coming in here with a man, comparing him to Mitch, acting like a foolish teenybopper.

Melanie Mason, the owner of the bakery, caught Karla's attention, raised her eyebrows, and nodded to Ian's back. She gave her a surreptitious thumbs up. *Perfect.* Karla turned her back on her friend and made her way to the table. *I'll finish my drink and leave. I don't need to see him again, and I certainly don't want my friends thinking I'm on the hunt.*

"I have a confession to make."

"What's that?" Karla took a seat.

"I looked through your cookbook. Some of the pictures had my mouth watering." He stopped to sip his coffee. "I think I'll have to stop by the bookstore and get a copy for myself."

His smile was impossible to resist. She met it with one of her own, her determination to hurry fading into the background. "Yeah, I sniffed bottled soap at the supermarket until my sense of smell was completely gone. But I ended up buying a bottle of the floral stuff for myself, figured it couldn't hurt to try something new. You'll have to call me and let me know how you like it." Karla wanted to suck the words back the second they snuck passed her lips. *I just invited him to call me.* She clamped her mouth shut and raised her cup to keep anything else from tumbling out.

Ian sat back and crossed his arms. He studied her with a look Karla could only describe as contemplative.

"About that, I'm going to guess that your daughter didn't relay my message the other night?"

"What message?"

Ian nodded and leaned forward to retrieve his cup. "I didn't think so." He took a deep breath. "I called you on Monday night. I wanted to make arrangements to get your book to you. I got your daughter instead. She...umm..." He twisted the Styrofoam cup in his hands.

Karla tilted her head while he fumbled. "She what?"

He fidgeted in his seat before clearing his throat and meeting her confused stare. "She pretty much told me to forget that I had your number."

Karla sat back. "Oh, you must have misunderstood. Bridgett would never be intentionally rude." She fished her phone out of her bag. "But, she did forget to mention it." Karla paged through her call log. She tilted her head. "When did you say you called?"

"Monday night."

"Hmm." Karla went back to the beginning of the list and started over. "I did forget to take my phone with me Monday night. Bridgett even met me at the door to give it to me and remind me that I needed to carry it when I left the house." She frowned at the screen. "There's nothing here. Are you sure you called the right number?"

Ian removed his own phone from his pocket, thumbed it to life, and recited a number. "That you?"

"Yes, but..."

He held out his hand. "May I see that for a minute?"

Karla handed it across the table, more confused by the second.

Ian swiped the screen a few times before meeting her troubled expression. "My number isn't in your phone."

"I know. It's very strange."

Ian continued to page through screens. "It's not just missing from your incoming list, it's missing from your outgoing list as well. It's been erased from both locations." He looked up with a frown of his own. "And my number has been blocked."

What...? "Blocked? I didn't...I mean...I don't even know how..."

"I didn't think you had. Your phone's been tampered with."

Karla's breath caught in her throat, and it had nothing to do with her unwanted attraction to the handsome man seated across from her. She searched for an emotional label for the feeling and finally landed on good old fashioned anger. *That selfish, silly girl* "Can you undo all of that?"

"If you'd like."

"Oh, I'd like." *The girl has gone too far.* Karla shook her head, forced to call it like it was. Bridgett was a grown woman, and she knew full well what she was doing. Ian finished with her phone, and Karla held her hand out. "Thank you. I need to go. I'm sorry my daughter was rude to you."

Ian raised a hand. "It's OK."

"No, it isn't." She stood and slipped her jacket back on. She wiggled her phone. "I'll be keeping this with me from now on. Call me any time." Karla made her way home, powered by the fumes of her anger.

~ * ~

Bridgett sat up in bed when she heard the noise of the garage door opening on the floor beneath her room. She looked at the clock and had about sixty seconds to wonder where her mother could have gone before eight-thirty in the morning. She cringed when her bedroom door swung open and bounced off the rubber stop.

"What were you thinking?"

Bridgett looked at her mother. What she saw sent her right back to high school. Mom's mouth was thin and tight, and her narrowed eyes flashed with the green fire of righteous indignation. Dad had teased Mom about *the look.* Bridgett hadn't seen it directed at her since the morning Mom found the crumpled fender on the car Bridgett hadn't had permission to borrow. She searched her mind, unable to find any offense worthy of it today... *except...* She squirmed under the sheets at the single *except.*

Karla crossed the room and stared down at Bridgett with her fists on her hips. "How dare you."

Bridgett swallowed and remembered a childhood lesson. Always find out how much Mom knows before you start volunteering information. "Mom, what are you talking about?"

Her mom ignored the question and tossed out one of her own. "Guess who I ran into at the bakery a few minutes ago?"

Bridgett's heart sank when the *except* rose up to bite her. "Umm...Callie?"

Mom's green eyes went to slits.

Bridgett knew the only chance she had was offense. "Your boyfriend?" The two words dripped with all the sarcasm she could muster.

Mom jerked back at the words and pulled in a deep breath before she answered. "Bridgett Alexandra Black, neither of us is sixteen, and this isn't high school. I don't have a boyfriend, but if you mean Ian McAlister, then yes, that's who I ran into." She stopped long enough to slip out of her jacket, and then sit on the edge of the mattress. When she spoke again, the struggle to contain her temper was evident in her voice. "Imagine my surprise to learn that he'd called here looking for me, only to be met with rudeness from you. Imagine my greater surprise to learn that not only did you neglect to deliver his message, you messed with my phone so I wouldn't know he called, and fixed it where he couldn't call again." She waited until Bridgett met her eyes. "Why on earth would you do that?"

Bridgett reached for her mother's hand. When offense failed, conciliatory tactics were the next best thing. "Mom, I love you. This guy could be Jack the Ripper for all you know. I just didn't think that you should—"

"Is that your decision to make?"

"Maybe not, but..." Bridgett tightened her grip when her mom tried to pull away. "Someone has to take care of you. Daddy's only been gone a year and you—"

"Stop right there. I know exactly how long your father's been gone. It's a reality I live with every single day." She met Bridgett's frown with one of her own. "Ian is a very nice man, suffering through his own loss. If we can be friends and help each other through that, why should it matter to you? You have you own life."

Bridgett released her mother's hand, crossed her arms, and glared. "Oh yeah. The life that Jeff just detonated in my face."

"And your answer to that is to come home and shovel the shrapnel of that explosion onto my life?" Mom shook her head. "I'm ashamed of you, Bridgett. You were raised better than that. But just in case you've forgotten. That isn't the way it works."

"But..."

"No buts." Mom stood and crossed to the door. "You need to listen to me. I'm a grown woman. If I decide to die in my grief...or have twenty men at my beck and call...that will be *my* choice and my business. I don't need anyone's permission, and I won't be guilted into it or out of it. Not by my friends"—she pointed a finger in Bridgett's direction—"and certainly not by you."

Bridgett flinched as the door snapped shut on her

mother's final words.

CHAPTER SEVEN

Muffins forgotten Karla retreated to her bedroom. She needed an emotional time out. Mitch might not be waiting to wrap his arms around her, but she could at least surround herself with the remnants of his presence...his things. Scant comfort, but she'd learned to live with it.

Karla closed the door, leaned back against it, and threaded both hands through her short hair. *Where did that girl come up with the idea that I need to be taken care of?*

As if God chose to answer her question, the sunlight flooding through the east facing windows chose that moment to illuminate the physical evidence of her husband's long absence. The dresser top held a small glass bowl where Mitch had emptied his pockets each evening. Five quarters, three dimes and a nickel glinted under a twelve-month coating of dust. Karla's gaze followed the beam of light to where it fell across his favorite slippers, sitting right next to his nightstand, where he'd left them the morning before the accident. From there, the sunbeam arrowed straight to the louvered doors of the closet. The leaves on the tree outside the window caused the light to flicker. The play of light looked like a big *open me* sign.

Karla shuffled across the room and threw open the

doors. Mitch's Sunday suits hung next to his work clothes in no particular order. Her hand reached out to stroke a sharp crease she'd pressed into a pair of denim overalls.

"Karla, these things are stiff enough to stand by themselves."

"I want you out of my hair, but you'll be neat when you leave the house."

"I'm going, I'm going." Mitch pulled her in for a quick kiss. "When I get home tonight I've got an idea for reorganizing your pantry."

"Over my dead body, now get!"

A sad smile pulled at the corners of Karla's mouth as she continued to finger the stiff fabric. "You were driving me a little crazy once you retired." The sob built under her rib cage and climbed to lodge in her throat. *How could I know you'd be gone so soon?*

She allowed her gaze to skim the things she'd refused to touch for the last twelve months. They'd provided solace in the past, but today? A single word inched around the sorrow blocking her throat and slammed through Karla's defenses.

"Things."

Cold. Lifeless. Things.

A shrine to the dead.

A shiver ran up Karla's back. No wonder her daughter felt compelled to run interference for her. The realization didn't excuse Bridgett's actions, but it did offer an explanation. When you were content to live in the gloom of a mausoleum, why should anyone think you capable of life in the sun?

It's time.

She straightened. *Father?*

To everything there is a season. I've allowed you your grief. It was necessary, but it's time to step out of those shadows.

Karla swallowed, speaking aloud to the quiet voice in her spirit. "I don't know if I can. My life still feels so empty."

Small steps, daughter. My grace is sufficient.

"I don't even know where to start..." Her eyes swept the closet and came to rest on a large plastic storage bag wedged into the far corner. Karla pulled it free, brought it into the room, and released the zipper. A mountain of frothy lavender and yellow billowed out. She lifted the new comforter and sheets free. Dainty daisies sprinkled across a field of delicate purple. Matching pillow shams, window sheers, and valances lay at the bottom of the package. The set had been a Christmas gift from her Secret Santa the December before she retired from her job, then stored away for the last seven years. Beautiful, but too *girly* for the space she shared with her husband, despite his insistence that she use it. *But now...*

She looked at the navy comforter and the matching curtains on the windows. Plain and unadorned except for the white stitching on the outside edges. *Should I?* Words from Callie's card echoed in her heart. *It's a passage, not a place to stay.* Maybe she wasn't ready to call her grief done, but a few baby steps in that direction sounded appealing all of a sudden.

A quick yank had the old comforter off the bed before she could change her mind. The white sheets and pillowcases, both printed with small blue flowers, came next. Karla stood back with crossed arms, staring at the striped bed skirt anchored under the heavy mattress.

Where did I put that...?

Returning to the closet with a sense of purpose she hadn't possessed in months, she rummaged through shelves and storage boxes, finally surfacing with a brand new eyelet bed skirt. "I knew when I saw you at that garage sale that you'd come in handy someday."

Determination fueled her like a rocket booster, lending her strength as she pushed, huffed, and scooted, finally managing to get the queen-sized mattress on its side next to the box springs. Rushing, because she didn't know how long the mattress would hold its precarious balance, Karla removed the stripes and replaced it with the double tiered, yellow eyelet. She circled the bed and gave the mattress a small shove, sending it almost squarely back into place with a single bounce. A few tugs had the mattress even and skirt perfectly aligned.

Her deep breath echoed through the room. "I'm committed now. I couldn't do that again today if someone paid me." Karla remade the bed, smoothing the sheets. Pleased by the feel of the cool linen under her hands, the cheerful colors brightened her mood almost as much as the room. She flipped the comforter into place, stuffed pillows into the ruffled shams, and propped them against the headboard. The end effect looked like something out of a home design catalog.

She liked it.

Karla clapped imaginary dust from her hands and shifted her focus to the windows.

Those curtains had to go.

She sped through hanging the window treatments, stopping only long enough to iron the filmy sheer panels before threading them onto the spring-loaded rods. Once the rods were snapped into place under the new valances, Karla stepped back to the door to study the completed project. She loved the overall effect, even though the change tugged at her heart.

She pushed the negative aside, grabbed a towel from the bathroom, and attacked the dust on Mitch's side of the room.

"Mom, are you all right in there?"

Karla paused when Bridgett's voice filtered through the closed door. She placed one fisted hand in the small of her aching back and with the other, positioned the framed picture of Mitch in its new place on her nightstand, next to her reading lamp. She blew her disheveled hair out of her face with a huff of exhausted breath as she straightened and looked at the clock. She'd been cleaning for better than two hours.

"I'm fine."

"May I come in?"

Karla caught her bottom lip between her teeth and looked around the room. *Transformed* was too light a word. Bridgett would think she'd lost her mind. *Stop it! If you're ready to move forward, people need to accept that. Even Bridgett.*

~ * ~

Bridgett paced outside her parent's room. *What is Mom doing in there?* Muffled thuds and bumps had been filtering through the walls for a while. Bridgett had chosen to ignore them. She and Mom both needed some time to chill after their confrontation. She stopped and crossed her arms. *But, I don't care what she says. I'm not letting some stranger she picked up in the cemetery take my daddy's place.*

"Come on in," Mom said.

Bridgett shoved the door open. "It's almost lunch time. If you aren't still mad at me..." Her words dwindled away. *Merciful heavens.*

Her mother motioned to the room. "What do you think?"

Bridgett took a step into the room and turned a circle. *It's hideous. I mean the dust was awful, but this...* "It's...different."

Mom crossed her arms, the frown on her face a clear challenge. "I needed a change."

Bridgett nodded. "It just surprised me. It's going to take some getting used to."

Her mom stooped and gathered the discarded bed clothes from the floor. "I'm taking these to the laundry room. What were you saying about lunch?"

"I was going to offer to fix us both something." She pasted a smile on her face. "I overstepped with that whole phone thing. I'm sorry."

"Apology accepted. I'd love some lunch. I need some energy to finish up in here."

"What else are you planning to do? Knock out a wall?"

"No walls, but I think the bed would look better over there." Mom motioned to where the chest of drawers stood.

"I can help you, but wouldn't it have been easier to do that before you changed out the bedding?"

"Not the bed, it's on castors, but that chest is heavy, even once I take out the drawers. While I have them out..." Mom hesitated.

Something in her eyes put Bridgett on alert.

"I need to clean out some drawers and then the

closet."

"You what?"

"I'm going to box up your father's clothing and take it to the church. They can keep everything stored until the spring garage sale."

"Mom..." Bridgett's response was a whisper. She swallowed, unable to meet her mother's determined gaze she fixed her eyes on the wall over her mother's shoulder. "Why are you doing this?"

Her mother dropped the laundry, put a hand on Bridgett's arm, and pulled her to the bed. She sat and patted the mattress beside her. "Sit down, sweetheart."

Bridgett sat but refused to meet her mother's eyes. "Mom, I'm sorry if what I did pushed you to all of this. I was trying to protect you. I might have gone about it the wrong way, but this..." Her sniff echoed in the room. "This is too much. Don't clean Daddy out of your life because I did something stupid."

"Is that what you think I'm doing?"

Bridgett lifted a shoulder and swiped at a tear.

"Bridgett, even if that's what I wanted to do, there's no way I could." She stopped and stared into the distance. "It's hard to explain, but it's time." Mom reached around her and picked up the Bible lying next to Daddy's picture. She opened it, pulled out a card, and handed it to Bridgett. "Read this. Callie gave it to me the other night."

Bridgett studied the card for a few seconds before handing it back to her mother.

"That's a very nice sentiment but —"

"It's time." She repeated, tapping the card on her leg. "I didn't see it when Callie and the girls gave me this. I didn't see it when Ian tried to befriend me. And it wasn't your stunt with the phone that pushed me over the edge either." Mom paused and slipped an arm around her shoulders. "It's not any single thing, but maybe a combination of the three. The Bible says that there's a time to mourn and a time to dance."

She stopped, angled away, and waited until Bridgett looked up. "I married your father when I was nineteen years old. We had almost forty-six wonderful years together. When he died he took part of my heart with him." Her eyes left Bridgett's and swept the room. "I've been in limbo for twelve months. I don't like it there very much. I may not be ready to dance, but I've decided to take some baby steps out of the cave I've lived in since your father died. I have to think that's a good thing."

Bridgett frowned at her mother through blurred eyes. "The room is yours to redecorate or rearrange as you please, and I'll help you box up Daddy's things if that's what you feel like you need to do. But...I still have serious reservations about you dating Ian McAlister. I'm not sure I—"

"Oh, dating, smating. What's gotten into you?" Mom stood and retrieved her pile of laundry. "Ian wants to enjoy an occasional cup of coffee with a friend his own age. We both need someone to talk to who can identify with the losses we've suffered. I'd hardly call talking about his wife and your father dating. We're both a little old for that sort of thing anyway." She jerked her head towards the door. "Let's get some lunch. Now that I have this project started, I'd like to finish it before the end of the day."

Bridgett followed her mom out of the room. She turned at the door for another look around. She hated it. *It's not your decision.* The truth of the words clenched her hands so tightly, the nails almost cut into her palms. *I don't care.* Why couldn't Mom be just a little more considerate of Bridgett's feelings? Was it so hard to see that she had enough change in her life right now? *I need stability, not more upheaval.* Her conscience prodded her but she ignored it.

"Bridgett?" Mom called her name from the bottom of the stairs.

"Coming." She followed her mother to the kitchen. She needed an ally to help talk some sense into her mother, and she knew just where to find one.

Two hours later, with lunch finished, the chest moved, and the bed repositioned, Bridgett volunteered to go pick up some boxes. She left her mother folding Dad's clothes. Boxes weren't her only errand though. It was time to have a conversation with her big brother.

Bridgett parked her car in front of the squatty little brick building that housed Garfield's police department. She pulled the door open and waved at the dispatcher, an old friend from high school. "Hi, Tara,

"Bridgett." Tara stood at the thick sliding window separating the entry from the squad room. "What are you doing home?"

"Oh, just spending a few days with Mom." She left her explanation there and studied Tara. "I thought you were long gone from Garfield. You always said you couldn't wait to leave small town life behind. When did you move back?"

"A few months ago. You know what they say, you can take the girl out of the country but..."

"Yeah, I get that. Home is home. Besides..." She motioned to the door she'd just entered. "Things have perked up some since high school. Downtown Garfield isn't the same dusty hole in the wall it was twenty years ago."

Tara leaned on the counter. "That's a fact. Civic pride is on the rise. Lots of new shops and stores." Her smile turned sly. "Have you been over to the new bookstore yet?"

"No, why?"

"You will never believe—"

"Tara, can you help me? I can't get the copier to work."

Tara turned to a young uniformed man. "Sure, Elliott, I'll be right there." She faced Bridgett. "Duty calls." She grabbed a piece of paper and scribbled a number. "Call me. We should go out and catch up."

Bridgett took the note and stuffed it in her pocket. "I'll do that. Is Nicolas back there?"

"Yep, your timing is great. He walked in about five minutes ago. I'll buzz you through."

"Thanks." Bridgett crossed to the door that would take her back to the office portion of the building and waited for the muffled snick of the automatic lock. She pushed the door open, nodded at a couple more old friends, and went to stand next to her brother's desk.

Nicolas acknowledged her with a nod and held up a finger to let her know his phone call was almost done.

"I have the bikes in storage. If you can fax some descriptions over, I'll see if any of them match." He nodded. "Hey, that sounds great, talk to you in a day or two." He cradled the phone and smiled up at Bridgett. "Hey, Sis." He stood and pulled Bridgett into his arms. "Do you want me to go kick Jeff's butt?"

Bridgett shook her head and fought tears. "No,

there isn't anything anyone can do as long as he won't talk to me."

Nicolas held her out at arm's length. "I'm praying for both of you."

Bridgett dipped her head and stepped out of his reach. She looked around the crowded room. "Is there someplace we can go to talk?"

"About Jeff?"

"About our mother."

Nicolas studied her for a few seconds. "Have you had lunch? I dropped Tyler off at his house so he could have a few minutes with Melanie and Gracie. I was about to go grab a burger."

"I ate with Mom, but I could be talked into a chocolate shake."

"Done. The Camaro is parked out back."

"Where are we going?"

"Lizzie's."

"We're going to drive two blocks?"

He nodded. "Red gets cranky if she doesn't get her exercise."

"You and that silly old car."

Her brother grabbed a set of keys out of his desk drawer. "Better not let her hear you say that. She has a new passenger seat ejector system. You could be her trial run."

Bridgett let the effort at humor pass, keeping her thoughts to herself as they made the short trip and settled into a corner booth of the mom-and-pop restaurant that was older than she was. They placed their orders with the gum chewing, teenaged waitress. Conversation filled the gap between order and delivery. Jeff's betrayal. Progress on Kate's Center. Once their food arrived, she allowed Nicolas a few minutes to eat undisturbed. Her brother's brain worked better when it wasn't running on empty.

Nicolas looked at her over his half-eaten burger. "Jeff's an idiot, Kate's an angel, but that isn't why you're here. What's on your mind, Sis?"

She swirled whipped cream into her shake with the straw. "We need to have a conversation about Mom. I'm worried about her."

He nodded. "It's been an uphill battle for the last few months. Has she done something to make you more concerned than normal?"

Bridgett pulled the straw free and licked the thick chocolate clinging to the plastic, suddenly worried that her brother might not see things in the same light as she did. *Could that possibly be because he's an adult and you're acting like a spoiled five-year-old?* She leaned forward on an elbow and took a deep breath. *I'll start small and work my way up.* "She redecorated and rearranged her bedroom today. I'm supposed to be out gathering boxes so she can pack up Daddy's clothes."

Nicolas laid his burger aside and stared down at his plate for a few seconds. "Well, good for her. Is the room nice?"

"It's purple."

"That doesn't surprise me. It's her favorite color."

Bridgett took a drink of her shake. "I don't think you get it. It looks like the giant purple people eater barfed on her bed."

Nicolas laughed at her comparison. "I doubt it's that bad."

"I helped her rearrange once she was done. I'll probably have nightmares."

Her brother shook his head. "Two questions. Does Mom like it?"

Bridgett nodded.

"Do you have to spend any time in there?"

"Not really, but—"

"But nothing. It's time she started getting her life together. I'm thrilled to see her making an effort."

"But she's packing up Daddy's stuff."

"And to that I say, praise Jesus!"

"Nicolas! He's only been gone a year. I need—"

"Hold up, Sis. Is this about what Mom needs or what you need?" Nicolas scooted the paper lined basket aside. "Look, you haven't been here. You have a life in Texas—"

"Had."

Nicolas reached across the table and took her hand. "OK, had. But the fact remains that you haven't been here except for short visits since Dad died. I have. I'm beginning to think there were a lot of reasons God moved me back here after I retired from the Air Force, even if I didn't know it was Him at the time."

He released Bridgett's hand and ran his fingers through his hair. "I've seen Mom grieve herself down to a shadow of the woman she used to be. I've worried, and fretted, and prayed every single day. So if she's ready to rejoin the land of the living, I say Hallelujah and what can I do to help."

Bridgett stared at her bother. A part of her wanted to agree with him, but mostly she just needed him to see what she was seeing. "So, it's OK with you if she has a boyfriend?"

Nicolas put his head back, his whole body shaking with laughter. "Boyfriend? Sis, there aren't a lot of secrets between that group of women who get together on Monday nights." He slurped his shake. "Kate told me about the guy Mom met at the cemetery. I gotta tell you, I think your use of the word *boyfriend* is more than a little exaggerated."

"He—"

"Don't get your panties in a wad over Ian McAlister."

Bridgett huffed, crossed her arms on the table, and leaned forward. "He could be an axe murderer for all we know."

"He isn't."

"How—?"

"Because after I got the scoop from Kate, I did what any self-respecting officer of the law would do. I ran a very discreet background check on Ian McAlister. From what I can see, he's a good guy.

"But—"

"No buts, Sis." His expression went from amused to serious. "You need to take a giant step back and let Mom find her way back into the light. If that means the occasional company of Ian McAlister, so be it."

Bridgett sat back. So much for an ally. *When did my big brother start sounding so much like my dad?*

~ * ~

Karla switched on the bedroom light. The drastic changes she'd made to the room earlier leapt out at her harsh and glaring under the artificial light. How was it possible to appreciate and regret something at the same time? She maneuvered around the room's unfamiliar layout, forced to think about routine tasks for the first time in years. Her eyes searched for the signs of her husband that had been there just this morning. They were gone, wiped away like writing on a chalkboard. *What have I done?*

With mechanical movements, she changed into a nightgown and then crawled into the bed. Karla swallowed a sob as she clasped Mitch's picture to her chest, turned onto her side, and wept. Baby steps might be a good thing, but they always came with plenty of bumps and bruises along the way.

CHAPTER EIGHT

Karla lay awake in the still quiet of pre-dawn that was neither day nor night. Her dreams had been a hodgepodge of disturbing images and sensations. Partly Mitch and partly, of all things, Ian McAlister. And that was just wrong...wasn't it? She peered up at the dark ceiling and spoke to whoever might be listening. "I promised to love my husband. I did...I do."

Till death do you part. I have new things for you, daughter.

"Bah!" These whispered conversations with God were a broken record the last couple of days. Move on, move on, move on. *Where, exactly, am I supposed to move on to?* Karla threw the covers aside and climbed out of the bed, half-afraid God would answer her question, half-afraid He wouldn't. She made up the bed, stacking the lavender and yellow pillows at the head of the bed. *It really is pretty.* Her glance landed on Mitch's picture. *Maybe tonight I can enjoy it without the tears.*

Karla crept past the door to Bridgett's room, trying not to wake her daughter. Some quiet time sounded appealing this morning. She descended the stairs, flipped on the kitchen lights, and paused in the doorway. She missed her husband twenty-four-seven, but if forced to pick just one time of the day special to both of them, it would be the moments spent across the morning table from each other. She rarely fixed breakfast, since Mitch so often met Benton and the rest of the crew at one of the local cafés before they started their day. Instead of food, they'd fallen into the habit of trading bits of morning news over their first cup of coffee. Hers gleaned from the Internet, his delivered the old fashioned way via the newspaper. Then they shared a quick prayer and a kiss, and he was out the door. She leaned against the counter and stared at the table. *Well, it was* my *favorite part of the day, anyway.*

She busied herself with coffee preparation. A cup for one made easier with the single cup brewer Mitch had bought for her just before he... She looked around the kitchen while coffee dribbled into her mug. Maybe the house was part of the problem. Everything in the place held a memory of her husband. Karla shook her head. Redecorating in here would require more effort than a new comforter. Karla pushed the brew button a second time to fill her oversize cup to the brim. While she waited, she plucked a verse from the promise box sitting on the shelf with the sugar and creamer. The random verse would get her devotion time started. There were times when that single verse launched a rabbit trail of study that took her all the way to lunch.

Karla held the card under the light and read the verse aloud. "Psalms 32:8. I will instruct thee and teach thee in the way which thou shalt go. I will guide thee with mine eye." She dropped the card as if it burned her fingers and raised her face to the heavens. "Nice try, but I don't think so. I agreed to baby steps, remember?" Karla picked up the discarded card, stuck it in the back of the stack, and chose another.

"Proverbs 4:25-26. Let thine eyes look right on, and

let thine eyelids look straight before thee. Ponder the path of thy feet, and let all thy ways be established."

What...? Karla shoved it back in with its predecessor, looked defiantly heavenward, and yanked out a third. "Isaiah 30:21 And thine ears shall hear a word behind thee, saying, This is the way, walk in it, when ye turn to the right hand, and when ye turn to the left."

The card fluttered to the floor. Karla reached for one of the bar stools flanking the counter and boosted herself on to it. She lowered her head to her hands. "What are You trying to tell me, Father?"

I have new things for you, daughter. Listen well.

Karla frowned. Cryptic was not a word she'd have applied to her Heavenly Father before today, but... "What new things?" She started when her phone rang. She snatched it up, glanced at the screen, and swiped the call open. It was a bit early for phone calls, even from Dave Sisko.

"Hello."

"Good morning. I hope I didn't wake you."

The voice of Valley View's youth pastor seemed a bit too chipper for a pre-eight a.m. call. "No, I'm awake. What can I do for you?"

"What would you say if I told you that God told me to call you?"

Karla pulled the phone away from her ear and looked at it. She brought it back to the side of her head. "Excuse me?"

"Yeah, took me a minute too. Listen, I know you're probably gonna think I'm crazy, but I've got an idea for a new afternoon ministry a couple of days a week. I was thinking about who might be available to help, and your name popped into my head, and I couldn't shake it. You can tell me to go away and I will, but I'd like to share my idea with you first, because calling you sure feels like a God thing."

Karla closed her eyes. *A new job?* She'd resigned from her Sunday school class and taken a huge step away from most *extracurricular* church activities since Mitch died. She'd remained faithful to her church attendance, she continued with the weekly Bible study, but the rest...

"Hey look, I'm sorry. I..."

This is the way.

Karla's head jerked up.

"...can call someone else."

"No!" The word leapt from Karla's mouth. She stared at the card lying on the floor. "I mean, what did you have in mind?" She listened as Sisko outlined his idea to open the gym a couple of days a week in order to serve a free lunch to area high school students.

"Nothing elaborate," he assured her. "Hot dogs and nachos, or barbeque sandwiches and chips, maybe a cookie or cupcake for dessert. I want to give the kids an alternative to hanging around downtown, but I need someone to spearhead the kitchen part of it, sort of a friendly grandma presence. God and I think you'd be just about perfect for the job."

"I...um..." Her heart urged her toward *yes*, but she buried the impulse under a layer of caution. "Can I think about it for a day or two?"

"Absolutely," Sisko said. "I still have some details to hammer out on my end. How about we get together after church on Sunday? I'll have more of the project worked out by then."

"That's a great idea."

"Outstanding. You have an awesome day, and we'll talk on Sunday."

Karla laid the phone aside, already knowing what her answer would be. She hadn't asked for time to think about it or pray about it because she didn't want to do it. It actually sounded like a lot of fun. *And that's a sudden turn around.* Her hesitation came from the fact that she was a stubborn old woman who didn't like to be bullied, even by God.

She picked up her rapidly cooling coffee. The phone rang a second time before she drank a single drop. This time when she looked at the screen a smile bloomed in spite of her restless night and the early hour.

"Good morning, Ian. Are you always such an early riser?" She no longer needed the heat of the coffee. His answering chuckle warmed her from the inside out.

"Not always, but I have to go to the airport in a bit to pick up my daughter and her husband. They're coming back from vacation. I was going through my wallet looking for their flight info and I came across a gift card I'd forgotten I had. It's a dinner for two at Southby's Steak House in Oklahoma City, and it expires in a week."

Listen well.

Karla sat up straight and gripped the phone, her breath shallow in her chest.

"I hope you won't think I'm being forward, but it seems a shame to waste the meal on just me. I was wondering if you'd like to join me for dinner on Saturday night."

"I..."

"Dinner between friends?"

Her heart trembled as her world tilted into a new

reality. She closed her eyes, took a deep breath, and jumped from the proverbial cliff. "I think I'd like that."

"I hoped you would. I'll make the reservation for seven and pick you up at six."

Karla swallowed and forced her next words around her constricted throat. "Do you have a pen? You'll need the address."

"I'll call you tomorrow at a more decent hour and get it. That way I have an excuse to talk to you again."

She wasn't prepared for the tingle of pleasure that spread to the very tips of her fingers and toes. It had been years since Karla had been flirted with, but a woman never forgets the feeling of being appreciated. "I'll talk to you then."

She laid the phone down a second time and looked at the clock. It was just shy of eight-thirty. She'd had a conversation with God, she had the offer of a new job at the church, and she had a date for Saturday night.

Karla heard sounds of life from the top of the stairs. The thought of breaking this news to her daughter turned her newly born contentment to ashes.

~ * ~

"Spill it, Dad." Hillie crossed her arms and sat back in the booth. Rachel mirrored her older sister's pose.

Ian studied his daughters from across the table. Twenty-two months apart and identical enough that they were often mistaken for twins. Blonde haired, blue-eyed mischief makers from the get go. Raising them had been the joy of his life.

"It?"

Two sets of eyes glowered at him, but it was Hillie

who took the lead. She'd consider that her right as the eldest. "Yes, *it*. Lunch on a Friday with specific instructions to exclude your sons-in-laws and grandchildren?" She nodded to Rachel. "We'd be worried, but we talked it over last night and decided that if you were planning to share bad news, you would have invited Michael and Dean to come along for moral support."

"That, and you would have picked a less public place," Rachel chimed in.

Ian squeezed lemon into his iced tea. "That's a pretty in-depth dissection for a simple lunch invitation."

"You can call it what you want, but you're stalling." Hillie's eyebrows lifted. "I'm still on vacation, so I can sit here all day, but Rachel has to be back in her office in forty-five minutes. So you need to get a move on."

The waitress picked that moment to bring their burgers and salads. While she served the food, Ian took a few minutes to look deep into his heart. *How will they take this?* His daughters were reasonable adults, but Alicia's death hit them hard. The fact that he was seriously attracted to another woman had brought a little light back into his life. They might not welcome the news so gladly. *I'm sixty-six years old. I don't need their permission to enjoy Karla's company.* But it would feel wrong to hide it from them.

Ian cleared his throat. "You're right, I did call this little family meeting to share some news." He glanced from Hillie to Rachel, and both of his daughters met his eyes intently. He took a deep breath. *In for a penny, in for a pound.*

"You girls know how much I loved your mother. I

miss her more every day, not less. But life moves on, and I've decided mine has been in a rut long enough. I'm lonely. I need more companionship than Polly can provide. I think I'm ready to look for some female company."

Both girls gasped in unison. They clasped hands on top of the table and turned to stare at each other.

Ian's eyebrows rose at their reaction. *Oops!* "Girls, I'm sorry if this news disturbs you. I—"

Giggling from across the table interrupted his apology. "Is this a generic notice of intent?" Rachel asked.

"Or do you already have a target for your affections?" Hillie finished.

Ian sat back and reassessed his position. At best he'd expected a bit of curiosity, at worst a few frowns and mild objections. He wasn't prepared for the mirth across the table. "You two are OK with this?" They both nodded and dug into their lunch as if he'd made a simple comment about the weather.

Hillie wiped her mouth and met her father's eyes. "We've wondered what was taking you so long."

Ian swallowed a bite of his burger. "What was taking me so long?"

"Sorry, Dad, that came out wrong." Hillie motioned to Rachel. "We've talked about this a few times. You're a handsome man with a lot of love to share with someone. We know how much you loved Mom."

"We've watched you grieve," Rachel added. "But we've seen you start to come out of it over that last couple of months. Mom told us that when—"

Ian stopped her with an upheld hand. "Your mom talked to you girls about this?"

His daughters nodded, and Rachel continued. "Mom told us that she'd made you promise not to grieve forever. She wanted us to know that you had her blessing when the time was right." Rachel laid a hand on her sister's arm. "I'll be the first to admit that there was more than a little dissension over that conversation."

Ian handed her a clean linen handkerchief from his pocket when her eyes filled with tears. Rachel took it, wiped her eyes and handed it to Hillie. "More because we had to accept that Mom was actually dying. We'd both been in denial until then."

Hillie stuffed a rogue pickle back onto her burger. "Enough of this maudlin stuff. Tell us about her. What's she like, when do you plan to ask her out?"

Father, thank you for these two. I don't know what I did to deserve them. "Her name is Karla Black. Her husband died the same night as your mother." He filled in a few more blanks, answered a few more questions, and shared the story about their simple gifts.

"Ah...that's so sweet. When do you plan to ask her out?" Hillie repeated.

Ian drained his glass of the final drop of tea. "Actually, we're going to dinner tomorrow night."

Hillie looked at Rachel and received a slight nod. "What time?"

"I'm picking her up at six, why?"

"We'll be at the house by four," Hillie answered.

"Why would you—?"

"Daddy," Hillie interrupted. "When was the last time you dressed for a first date?"

Ian studied his daughters. The speculative light in their matching eyes brought a shiver to his sixty-six-year-old heart. "Nearly fifty years ago, but I think I can manage."

Hillie shook her head. "Wrong answer."

"Trust us, you're gonna need our help with this," Rachel added.

Ian rolled his eyes and shook his head. "Is there any way to talk you two out of this?"

"Only if you cancel your date," Hillie answered.

"That's not an option, and you both know it."

"Didn't think so." Rachel lifted her glass and waited for her sister and father to do the same. She extended hers over the table and grinned when the three glasses clanked together. "To Daddy and new beginnings."

CHAPTER NINE

Karla entered the kitchen on Saturday morning and found Bridgett there ahead of her, the remnants of her coffee and breakfast to one side, her nose buried in a book. Her daughter shifted a bit to better place her back to Karla and flipped a page.

This was the second morning of Bridgett's silent treatment in response to the news of Ian's dinner invitation. Bridgett was her only daughter, and Karla loved her with every ounce of a mothers soul, but if the girl thought she could come home with her own life in shambles and run Karla's...well...she couldn't. *I wonder if she knows that the more she acts like a spoiled brat, the more determined I am to show her who's in charge?* The thought felt petty. Karla was beyond caring.

Karla's phone rang, and she fished it out of her pocket. "Hello."

"It's Callie. Are you ready?"

"Just getting a cup of coffee. What time will you be here?" She saw Bridgett glance up for half a second, and right back down. *The girl has no clue who she's dealing with when it comes to stubborn. Everything she knows, she learned, or inherited, from me.*

"Leaving Kate's now. We'll be there in about ten minutes. Let me tell you, you are a hot topic for discussion this morning. Text messages are flying. If Sam and Terri weren't huge with child and Pam hadn't committed to chaperoning Megan's field trip today, they'd all be meeting us at the mall. As it is, I have a whole list of suggestions regarding new clothes and makeup."

Dear Lord! Karla popped a slice of bread in the toaster. "Callie, we promised not to go crazy today. It's one dinner."

Callie laughed. "I said we had a list. I didn't say we'd use it. Suck it up, girlfriend. One dinner or six, you've needed a shopping trip for months. Looking nice for Ian tonight is just icing on the cake."

"Whatever. See you in a few minutes." She shook her head. *A winter coat, one dress. Maybe shoes, but that's it.* She carried her breakfast to the table on a paper towel and sat with her coffee.

Bridgett turned in her direction and spoke to her for the first time in more than forty-eight hours. "Mom, please don't do this."

"I'm going shopping."

"You know what I mean."

"Yes, Bridgett, I know what you mean. I'm going to tell you the same thing I told you Wednesday...and Thursday. It's time for me to move forward."

Bridgett snapped her book shut and slammed it on the table. "You don't need a man to do that."

Karla rubbed her forehead. "You know what?" She spread her hands. "I agree with you. I don't *need* a man, but what if I *want* one?"

Bridgett gasped. "You *are* thinking about replacing Daddy."

"Oh grow up! I'm not replacing anyone. I'm going

to have dinner with a nice man, a man who makes me feel like a woman, something I didn't even know I missed or would ever want again until now."

"You're going to have dinner with some ghoul you met over Daddy's grave!"

Karla heard a car in the drive and rose to put her cup in the sink and her untouched toast in the garbage. Words failed her, and maybe that was a good thing, since Bridgett seemed to be an expert at twisting them. She picked up her purse and plucked a light jacket from the hook next to the back door. She turned to say goodbye, but swallowed the impulse when she met Bridgett's belligerent stare. She left the house and allowed the slamming door to accent her departure. The action would have earned one of her children a reprimand and a return trip through the door to close it properly. Karla was too fed up with Bridgett's childishness to care about protocol.

The day flew by in a blur of stores, fruitless arguments for retail restraint, and credit cards nearly melted from such vigorous use after such a long season of neglect. Karla returned home seven hours later, lighter in both spirit and wallet. She navigated the walk carefully in the flimsy flip flops provided by the nail salon. She set the bags on the porch and dug for her keys. *Why did I let Callie and Kate talk me into all of this stuff?* She managed to get the door open and spoke to her friend and daughter-in-law without turning around.

"Let's get this mess upstairs." She took the stairs one at a time, afraid of tripping on the plastic shopping bags that dangled from her arms and bounced around her legs. *A coat and a dress?* Oh, she'd bought those things along with three pair of shoes, four additional dresses, assorted skirts, pants, and tops. She also had a fresh conviction that her friends, Callie the Shopenator and her faithful sidekick Kate the Buy-it Girl, received a secret commission from every store in the mall.

Karla nudged the bedroom door open and hefted her load up onto the bed. Callie and Kate followed her through but froze at the threshold.

"Oh wow." Kate turned in a circle. "Karla, this is beautiful."

"When did you do all of this?" Callie asked.

Karla shoved sacks out of the way and sat on the edge of the bed. "A couple of days ago. I just...I walked in and really saw it for the first time in months. I'd allowed it to become a shrine." She swallowed around a sudden lump of emotion. "I think I went a little crazy." She looked at the bags littering the bed and the floor. "Sort of like today." She glanced down at her hot pink toenails. "I mean really, a pedicure. Who's going to see it?"

Callie sat next to her and threw an arm around her shoulders. "Maybe no one, but that isn't the point. If it snows tomorrow, heaven forbid, and you walk around for a week in winter socks and boots, you'll know that underneath it all your toes are saying I am woman, I am pretty." She squeezed her friend in a half hug. "Trust me, it's a total confidence builder."

Karla wiggled her toes and watched the glitter top coat sparkle in the light. "If you say so."

"I say." Callie scrambled to her feet. "Now, let's get this stuff unpacked. You have ninety minutes before your date gets here. We need to make every minute count."

Karla's breathing hitched as the blood drained from

her head and pooled in her toes. She placed both hands over her racing heart and took a shuttering breath.

Kate crouched in front of her. "Karla?"

Callie turned. "Karla, you're white as a sheet. What's wrong?"

"I'm going on a date...with someone who isn't Mitch." She looked up through a haze of tears and shook her head. "I don't think I can go through with this."

Callie sat down and took Karla's hand in hers. "Take a couple of slow deep breaths for me." She waited while Karla did as she instructed.

"Now you were fine thirty seconds ago. What changed?"

Karla looked into the eyes of her oldest friend. "I'm terrified." The bed dipped on her other side as Kate took a seat, but Karla kept her eyes locked on Callie's blue ones.

"Terrified of what?" Callie asked.

Karla shook free of Callie's hand and rose to pace next to the bed. "Oh, you name it. Of liking this man, of not liking him. Of developing feelings for him and him not liking me, or the other way around. Of saying or doing the wrong thing. Of betraying Mitch's memory and love." She twisted her fingers together and rolled her eyes to the ceiling. "Of being the foolish, needy old woman Bridgett seems to think I'm turning into."

Kate held up a hand. "Bridgett said that to you?"

Karla wrung her hands at her waist and watched Callie and Kate exchange a look. Callie patted the empty mattress between them.

"Come sit." Once she did Callie continued. "First of

all, there is nothing you could do or say to betray a single minute of what you and Mitch shared. Admitting that you're lonely isn't disloyal to Mitch, it's a testimony to the wonderful relationship that you had with each other. If you hadn't been happy, you wouldn't miss him so much." Callie's expression turned thoughtful. "What are your expectations for this evening?"

Karla chewed her lip as she tried to sort through the hodgepodge of feelings and nerves running rampant through her belly. "All I want is a nice meal with a new friend. Ian and I are in the same place. We can relate to each other. Beyond that...I don't know if there is a beyond that." She stopped and placed a hand on her stomach as butterflies strapped on clogging shoes and danced an Irish Jig on top of her lunch. "But I can tell you this. God's been pretty insistent over the last few days that I need a change in direction. I don't know what I want out of tonight, but I do want what God wants me to have."

Callie reclaimed one of Karla's hands and reached toward Kate. "That's the best thing you could want, so let's start there." The three women bowed their heads over their joined hands.

"Father," Callie began, "thank You so much for the wonderful day we've had together as friends and sisters. Lord, we're coming to You for a special favor this evening. Karla is Your daughter, and she sincerely wants Your will for her future. Calm her nerves and heart and be a light to her path. Strip the worry away. Allow her to relax and enjoy her time with Ian tonight while she rests in the knowledge that You hold her future in Your hands." Callie squeezed Karla's hand. "Amen."

"Amen," Kate said. "And just so you know, worrying about the rest of the things you mentioned doesn't make you foolish or old. It makes you human and female."

Callie chuckled. "Not just female. I'd bet money that Ian McAlister is spending some time fretting over the exact same things. It goes with the territory."

Karla sat a little straighter. "Do you think?"

~ * ~

Rachel covered her eyes. "Oh, Dad, you're killing me."

Ian looked down at the black suit and white shirt that had served him well throughout the years. "What?"

Hillie shook her head. "You look like a preacher."

"Or a mortician," Rachel added. "Is black the only color suit you have?"

"I have charcoal gray."

"Oh, goody...light black." Rachel's head-shake matched her sister's.

Ian squirmed under the studious eyes of his daughters. He didn't like what he saw brewing between them.

Hillie made a motion with her hands. "Just wait right there. I've got to run out to the car."

Ian looked at his watch. "Girls, I have to pick Karla up in thirty minutes. The black is fine."

"No," Rachel said. "It isn't. Do you have a pair of nice khakis?"

"Yes."

"Go put them on and change into the pale blue shirt I gave you for your birthday."

"But—"

Rachel shooed him out of the room. "Just go. Hillie will be back in a minute with the final two things you need."

Ian retreated to his room. *I'm nothing but a big dress up doll to them tonight.* His shoulders hunched as Rachel's voice followed him out of the room.

"And get that red and navy striped tie that came with the shirt."

He opened his closet and shoved hangers aside until he found the tan khakis and the specified shirt. He tossed them on the bed. His daughters' would be the death of him this evening. *I should never have told them about my plans ahead of time.* He stripped off the suit and hung it back in the garment bag emblazoned with the name of a local men's shop, his movements accented with mumbled objections. "I paid a lot of money for this suit. It should be adequate for any situation." He yanked the zipper up. "But no, these girls think they have all the answers. Young scallywags!"

Giggles filtered through the closed bedroom door. "You do know that we can hear you, right?" The door opened a fraction and a hand holding a navy blue jacket filled the gap. "Put this on before you come out."

Ian accepted the offering without a word, tugged it on, and returned to the living room. The flash of a camera blinded him for just a second.

"What...?"

"Pictures, Dad. We need lots of pictures."

"Oh, good grief."

Hillie laughed as she stepped forward to straighten his lapel. "Remember all those prom pictures you took of us over the years?"

"Prom?" Ian sputtered. "That was more than twenty years ago."

"Paybacks bite, don't they?" She stepped back and studied him with a critical eye. "Perfect. Thank goodness you and Michael are the same size."

Ian considered his attire in the reflection from the large mirror hanging over the mantle. On a scale of one to ten he'd give it a seven. He twisted to get a better look. "You don't think it's too casual?"

Rachel moved forward to smooth a stray tuft of hair. "Dad, it's Saturday night at a high end family restaurant. Trust us on this. You look exactly right. Now, you better get going. You have fifteen minutes to get across town."

"But don't forget these." Hillie thrust a bundle of multicolored flowers into his hands.

Ian clutched the green paper wrapped around the stems. "For me? You shouldn't have."

"Cute, Dad. They're for Karla."

"Hillie, they're beautiful, but—"

Hillie stepped back. "Do you want to impress this woman or not?"

Ian drew himself up. "Young lady, I'll have you know, I was impressing women before you were born. How do you think you got here?"

His daughters' giggled and pushed him towards the front door, flowers and all. Ian started down the walk to the driveway. He opened the car door and took a single look back. His girls stood in the door, cheesy grins on their faces, arms wrapped around each other's waists. They waved at him.

"Have fun."

He ducked into the car. Heaven help him, it did

remind him of the prom.

The heat and humidity of the domed botanical garden provided a welcomed change from the chill of the late October night. The air was heavy with moisture and the fragrance of exotic flowers. A brook babbled down the center of the attraction and sported an occasional duck or frog. Flashes of colorful wings broke the green as butterflies and birds hopped or fluttered from branch to branch.

Karla climbed the half dozen steps to the platform that overlooked a small waterfall. She leaned on the railing and smiled when Ian did the same. "I can't believe you've lived in Garfield for as long as you have and you've never made this trip before now."

Ian shrugged. "I don't spend a lot of time in Oklahoma City. Alicia and I always enjoyed Tulsa, and since that's where Rachel and her family lived for a while, a trip east made more sense than west. And the two-hour drive gave us an excuse to make a day of it."

"You must be glad to have them living closer to home."

"Absolutely."

Ian leaned up on one elbow and tilted his head in Karla's direction. "So tell me about your family. I know your daughter Bridgett is home for a while. Is she your only child?"

Karla took a deep breath of the scented air before she responded. She turned towards him and the sight of his kind, rugged face, totally attentive on her, did funny things to her nerve endings. *I'm really having a very good time.*

"Karla?"

"Sorry, just...taking in the atmosphere. No, Bridgett is our second child. Our eldest, Nicolas, is a detective on Garfield's police force. Lucas lives in Wichita, Kansas, with his family. Andrew, the baby, lives the farthest away. He and his family live in Houston."

"Three boys and a girl?"

Karla nodded.

"You and Mitch were very blessed."

A lump of emotion formed in Karla's throat at the mention of Mitch's name. She forced it down and away. "We always thought so."

Ian frowned. "I'm sorry. I didn't mean to make you sad."

"You didn't. It's actually getting easier to talk my way through the grief. You understand where I'm coming from, and that makes a huge difference."

Ian straightened from the railing seemingly content to allow her comment to pass. "Where to next?"

"Oh, the path winds around for quite a while. Are you game?"

"Lovely company and new sights to see? Lead on." He went down the steps first and then offered a hand to help Karla descend. When she reached the bottom, he pulled her hand through the crook of his arm and covered it lightly with his.

The easy intimacy of the gesture sent heat flooding through Karla's limbs. Her knee jerk reaction was to pull away, but she tamed the embarrassment long enough to realize that she liked her hand right where it was.

CHAPTER TEN

Bridgett paced the living room as she dialed Jeff's phone for the twentieth time that evening. Her anger mounted with each unanswered ring. *My mother is out running around like a teenybopper, and my husband thinks he can just...* The call rolled to Jeff's voice mail. Frustration erupted. "Pick up the phone, you weasel! You have to talk to me sometime. I'm not going to be treated—"

"Bridgett."

She fumbled the phone at the sound of her husband's voice instead of the recording she'd been listening to for days. "Finally." She sank onto the couch and ran a shaky hand through her hair. "I was beginning to think you were going to ignore me forever. We have to talk this out, Jeff. You have to tell me—"

"Bridgett, you have to stop."

"Stop? Stop what? You walk out on twenty-three years of marriage without any sort of reasonable explanation, and I'm just supposed to wave as you leave? Not likely." She took a deep breath, prepared to delve into problems she hadn't known existed last week. "Now, let's—"

"I didn't take your call to discuss things that conversation can't fix. I answered because I need to let you know that I spoke with my lawyer yesterday—"

"Jeff." Bridgett's grip on the phone intensified, her hand shook in concert with her accelerated pulse. "Please—"

"I spent the day over at the house clearing out all of my personal belongings." Jeff's tone was all business.

"I don't understand any of this."

Jeff continued, undaunted by the pleading in her voice. "Our marriage is over, but it's not my intention to leave you without resources. I've made arrangements to pay off our mortgage and have the deed transferred into your name. Keep it or sell it, I don't really care which. I've also established an account that you can draw from to pay the utilities, taxes, and insurance for the next five years if you decide not to sell. The funds will be dispersed through my lawyer. You only need send him the bills once a month. I've done this in lieu of alimony. I wanted to give you ample time to decide on a plan for your future and secure a degree if that's what you wanted."

Bridgett stammered for words as her well-planned future crumbled at her feet. "Jeff, I still love you. We raised a family together. You have to tell me what's at the root of all this."

"We both know you won't be satisfied with what I have to say."

"Say it anyway."

A sigh echoed through the phone, and Bridgett could picture him pacing. One hand in the pocket of his pants, concentration lines on his face as he looked for words. She wasn't prepared for the ones he found.

"I've decided I want more out of life than what we have. Your dad's death showed me how short and unpredictable life can be. If I want more, I have to take it now." A second harsh breath crackled across the connection. "I'm sorry, Bridgett. There's nothing you can say to change my mind. Our marriage is over."

She heard weariness in her husband's voice. Weariness laced with the steel she'd always admired—until now.

"You should get the divorce papers early next week. Once I disconnect this call, the number will no longer be valid. If you have questions about the settlement, you need to address them to my lawyer."

"Jeff..."

"Goodbye, Bridgett."

The hollow silence from the phone told Bridgett that he was gone. *In more ways than one.* She stabbed the numbers in an effort to reconnect the call. Silence greeted the attempt, and a look at the screen showed "call failed." The phone slipped from her numb fingers and bounced on the carpet. She longed for that numbness to encompass her heart, but instead, she felt the pain as every crack widened into a soul deep abyss.

A deep breath failed to stem the pain or the tears. Bridgett crumpled onto the couch and curled into a tight ball. Jeff was right. His brief attempt at an explanation hadn't satisfied. Questions ripped from her throat as she wept aloud. "What did I do? What is he doing? How can he just tear our lives and our family apart? God, I..." She gulped back the words that were dangerously close to a prayer. God didn't care about her, past, present or future.

Time passed, and she stilled as the tears dried and her breathing evened out. *So it's over, just like that? I have to talk to the kids. I have to decide what comes next. I have to...*

She rolled over and looked up at the ceiling.

"Oh, Daddy, I wish you were here. You were always so wise and strong. I wish you could come back, just for an hour, just long enough to let me cuddle in your lap and hear you tell me that everything was going to be OK. Things just aren't the same..." She stopped as her voice cracked and two more fat tears rolled from her eyes. "Everything's falling apart without you here."

Car doors slammed in the drive and brought Bridgett upright. She swiped at her damp cheeks with her sleeves. She'd meant to be in bed long before Mom got home. She lowered her head into her hands. Of all the things she needed right now, watching her sixty-five-year-old mother moon around over some man wasn't one of them.

She rose to hurry up the stairs, but curiosity got the best of her. *I'd at least like to know what this creeper looks like.* She crossed to the small window next to the door and shifted the blinds just enough to get a view of the porch.

Bridgett watched her mother come up the walk on the arm of a tall, silver-haired man. He was taller than her mom by a good foot. *They look like Jack and the Giant.* Her focus narrowed to the spot where her mother's hand rested on the sleeve of Ian McAlister's jacket. The muscles between her shoulder blades tightened at the sight of the physical contact. *Just friends my big toe!* Her eyes remained riveted on that spot as they approached the porch. At the base of the steps, the creeper pulled his arm free and placed his hand on the small of her mom's back as they both ascended the four steps to the front door. *How can she allow him to put his hands on her? They just met.*

Bridgett shifted her position to keep them in view. She gasped when Ian angled her mother towards him and rested his boney, claw-like fingers on her shoulders. Their whispered conversation didn't make it through the door, no matter how she strained to hear, but the sound of sudden masculine laughter lit a fire under every nerve in her body. Horror mingled with disbelief as the creeper placed his hands on either side of her mom's face and leaned close. "Oh no, he doesn't dare!"

~ * ~

Karla smiled up into Ian's eyes. *I thought Mitch was tall. This man towers over me, but I don't feel the least bit intimidated.* "I want to thank you for a very pleasant evening."

"Entirely my pleasure. I need to get out of my cave more often, especially if I can have a beautiful woman on my arm." He tilted his head. "Has anyone ever told you that you have the most striking eyes? Even here under a dim porch light, they glow like emeralds." Laughter followed his words, echoing on the night air. "And that's just about the corniest thing I ever said to a woman. I'm sorely out of practice."

Karla beamed at the compliment. "Nonsense, it was a very sweet thing to say." Nerves churned Karla's stomach when Ian's hands cupped her face. *Is he going to kiss me? I'm so not ready for that. I may never be ready for that.* Karla closed her eyes as his face grew closer. *I don't... How do I...?* When Ian's lips brushed the spot between her brows instead of her lips, she relaxed. *He's such a gentleman.*

117

Something loosened inside her chest. *Is it possible for me to be more than Mitch's wife?* She mulled that question as she stood in Ian's loose embrace, his forehead, resting on the crown of her head. *Do I want to be?* She wasn't prepared for the sense of contentment she felt in his presence. She was equally unprepared for the storm that boiled out the front door.

"What in the name of all that's holy do you two think you're doing?" Bridgett's eyes were mere slits, her voice a rough snarl. "Get your hands off my mother!"

"Bridgett!" Karla took a shocked step back even as Ian's hands slipped back to her shoulders.

She ignored Karla and faced Ian. "Get. Your. Hands. Off. My. Mother." Bridgett's voice shook with suppressed anger. When Ian's hands dropped to his sides, Bridgett turned to Karla.

"Of all the... It's not enough for you to go traipsing around town with this...this...*person.* Are you actually going to pretend that it's OK to let him slobber on you while you stand on the porch of my father's house?" She waved a hand in the night air. "While God and the neighbors watch?" Bridgett crossed her arms. "Over my dead body." She held Karla's gaze but addressed Ian. "You need to leave."

Ian took Karla's hand. "Do you need me to stay?"

Bridgett glared daggers at him "She doesn't need anything from you, tonight or ever."

Karla lost the tenuous grip on her temper. "Bridgett, you need to shut up and go back in the house." She faced Ian, grateful for the dimly lit porch. If the heat radiating from her neck and face were any indication, she knew her complexion had gone an unattractive shade of red with a mixture of embarrassment and anger. "I'm so sorry our evening is ruined. I apologize, again, for the unmerited rudeness of my daughter."

Bridgett crossed her arms over her chest. "Don't you dare speak for me."

"Bridgett."

"Fine."

Bridgett pushed back through the door and slammed it behind her, leaving a stunned and speechless Karla rooted to the boards of the porch. Ian shuffled his feet. The noise jerked Karla back to the here and now. *Stop staring at the door like a dolt. He probably thinks you've gone off the deep end with your daughter.*

"Ian, I..." She searched beneath the humiliation, looking for adequate words, finally giving into a helpless shrug. "Beyond I'm sorry, I don't even know what to say."

He studied the porch, head down, clasped fingers bouncing against pursed lips. He met her gaze and instead of annoyance, she found compassion in the depths of his blue eyes. "You don't need to say anything, dear heart. She's grieving. We both know that can't be rushed or wished away."

Karla shook her head. "You're much too generous. She's a spoiled brat. A daddy's girl in every sense of the word. I understand that this year has been hard, but grief or not, her behavior toward you has been unconscionable. I won't stand for it."

Ian nodded. "You're her mother. You'd know best in this situation." He grinned. "I feel sorry for her, though. Running afoul of our mothers is never a good thing. I can remember more than one occasion where I came out on the losing end of that equation." He took her hand in his. "I had a splendid time this evening. I refuse to let a moment of unpleasantness define the whole. May I call you next week?"

"I'd like that a lot." This time it was she who raised a hand to his cheek, the scrape of whisker stubble against her palm a pleasant sensation. "You've a kind heart, Ian."

He captured her fingers in his and brushed her knuckles with a quick kiss. "You better get in there before she decides to come after us again. Promise you'll call me if you need to talk."

"I will."

Karla watched as he made his way to the car, raised his hand in her direction, and slid behind the wheel. She turned to the door, straightened to her full five feet, and drew in a sustaining breath. *Mitch, I wish you were here.* She shook the words off. It was time she learned to fight her own battles, and fight she would. But Ian's gentle words and attitude had managed to take the edge off her temper. Bridgett would get a lighter response to her insolence than she deserved.

She pushed open the door. Bridgett sat across the room, her posture rigid, arms crossed, one foot tapping the floor impatiently. Anger rolled of her like heat from hot asphalt. A tendril of that heat stretched across the room and wrapped around Karla's neck like a too tight scarf. It squeezed the calm right out of her.

She dropped her purse to the floor. "Would you like to tell me what that show of yours was all about?"

Bridgett lunged to her feet. "My show? You mean the one that followed yours? How dare you let that man grope you in public? Daddy would be so ashamed!"

The vindictiveness in her daughter's words

threatened to knock Karla back a step, but she stood her ground. She'd reached the point of dry anger. Mitch had nicknamed those times when she was too angry for tears *the Sahara wrath*. He'd learned it wasn't a good place to be. Bridgett was about to get her first lesson.

"Grope? He had his hands on my shoulders."

"He had his mouth on you."

"Bridgett, the man kissed my forehead."

"Whatever." She shook her head. "I'm ashamed of you right now. Daddy's only been gone a year, and I come home to find you chasing after some man you barely know. *We're just friends.*" She snorted. "I don't know where you two went tonight, but I hope no one we know saw you out acting like some lovestruck teenager."

Karla stared at her daughter too angry to speak.

"Look at yourself." Bridgett's eyes traveled from the top of her mother's silver hair, past the new dress, and stopped at the toes peeking out through the open end of her new shoes.

By the expression Karla read on her daughter's face the assessment wasn't flattering.

"New dress, new shoes, I don't believe I've ever seen you wear that shade of eye shadow before. If browns were good enough for Daddy, they should be just fine for the creeper." Her gaze went back to Karla's feet. "Hot pink, Mother, seriously? It's mortifying."

"I beg your pardon?"

Bridgett nodded. "When I was growing up, how many times did I hear you tell me to act my age? Allow me to give that advice right back to you. You're sixty-five-years-old. You need to act your age."

"Bridgett, when I told you to act your age, it was

generally because you were whining in the cereal aisle, or pouting over a pair of name-brand jeans."

"Exactly. I thought I wanted something that wasn't good for me, or something I didn't need. The same principle applies here. Regardless of what you might have talked yourself into, the last thing you need in your life right now is another man."

Karla leaned back against the door and crossed her arms. "Who are you to make that decision for me?"

"Mom, I know that tone. I know you're angry." Bridgett stopped to take a deep breath. She raised her hands and massaged her temples as she paced a few steps away. When she turned, Karla saw the struggle for calm on her face. "Look, I've handled this badly. I was rude, and I'm sorry, but I love you, and I'm concerned about you."

"Concerned?"

Bridgett nodded. "You're lonely. I get that, but I'm home now. You don't have to be cooped up here by yourself any longer, and you don't need to cozy up to some man for company. If you feel like you're ready to get out more, we can go anyplace you want. And hanging out with me won't ruin your reputation."

"My rep..." Karla shoved herself away from the door and took a step toward her daughter. She roped in her anger before she took the second step. "What does my reputation have to do with any of this?"

"Everything, Mom. You're a pillar in our little community. Everyone in Garfield knows they can depend on you for wisdom and stability. If you go chasing after this man, you'll ruin that. You need to ask yourself if he's worth it."

You willful, manipulative... The words flashed through

Karla's mind, and she bit her tongue before they had a chance to spill out of her mouth. *One, two, three, four...* She never made it to ten. Fury bubbled in her stomach like a live volcano. She had two choices. Strangle her own flesh and blood, or surrender the field of battle. Neither appealed, but she chose the lesser of the two evils.

"I'm going to bed."

"I think that's a good idea for both of us. Will you at least think about what I said?"

"Trust me, I'll give it due consideration." Karla climbed the stairs, muttering under her breath. "That girl, that girl, that girl." But somewhere between the first floor and the second, a small seed of doubt began to bloom in her heart. *Maybe I am just a foolish old woman.*

By the time she reached her bedroom, newborn self-confidence oozed out of her like air from a pin-pricked balloon.

Her hand brushed at the fabric of her new burgundy dress as she hung it in the closet. A closet empty of her husband's things. She stared at the bare racks and a tear streaked down her cheek. *What have I done?*

She crawled into bed, tugged the comforter to her chin, and stared at the picture of Mitch. She reached to pull it into her arms, the motion arrested by the echo of Bridgett's words. *Daddy would be so ashamed.* Her groan of pain filled the dark room. "Mitch, I never meant to dishonor you."

The space in her heart, so recently filled with happiness, emptied out. Grief and shame flooded in to fill the void. Her harsh whisper filled the dark room. "Mitch, I miss you so much. I'm so lost without you and so tired of being lost. I wish...I wish God would just take me." She swallowed back the words, rolled away from the picture she had no right to look at, and wished for morning.

CHAPTER ELEVEN

Sunshine poured through the windows on Sunday morning. The light and warmth lit up the room but failed to penetrate Karla's heart. She rolled from the bed, achy from a restless sleep, eyes swollen and gritty from the tears shed off and on through the night. Heart heavy and feet leaden, she trudged to the closet to find something to wear to church. Her hand caressed the new burgundy dress then moved to brush the bright fabric of the three other new outfits. *Burnt orange, pale green, and hot pink, to match her toes.* Her fingers lingered on the soft green sweater that topped her favorite new acquisition. The one she'd planned to wear this morning. Her chest ached as she reached beyond the new and selected an old but reliable black jacket and skirt. The jacket hung off her shoulders, and the elastic of the skirt had a safety pin cinching up the excess at her waist. She couldn't work up the energy to care. *Better a dowdy frump than a foolish old woman pretending to be something she's not.*

Callie would have a hissy fit later, but neither Callie nor the others could feel the renewed pain in her soul this morning. Bridgett was right. It was too soon. *A hundred years from now would be too soon.* And Karla was done trying to fit the square peg of her life into the round hole of her friend's expectations...or Ian's.

She dressed in silence, brushed her teeth, wrestled her hair into some semblance of order, and ignored the makeup caddy sitting on the counter. No need to primp. The only man she'd ever wanted to impress wasn't around anymore.

As ready to face the day as she was going to get, Karla moved out into the hall. She paused at Bridgett's door, hand raised to knock to get her daughter up for Sunday school. Karla's hand fell back to her side. The girl was an adult with her own transportation. She knew where Valley View was. She could get herself up and around, or not. Karla really didn't care either way. If Bridgett did show up for church this morning, Karla hoped her mood had improved, because Karla's heart couldn't take much more abuse. *She'll be fine now that you've caved to her way of thinking.* Karla brushed the thought aside. It wasn't about giving in it was about being who she was. It was about accepting the life she'd been given.

Daughter, you should wear the green. It's always been one of your best colors.

Karla rolled her eyes at the ceiling and shuffled down the stairs, her words mumbled under her breath. "So You care about dresses now? Where were You last night? Where were You twelve months ago?"

Her conscience pricked her, and she filed her sarcasm away along with her *almost* wish of the night before. She couldn't remember a time in her life when she hadn't believed in a God who knew best. She certainly had no plans of abandoning her faith now. But this last week had been a tidal wave of conflicting emotions. She was drowning in them and longed for direction.

"So, how about it, Father. Who's right? Bridgett, Ian, my friends?" Karla's shoulders drooped when no answer came. *That's helpful.* She dropped the little cup of prepackaged coffee into the brewer, pushed the button, and crossed to the refrigerator. She'd skip the Sunday morning fellowship. If she ate breakfast at home, she could duck the inevitable questions from her friends. If she were lucky, she could sneak out the side door of the auditorium when church was over and avoid a conversation with them all together.

Karla ripped the top from a container of yogurt. The strawberry concoction was bitter in her mouth, and she tossed the whole thing in the trash. One more day with no taste for food, she'd stick with coffee. *When was the last time I truly enjoyed a meal?* The answer was easier to find than she'd anticipated. *Last night with Ian.* "Yeah." She stirred creamer into her cup and watched the dark liquid consume the swirl of color. "And then I came home."

Karla leaned against the cabinet, overcome with a soul-numbing lethargy. A tear rolled down her cheek. "Father, I don't think I can do this. I'm so tired of not knowing what comes next. My friends think I've grieved long enough. My daughter thinks I've lost my mind. Ian...I don't know what Ian thinks, but I think I could like him a lot under different circumstances."

Habit drew her hand to the promise box. She plucked out a card, held it under the light, and read it aloud. "Psalms 27:13-14. I had fainted unless I had believed to see the goodness of the Lord in the land of the living. Wait on the Lord: be of good courage, and he shall strengthen thine heart: wait I say on the Lord."

"The land of the living?" The words slammed into her soul and stole her breath. Her almost wish of the previous night came back to haunt her. "Father, I know that you know our every thought, but—"

Wait to see My goodness, daughter, in the land of the living. Wait on Me.

She laid the card on the counter. Waiting wasn't her best thing, and it certainly wasn't the answer she was looking for, but... She picked it back up and read it again. There was a promise in there too, wasn't there?

Her phone buzzed with an incoming text. *Thinking about you this morning. Hope all is well. Lunch?*

The floor above Karla's head creaked, and she whipped the phone behind her back like a guilty toddler with chocolate covered fingers. She poured her coffee down the sink and rinsed her cup. Her friends weren't the only people Karla planned to avoid today. *What about Ian?* She looked at the phone screen, and her lips twitched up in a sad smile. Lunch with Ian sounded wonderful, but until she had things settled in her own mind... *Are You listening, God?* She'd avoid him as well.

Two hours later, Karla drew in a deep breath of relief as she rounded the block wall that lined the walkway between the parking lot and Valley View Church. Her late arrival meant she'd had to park in the far corner of the property, but if that's what it took to get through the morning without addressing questions she had no answers for, she was good with that.

She couldn't remember the last time she'd intentionally avoided her friends, but...Karla stopped in her tracks, her gaze riveted on her car. Five women dressed in their Sunday best lounged against her vehicle, all looking in her direction, all wearing expressions that told Karla her thoughts of a successful escape were premature.

Callie stood straight at Karla's approach. The breeze tugged at the flowing edge of the red, black, and white tunic that topped her friend's black slacks. "You really didn't think we'd let you just sneak out, did you?"

Karla swallowed back her frustration and closed the distance to her friends. "It was worth a shot."

Terri crossed her arms over her pregnant belly and hunched deeper into her sweater. "That depends on who you ask. It's the coldest day we've had so far, and you made two pregnant women chase you to your car for news."

Samantha chuckled as she dug in her purse. "Don't listen to her, Grams. Her blood sugar is probably a little wonky." She held out a package of peanut butter crackers. "Here you go, Mom. Eat these, you'll feel better."

"Thanks, Sam." Terri ripped open the snack while she eyed Karla from head to toe. Her frown deepened. "I thought you went shopping yesterday."

"Yeah," Pam chimed in. "We got the full report on yesterday's retail therapy session." She motioned to Karla's outfit. "What's up with the black?"

Karla smoothed the front of her jacket. "What's wrong with what I have on?" She motioned to Kate, also dressed in a black jacket and skirt. "I don't hear you ragging Kate about her clothes."

Kate cleared her throat. "I bought this yesterday, and it fits. The one you have on is at least ten years old and three sizes too big for you. What gives?" Kate swiped at her phone and held up a picture of Karla dressed to go out the previous evening. "Who are you, and what have you done with my mother-in-law?"

Karla ducked her head as the other women crowded around the phone to admire the picture. "That's a fairy tale. Cinderella going to the ball. We all have to come back to reality sometime."

Five pair of eyes snapped to her face.

Kate lowered the phone. "Oh, Karla, was it horrible?"

Callie slipped an arm around Karla's shoulders. "What happened? Ian always seemed like such a nice guy."

"He's great."

"Then why...?"

Karla shook her head. "I don't want to go into it, OK? Ian McAlister is one of the sweetest men I've ever met but...but..." Her words died as tears stung her eyes. She swallowed them back. "Just let it be, OK?"

Terri took a step forward and took Karla's hand in hers. "Karla, look at me."

She did, reluctantly.

"Do you remember when Steve and I were just starting to date...and fight? I was so upset and hesitant to share. You were the one who reminded me that we're sisters, not interested in gossip, but interested in loving and supporting each other. You were there for me. You guys helped me figure things out." Terri stopped long enough to dig a clean tissue from the pocket of her sweater. She pressed it into Karla's hand and waited for her to dab at her eyes. "Let us be there for you."

Karla looked from her friends to the congregation beginning to stream from the doors of Valley View. "Your husbands—"

Pam shook her head. "Our husbands will survive on their own for a few more minutes. But I do think we need to take this someplace more private, and warmer, than the parking lot."

"My classroom?" Callie suggested.

Nods of assent met her suggestion and Karla found herself surrounded by women bent over cell phones as text messages were sent to spouses. But more than that, she began to see the answer to the promise of strength that God had given to her over her cup of morning coffee.

~ * ~

Karla was the first through the door, claiming the seat at the back end of the table. The rest of the women filed into the room and followed suit. Callie closed the door and leaned against it, her arms crossed. She studied Karla with an intensity reserved for lifelong friends before she nodded and pushed away from the door.

"I think we should pray before we get started." She held out her hands, waiting as each one took the hand of the one next to them. When the circle was complete, she bowed her head. "Father, thank You for friendships that have stood the test of time. We need Your wisdom today to listen and advise. And Karla needs courage from You to share what's weighing on her heart this morning. Help us all find the direction we need in You."

Amens echoed and dwindled as Callie boosted herself up onto the corner of her desk. She crossed her ankles and looked at Karla with a no nonsense expression. "OK, Karla, spill it. If you had a great time with Ian last night, why do you look like death warmed over this morning?"

Karla mulled her answer, allowing her gaze to roam the room from one friend to the other. This group of women had never let her down. They wouldn't start now. She searched her heart for the most pressing question. No matter where she started, they wouldn't think her vain, silly, or petty.

She took a deep breath. "Do you guys think I'm a foolish old woman?"

"What?" The question came from Callie. The single word puzzled, and drawn out into three syllables.

"Karla, we'd never..." Pam swallowed, obviously looking for words.

"I have a better question." Kate leaned forward. "Who? Who put that idea in your head?"

Karla shook her head. "Who isn't nearly as important as honesty." Her hands twisted in nervousness under cover of the table. "I loved...love Mitch. I'd give anything if the last twelve months could vanish like they never happened, but they won't." She looked up. "I know you guys think I've mourned long enough. And I know what I said a week ago about my life being over. I meant it when I said it, but God has been whispering new things in my ears all week.

"I went out with Ian last night. He's the most gentle and attentive man I've ever spent time with." She focused on the table in front of her. "But—and I need you to be truthful, even if you think it might sting. Am I a foolish old woman to think that I can start over at this stage of my life? Am I completely off course in believing that God might be nudging me towards a second chance at happiness?" She closed her eyes, Bridgett's accusations ringing in her ears. "Am I ruining my reputation by being friends...and maybe more...with Ian?"

"Do what?" Terri's question came out as a confused squeak.

Karla ignored her pregnant friend and focused on Kate. "Am I betraying my children?" She turned to Callie, her oldest and dearest friend. "And tainting Mitch's memory by deciding that I've had enough loneliness?"

Kate smacked the table. "This has Bridgett's fingerprints all over it."

Karla offered no confirmation or denial. She sat back, her stomach churning, waiting for answers.

Callie shoved herself off the desk, crossed to the head of the table and leaned on it with both hands. "Ladies, our friend needs to hear the truth. Please feel free to stop me if I get off track."

She stared at Karla for a few seconds, and Karla could almost feel that gaze reaching into the depths of her heart.

"Karla, you're a beautiful, vibrant woman—body, soul, and spirit. We live in a world where sixty-five is not the end of life, but the prime of life. I know you hurt every day. We all know how much Mitch meant to you. And yes, we do think it's time for you to exchange your grieving for some joy, but more important than our opinion, if you feel like God is opening a door for you, you need to step through it."

"Amen," Kate added. "And Bridgett needs a thrashing or a tongue lashing. Once I talk with Nicolas, she's likely to get both."

"I didn't—"

Kate held up a hand. "You didn't need to."

Samantha had been a silent observer through the whole conversation. Now she leaned as close to the table as her pregnant belly would allow. She raised her eyebrows. "You like him?"

"More than I thought I could. I don't know if there's anything beyond *like* there. It's way too early to tell, but I'd like to explore the possibilities." She remembered the unanswered lunch invitation. "Shoot!"

She held up her phone in response to the puzzled looks and cocked heads. "He texted me this morning with a lunch invitation. I was so confused about things, I ignored it."

"Text him back right now." Callie demanded. "Better yet, call him."

Karla shook her head. "Callie, I can't. Look at me. I'm not dressed to go out. I barely touched my hair, and I didn't put on any makeup. I look just like what I felt like this morning. A used up old woman."

Callie shook her head. "You text him back and tell him that you would love to have lunch. Ask him to pick you up out front in thirty minutes." She motioned to the door. "Pam, lock that." She whipped the red, black and white shirt over her head and tossed it to Karla. "Trade me tops. Your skirt will look fine with this. Ladies dig out those cosmetic bags, and let's see what we have to work with. We have an emergency makeover to perform."

CHAPTER TWELVE

Bridgett heard footsteps pounding up the steps of the porch seconds before the door to her mother's house flew open.

"Bridgett."

Her book fell to the floor as one hand covered her chest. "Nicolas, you scared me to death!"

"Get in the car."

"What?"

Nicolas put his fisted hands on his hips. "My car, right now. We need to talk, and I don't want to be in the middle of this when Mom comes home from her lunch with Ian."

Bridgett lunged from the chair, her pulse pounding in her ears. "She what? Repeat what you just said."

The expression on Nicolas's face reminded her of the time he'd caught her kissing Robert James behind the church gym just days after Robert beat him out as pitcher of the Garfield High baseball team. Way too much big brother testosterone and righteous indignation for Bridgett to come out on the winning side.

"I said, Mom is having lunch with Ian, and I need to have a conversation with you. Now move your skinny, meddling little butt out to my car, or I will throw you over my shoulder and carry you down the walk."

"You wouldn't—"

"Your choice in three seconds. One...two..."

She held out a hand as he took another step in her direction. "OK, you big bully, good grief. Will you at least give me time to get my shoes and a jacket?"

"Get a move on. You won't like it if I have to hunt you down."

"You don't scare me."

His expression hardened.

Bridgett fled the room, muttering with each step. "Pushy, overbearing jerk. I'm not fifteen anymore,"

"I can hear you."

"I wasn't trying to keep it a secret." She stomped up the stairs, pushed through to her room, and grabbed her sweater from the foot of the bed. *Mom must have gone crying to Nicolas at church this morning.* She slid her feet into loafers. And wasn't that just the perfect addition to the stress overflowing her life right now? Her husband off doing God knew what, her son intentionally putting himself in harm's way in the service, her brother ready to strangle her, and despite her heartfelt warnings to the contrary, her mother off mooning around after some man. A tiny voice of reason eked up from somewhere. *You need to stop transferring your problems onto your mom's plate. She taught you better.*

"Bridgett!"

"I'm coming!" Her hollered answer drowned out the stray thread of logic. She slammed from the room like the fifteen-year-old she claimed not to be and hurried down the stairs. "All right, already."

Nicolas pointed in the direction of the front yard, and Bridgett headed to his car without another word.

She yanked the seat belt into place and shoved the lock into the buckle. Once her brother was settled behind the wheel, she broke the silence. "Where are we going?"

Nicolas's mouth was a grim, hard line. "Someplace public so I can't act on the impulse to wring your neck." He gunned the engine of the red Camaro and left rubber streaks on the pavement and tire smoke in the air.

Bridgett sat back and crossed her arms. "I hope you get a ticket."

He glanced at her from the corner of his eye. "You just need to be quiet until we get where we're going."

Bridgett huffed and angled her back to her big brother. She watched Garfield's scenery pass by her window. So little had changed in the little community since she'd moved away, but so much was different. The bookstore caught her eye, and she remembered Tara's suggestion that she visit. Maybe she needed to come exploring in the next day or two. She glanced at her brother when he slowed to pull into the Sonic parking lot. "May I speak now?" Sarcasm dripped from her words.

Nicolas maneuvered the car into a stall and cut the engine. He twisted in his seat until he faced her. "Only if you can tell me what the heck you were you thinking last night?"

"Nicolas, I don't know what Mom said to you—"

"Mom didn't say anything to me, and before it comes out of your mouth, she didn't blab to Kate either. She did, however come sneaking in to church this morning, almost late and looking worse than she did the morning after Dad died. It didn't take a degree in criminal investigation to know something was up.

After our talk the other day, and knowing that she went to dinner with Ian McAlister last night, a five-year-old could have put two and two together." He stopped to scrub a hand across his face. "Didn't you hear anything I said over lunch?"

"I heard every word. You weren't there last night, I was. That man was all over our mother, and she wasn't trying to stop him."

Nicolas shook his head. "Sis, I know that you have some issues in your own life right now—"

"You don't know nearly as much as you'd like to think." *You'll get divorce papers in the mail next week.*

"What does that mean?"

"Like you even care, just forget it."

"Fine, if you don't want to talk to me, I can't force you to, but where Mom is concerned, you are seriously out of line. Our mother is beginning to show signs of life after a year of grief. If dating King Kong makes her happy right now, I'll buy stock in bananas to keep him around." Nicolas looked at her with disbelief. "And seriously. I know and trust Mom. I doubt that any contact between her and her new friend could be even vaguely classified as improper."

Bridgett met his gaze head on. "If you aren't interested in my side of the story, why did you drag me out of the house?"

"I brought you here to try and talk some sense into you. In the absence of sense, at least have a little compassion. Dad is gone. That's a sad reality, and none of us likes it, but clipping mom's wings isn't going to bring him back. I can't tell you how to mourn any more than you can tell Mom how to. But you need to take a giant step back and let her find some happiness. If you can't take that advice, then feel free to take yourself back to Texas. You have problems of your own to work on. I'll take care of Mom."

Bridgett sputtered. "How... You can't tell me how to live my life."

"No?"

"No!"

Her brother's smile was victorious. "Then stop trying to tell Mom how to live hers."

~ * ~

Ian tossed greens and tomatoes in a bowl while Karla circled the kitchen for the third time. He watched her from beneath lowered eyelids. Her black pumps clicked on the tile floor and the red and black top she wore floated attractively around her with every step she took. He kept that to himself. She already seemed as nervous as a worm in a bass boat. He had no doubt the knowledge that he found her captivating would send her running for the door.

"Are you sure there's nothing I can do to help?"

He shook his head. "Steaks are on the grill, potatoes are in the microwave." He met her gaze. "Is relaxing on the list of things you'd be willing to do?"

She paused on the opposite side of the kitchen island, snagged a grape sized tomato from the grocery carton, and popped it in her mouth.

Ian ducked his head to hide a grin. Alicia used to do the same thing when they cooked together. The memory flooded him with contradicting emotions. *Alicia, I've brought a new woman into your favorite space. I wonder how you'd feel about that?*

You have my blessing to love again.

Karla answered him before he had time to dwell on the sadness of the remembered words.

"I'm just a little uncomfortable with a man doing the cooking, I guess. That was not Mitch's forte, even grilling." She laughed.

The sound simply lifted his heart.

"He could put on a grand show if there were other guys around," Karla continued, "but I took care of it most times. Besides that, if I'd known your lunch invitation meant so much trouble for you, I wouldn't have accepted."

"It's not a lick of trouble, and eating in wasn't my first intention, but I thought about last night on my way to pick you up. I hoped you might be more comfortable with something less public."

"Ian, I'm so sorry—"

"Let's not go there, my dear. I only wanted you to know what drove my decision." He dipped into the carton and offered her another tomato. "Besides, I got used to helping Alicia in the kitchen...I found I liked it." He glanced at the clock. "I'll be right back." He grabbed a set of tongs and a plate and stepped out onto the back patio to retrieve their steaks. When he came back in he saw that Karla had found the silverware and was busy setting the table.

"We're a pair, aren't we?" she asked.

The microwave dinged, and Ian turned to remove two large potatoes. He placed them on plates before looking up. "How so?"

"You've gone to all this effort, and all we can talk about are Mitch and Alicia." She finished with the table and came back to the counter. "It's strange and comforting at the same time."

"I think that's as it should be. They were a part of our lives for too long to be ignored, and the more we share about them, the more we'll share about ourselves." He reached across the counter and captured her fingers. "I want to know about your life, Karla. The good and the sad. Don't ever hold back a memory on my account."

Karla squeezed his fingers. "That's—" She jumped and stumbled back a step or two. "Oh, my gracious. What in the world?"

Ian came around to her side of the island and laughed at the site of Polly weaving figure eights between Karla's ankles.

"Sorry, I should have warned you that I share the house with a nosey feline."

"That's OK, she... She?"

Ian nodded.

"She just startled me." Karla stooped down and scooped up the ball of white fur and brought her nose to nose. "Aren't you a pretty baby?" She cradled the kitten in her arms and hitched herself up onto one of the tall stools that sat under the bar.

Ian's brows came up as the air filled with the noisy rumble of the cat's purring.

Karla must have caught his expression. She edged back from the bar. "I'm sorry, I should have asked before I plopped her down here while you were cooking."

"What...? No, you're fine. I brush her every day, so her shedding is minimal. I'm just a little surprised. She's normally very aloof with strangers. She won't even come out of my room when the girls are here." He stopped and took in the contented combination of woman and cat. "Do you have a fur baby?"

Karla continued to stroke the cat as she shook her head. "No, we had several dogs while the kids were growing up. The last one passed seven or eight years ago. Mitch and I talked about adopting a small breed once or twice, but we were still working full-time jobs, we couldn't justify getting a new puppy and leaving it penned up all day." She grinned when the kitten turned to paw at her fingers. "He was allergic to cats, so that was never an option." Her hand stilled on the vibrating animal, and she closed her eyes. "This is very relaxing. I bet the two of you aren't the least bit spoiled."

"Not at all spoiled." Ian washed his hands, sliced open a yellow bell pepper, and scooped out the seeds. "Polly never lets me forget who's boss."

"What an unusual name for a cat. How did you come up with that?"

Ian nodded toward the kitten as he diced the pepper. "With that black patch over one eye, pirate names were the first thing that came to mind. Blackbeard and Captain Kid didn't quite fit."

"So you named the poor baby after a cracker-greedy bird."

Ian chuckled. *Does she have any idea how much I've missed meal time banter?* He carried the salad to the table. "I suppose you could have done better?"

~ * ~

Karla regarded him with a smug grin. "There were women pirates, you know. Anne Bonny, Mary Reed, Grace O'Malley, Rachel Wall." She lifted the sleepy kitten from her lap and stared into the furry face, taking in the black patch. *Pirate indeed.* "She looks like a Mary Grace to me."

"I'm impressed. History buff?"

"Not so much. One of the granddaughters wanted to be a pirate for Halloween a few years back. Since the most popular are men, we had the same issue finding a name. We went looking for costume ideas online, and some of the names stuck."

Their lunch looked complete. Karla set the kitten on the floor and patted her behind to send her on her way. She loved the way the top she'd borrowed from Callie billowed and flowed with her every move. It looked so graceful and made her feel more feminine than she'd thought possible. *Maybe if I stick it in my closet, Callie will forget I have it.* "Not likely."

"Excuse me?"

"Oh nothing...just thinking out loud."

She moved to the sink to wash her hands. When she turned, Ian stood behind a chair, ready to assist her, the perfect gentlemen. Karla crossed the room and took the seat he offered. "Thank you."

"My pleasure." He scooted into the chair across from her and held out a hand.

Karla laid her fingers in his and bowed her head as he blessed the food. She looked up to find his eyes locked on her with an intensity that stole her breath. She looked back down, lifted her napkin, and spread it in her lap, all in a bid for an extra calming breath or two...or five. She picked up her fork and met his gaze, hoping that he didn't notice the tremor in her hand. "Dinner looks amazing."

"You surpass anything on the table. I've been

admiring that lovely blouse all day. You're beautiful in red. Did you get that on your shopping trip yesterday?"

Grateful for something to talk about that wouldn't stain her cheeks or accelerate her heart rate, Karla grinned. "Do you like it? I was just wishing that I could figure out a way to keep it."

He tilted his head, fork midway between his plate and his mouth. "Did you steal it?"

On solid ground at last, Karla shook her head. Dinner was filled with laughter as she shared the story of friendships, impromptu makeovers, and borrowed clothes. The memories had tears of mirth streaming from her eyes as she laid her fork aside. "I had one woman standing over me with a fold up brush that wouldn't stay open, another circling the room minus her shirt, two arguing over makeup choices, and one prowling through Callie's desk looking for a snack."

"And they did all of that just so we could have some time together?"

Karla nodded.

"I'll have to thank them. I know Callie from the doctor's office, but I'd like to meet the rest of them."

She stood and took her plate to the sink. "I'm sure you will if you hang around me for very long." *The Fall Festival.* Karla tilted her head and considered the annual family event that was coming up in just three days. Not a service, but plenty of food, lots of noise, and a perfect opportunity to introduce her new friend to her old friends in a casual environment. She glanced back at the table where Ian was gathering up the dinner items that needed to be returned to the refrigerator. *Am I ready to take that step?* How would it feel to take a new man amongst Mitch's friends? A part of her heart quaked at the thought, but other part admitted that the idea had a certain amount of appeal. "I have an idea if you're interested."

The steak sauce clattered into an empty space in the door shelf. Ian straightened. "Does your idea involve spending more time in the company of the lovely Karla Black?"

His comment accelerated her heart rate and forced her to take a breath before she could answer. Composure restored, she plunged ahead. "Our yearly Fall Family Fun Festival is this week. If you don't have any plans for Wednesday night, you could come with me."

Ian's expression turned mischievous. "Are you asking me out?"

Heat inched its way up her neck. "Maybe." *Where did that come from? I don't flirt.* Karla turned back to the sink, twisted the water on, and rinsed her plate. *What's gotten in to me?*

Ian joined her at the sink, deposited his own plate, and turned Karla to face him. "I'm sorry. I didn't mean to embarrass you."

Karla looked up and away. The intensity in his stare was un-nerving, turning the normal blue of his eyes two shades darker. Karla swallowed hard as he placed his hands on either side of her face.

"I'd love to attend the festival with you and meet your friends. They have my undying gratitude for talking you in to returning my call this morning."

"They...um...they'd enjoy meeting you too. They think our friendship is a very good thing."

His eyes bored into hers. "I don't want to scare you away, Karla, but I'm hoping that God has much more than friendship planned for our future."

He leaned forward, and Karla's stomach took a nosedive to her toes. *He's going to...* When his lips touched hers, her knees turned to mush. Her heart and mind clashed in battle, one urging her to push him away, the other willing her to draw him closer.

Ian must have sensed the internal skirmish, because he wrapped his arms around her and bound her in a firm, gentle embrace. Enduring Ian's kiss melted into enjoyment, the desire to flee transitioned into a longing to be held, just like this, forever. *He isn't Mitch, but that's OK. I need him to be different. He's taller, his cologne is woodsy instead of leather, he tilts his head in the opposite direction.*

How long is a kiss?

How long is a thought?

Karla lost track of both. But somewhere between the first touch of his lips and the moment he lifted his head, her heart broke free of the grief of the last twelve months and simply soared.

Ian lifted his head and stroked her cheeks with his thumbs. "That wasn't so bad, was it? Now let's get you back to your car."

CHAPTER THIRTEEN

Karla popped her breakfast into the toaster, shoved the lever down and, and inhaled as the scent of warm bread and Asiago cheese filled the kitchen. The rumble from her stomach took her by surprise. She was actually hungry, so eating would be a joy this morning, not just necessary fueling. *But not too much.* The toaster popped up. She laid the delicately browned bagel on a plate and studied the back of the cream cheese container. She measured out half of the recommended serving and divided it between the two halves of the bagel. With all of her heart, she would have chosen a different way to lose fifty pounds, but now that it was gone, she didn't intend to invite it back.

She sat at the table, content in her own skin for the first time in months. *It feels so good to be me again.* An incoming call sent her phone dancing across the wooden table. Karla snatched it up and looked at the display, mildly disappointed that it wasn't Ian but happy to take the call.

"Good morning, Dave."

The youth pastor's habitual good humor reverberated in his response. "Good morning to you. No need to ask if I woke you today. You sound very chipper."

"I'm feeling pretty chipper this morning. What can I do for you?"

"Well, I missed talking with you yesterday about my lunch idea and—"

"Yes." Karla waited when her single word answer produced several seconds of silence on the other end of the connection. She could picture Dave Sisko rubbing a hand through his sandy blond hair.

"Yes..."

"Yes, I want to help with your lunch program. It's time I crawled back into the light and I can't think of a better way to get back in the groove than working with the youth."

"Groove?" Sisko laughed. "Well, if the kids don't do anything else for you, they will update your vocabulary. Seriously though...I'm so glad that you're willing to help. Like I said last week, I've got some details to work out, but having you on board clears a big hurdle. I promise we won't take more than five or six hours out of your week."

"Whatever you need, Dave, I'm here for you and looking forward to it. Let me know once you get it all ironed out, and we'll see where it goes from there."

"Well, OK. I'll get back with you later in the week. Thanks and have a great day."

"Planning on it. Talk to you later."

"What are you planning?"

Karla disconnected the call and looked over her shoulder to see a dressed but drowsy looking Bridgett standing in the kitchen doorway. "Good morning." She held up the phone. "Dave Sisko has a new project he's working on. He asked for my help, and I just accepted."

Bridgett nodded. "Oh, won't that be fun?" She shuffled into the kitchen wearing blue jeans, a sweatshirt, and socks. "Is that where you're headed?"

"What?"

"You're up, you're dressed, and your hair and makeup are done. It's only"—she looked at the clock— "nine. Are you meeting Sisko?"

Karla sipped her coffee. "Not today. I just got tired of shlumping around the house like a slob. It's past time for me to rejoin life. I think Sisko's plan will help me do that."

"That and Ian McAlister."

"Bridgett—"

Her daughter held up a hand. "I'm really not trying to start anything. I've expressed my opinion, you've chosen to ignore it. You're a grown woman."

Karla motioned to a chair. "Can you sit down for a few minutes and have a talk without temper? I think it would do us good to clear the air on a few things."

Bridgett's sigh filled the room, but she pulled out a chair and sank into it. She eyed Karla's breakfast. "Any more of those?"

"Last one." Karla plucked a napkin from the holder in the center of the table, laid half the bagel on it, and slid it across the table. "But, I'll share."

"Thanks." Bridgett picked at the crispy edges with downcast eyes. "I'm sorry about Saturday night. I'm not taking back anything I said, but I was harsher than I needed to be. I was upset. Jeff finally answered one of my calls—"

"Oh, sweetheart." Karla laid a hand on her daughter's arm. "That's wonderful. I'm so glad you finally had a conversation. Were you able to get anything resolved?"

"Depends on your definition of resolved. It wasn't much of a conversation." She gave Karla the highlights. "He still maintains that our marriage is over." Bridgett closed her eyes, and two fat tears spilled from the corners. "He told me to expect divorce papers in the mail sometime this week."

"Oh, baby..." Karla stood, circled the table, and gathered her daughter into her arms. "I'm so sorry."

Bridgett clung to her mother like a panicked three-year-old. "Mama, why is he doing this? If I could just understand why. I thought we were solid. I thought we were looking forward to the same things."

Karla rubbed her back. "Let it out, sweetheart." *Jesus, give me wisdom for my baby. She's so hurt.* When Bridgett's sobs subsided, Karla pushed her back into her chair and scooted closer. She took both of Bridgett's hands in her own. "Baby, look at me."

Bridgett raised her tear-reddened eyes and met Karla's gaze. "Are you talking to God about any of this?"

Her daughter lowered her head and focused on her hands.

Karla tugged and waited for Bridgett to look back up. "What sort of response is that? Your father and I taught each of you kids that prayer is the most important resource you could ever have in this life. God will have answers for you if you'll ask. He can make a difference in Jeff's heart where you can't."

Bridgett's blue eyes turned to frost. "Yeah, well, let's see. God snapped my father out of my life, my husband's been a stranger for most of the last twelve months, and despite my prayers for a change of heart,

David chose the Marines over college. Now, my husband wants a divorce because life's too short to spend the rest of it with me. I'd say any prayers I'm praying at this point aren't making it much past the roof."

Karla sat back. "You know better than that." She studied her daughter. "Sweetheart, take my life as an example. I've been a wreck since your father's death. I've had my own bouts with unbelief. I know you don't approve of my friendship with Ian, but God has gradually begun to show me that he has a second chance for me. My life did not end the night of the accident." She reached up and tucked a strand of hair behind Bridgett's ear. "The one thing God won't do is change our will. If Jeff continues down this path and forces a divorce on you, that doesn't mean your life has to be over. If you'll ask, I know God will show you a new path. He never runs out of chances."

Bridgett pulled away, shoved her chair back, and lunged to her feet. "You don't get it, do you? I don't want a second chance or a new path. The original version of my life was more than good enough."

"Bridgett—"

"No!" She slapped both hands on the table and leaned into her mother's space. "I want my life back the way it's supposed to be." Her eyes flooded with tears, and her voice broke. "Before God and Jeff decided to screw it up." Her hand raised in a gesture of surrender. "I guess that's too much to ask."

Mother and daughter stared at each other in silence for a few seconds. Karla searched her heart for something to say. Some word of wisdom or encouragement. The doorbell rang before she came up

151

with anything.

Bridgett shook her head. "Stumps you too, huh?" The bell rang a second time. She motioned for her mother to remain seated. "I'll get it."

~ * ~

Bridgett left her mother at the table, mumbling under her breath as she made her way to the door. "She thinks God has the answer to all life's problems. Well, I've never heard of Him bringing someone back to life a year after the fact." She glanced up. *That's the only way to fix this. That and bringing Jeff to his senses.* Something neglected tugged at her heart and urged words heavenward. "Please bring Jeff..." The half formed prayer died on her lips when she swung the door open to find the postman on the steps.

"I have a registered letter for Bridgett Morris."

His words sucked the air out of her lungs. Her hand gripped the edge of the door, and her gaze locked on to the manila envelope in the man's hands. *You should get the divorce papers sometime next week.* She tried to force words past her constricted throat and failed. Instead, she pried her hand from the door and held it out, dismayed at the way it shook.

"Are you Bridgett Morris?"

She nodded. "Yeah...I..." She cleared her throat. "I mean, yes, I'm Bridgett Morris."

He allowed her to take the envelope and offered a clipboard as well. "Sign here, please."

Bridgett scribbled her name, nodded in response to his "Have a good day," and closed the door. She turned to lean back against it, her eyes drawn to the return address. Mason, Byers, and Anderson, Attorneys at Law. She swallowed. *I should open it.* "I don't think I can."

"What?"

Bridgett looked up to find her mother standing in the entry.

"Who was at the door?"

Bridgett focused on the envelope a second time, hard pressed to single out the predominate emotion among the anger, failure, and despair warring in her heart. Despair finally crippled her. Back against the door, she slid to a seat on the floor and held the envelope out to her mother. "I don't think I thought he was really serious."

She surrendered the paperwork to her mother and crumpled into a ball as her life hit rock bottom. "I don't understand."

Strong arms wrapped Bridgett in the comfort of childhood and rocked. There were no words on either side for several weepy moments. Mom finally broke the embrace and leaned back, she rubbed Bridgett's arms up and down.

"Tell me what I can do for you."

"Explain to me how this could happen?" Bridgett stared at her mother through a veil of tears. "If I could understand, maybe I could move on, but this last year, the last two weeks...how could He do this to me?"

"Sweetheart, I can't explain Jeff's ac—"

"Not Jeff, God." Bridgett pulled away and crawled to her feet, weary beyond her forty-three years. She offered a hand to her mother and waited until the older woman gained her feet. "You taught me my whole life that God loved us, that God wanted the best for us, that trusting God with our lives was the best way we could live." Her restless feet carried her around the room. "For as long as I can remember I prayed for you and Daddy every day, for health and safety. He snatched Daddy away without even giving me a chance to say goodbye. Six months ago, when David first started making noise about joining the Marines after he graduated, I begged for God to change his mind. I wanted my baby boy safe in school, not facing down terrorists in countries I can't even find on a map." She faced her mother with her hands on her hips. "And where is David? In a Marine boot camp. Why? Because he says that's where he feels God wants him to be." She swiped at her tears.

"And now, as if I needed any icing on my cake of despair, after being a Christian my whole life..." Her words trailed off as an ugly truth tugged at her heart. She hadn't cracked the cover of her Bible in months. Her church attendance had gone by the wayside in the face of Jeff's busy schedule, and prayer? Did "why did you steal my father" and "please change David's mind" really count? She brushed the momentary self-doubt aside. *What difference does it make anyway?* "My husband suddenly decides he wants a divorce, and I have squat to say in the matter." She glared at her mother. "Sorry, but I'm not feeling the love."

"Bridgett, I also tried to teach you that serving God doesn't mean we get everything we ask for. He's God, not a fairy godmother or a genie in a bottle. Christians aren't immune to problems, but they have divine help and guidance as they work through them." She stopped, and Bridgett could almost see her organizing words in her mind. "I can't answer your questions about Jeff. As far as David is concerned, mothers worry. It's what we're hardwired to do, but you should be proud of him. Both of his choice and his calling."

She frowned when her mom's mouth quivered slightly. "I'd give anything to have your father back with us, but that's not possible. The best I...we...can do is go to him when the time comes. Don't let these things steal your faith."

Bridgett took a deep breath. *Too late.* She shook her head. "Mom, you can sugarcoat my circumstances in all the platitudes you want, the truth remains the truth. I've been jilted, in more ways than one." She picked up the discarded envelope, broke the seal, and slipped her wedding rings inside.

"What are you doing?"

"Accepting the inevitable." She tossed everything on the sofa, slipped her feet into the tennis shoes resting on the rug by the front door, and dug her keys out of her pocket. "I'll be back after a while. I need some air."

~ * ~

Karla sat in silence as Bridgett left the house. Her heart ached for her child and the soul-deep bruises that couldn't be made better with mommy kisses. She lifted her eyes and took her own advice. "Father, show her the way through this valley. I don't know what you're trying to teach her, but she can't learn anything with her heart so full of pain and bitterness. Please lift her up."

She picked up her Bible, but she was too restless to read. Maybe Bridgett had the right idea. Getting out from between these four walls seemed like a great idea.

The phone beckoned. Maybe Ian...

The thought dwindled. She liked Ian, but running to him with her problems certainly didn't feel right, they barely knew each other. She raised her hands to her lips and remembered yesterday's kiss. Well, maybe more than barely, but...

You're all dressed up. Seems a shame to waste it.

Karla looked up. Dating advice from her Heavenly Father? She'd never known God to meddle in her life quite as forcefully as He had this past week. She shook her head. *I probably shouldn't assign God's voice to my own wishful thinking.*

Stubborn children. Where one won't listen...

The phone rang on the heels of those words. The display glowed with Ian's number. She answered the call with her eyes fixed on the ceiling. "Hello."

"Are you tired of my company yet?"

"No..."

"Good. I had a sudden urge to call you. Could I buy you lunch?"

CHAPTER FOURTEEN

Bridgett drove with no particular destination in mind. Her actions were jerky and mechanical, the road viewed through tears that streaked down her face and dripped from her chin in a steady stream. *My whole life is a failure.* Those six words bounced from her head to her heart and back again. Each time they landed, they dredged up another piece of evidence in their favor. Her words filled the car in a harsh whisper as she rehearsed the list aloud. "I failed as a mother." David was off on a path of his own choosing. One that would likely get him killed in the name of service and nobility. "I failed as a daughter." *Protecting Mom is the last thing I can do for Daddy. She obviously values my opinion about as much as a dog values fleas.*

She turned a corner, the action bringing her bare left hand into view. The image of a legal sized manila envelope coalesced in her mind. "I failed as a wife, even if I don't know how it happened." Fat white clouds dotted the robin's egg blue sky. Her eyes lifted for a second. "I guess I failed as a Christian too." A harsh exhale punctuated her words. "Frankly...that's the least of my worries."

There had to be something she could do. A way to get Jeff to talk with her face to face. If she could look him in the eye, maybe she could get some answers. A modest sign on a neat lawn caught her attention. Harrison Lake, Attorney at Law. She almost stopped in the middle of the road. *Well duh...*

Jeff's betrayal had taken her so off guard that she'd ignored the obvious. She didn't have to sign the papers she'd received this morning. In fact, she didn't have to accept Jeff's wishes on any of this lunacy. She'd call Pam's husband and hire him to contest this whole thing. That wasn't a guarantee of victory, but it insured a face-to-face meeting with her absent husband. The truth was out there, and she'd find it, even if it meant an expensive legal battle. *So there, Jeff Morris. Things won't be as tidy and impersonal as you'd like!* Having the beginnings of a plan felt right, but instead of drying her tears, it induced a fresh flow as she drove through her hometown and wished for the last twelve months to disappear.

Her meandering path spit her out on the edge of the four-block strip that Garfield claimed as its main street. Bridgett paused at the single stoplight and considered her options. She had two. Explore or go home. Divorce papers or coffee?

"Now there's a tough choice." The light turned green, and she took the right turn onto Main Street. She cruised the length, taking time at each of the four-way-stop intersections to check out the new offerings on the block ahead. Her mouth tipped up in an automatic smile when she saw Kate's car parked in front of the old newspaper building. The new signage was discreet and dignified, proclaiming the Wheeler-Archer Foundation open for business.

Bridgett's stomach rumbled, reminding her of the

bagel she'd barely touched. It was almost eleven, and her inspection had yielded plenty of opportunities for food and drink. After she ate, browsing through the gift shop and the bookstore would provide further distraction. And when those distractions were exhausted, she'd think about the unthinkable waiting in an envelope at her mother's house.

At the end of the fourth block, she turned around and made a quick decision between the Ground Zero Coffee shop and the Sweet Moments Bakery. The bakery was owned by her mother's friend. Right now Bridgett needed space to lick her wounds, not a conversation about why the wounds existed.

Parking wasn't an issue this early in the day, and her choice became more appealing once she spotted the chalkboard in the window listing a soup, salad, and sandwich of the day. She wasn't much on salads, but a chicken salad sandwich and the butternut squash soup sounded more than a little yummy on a cool fall day. A hissing noise above her head had her looking up as she pushed through the door. A giant clock in the shape of a grinning coffee mug showed the time to be straight up eleven. Coffee scented steam boiled from hidden vents around the numbers.

OK, that's weird. She looked around the half empty shop. Pumpkins, some carved into jack-o-lanterns, sat in the middle of each of the dozen tables. Several wreaths made from colorful fall foliage decorated the walls and acted as frames for masks of scarecrows, witches, and ghosts. Bridgett had no issue with the spooky fun of Halloween but one of the masks flashed blinking red eyes in her direction. She sucked in a breath, tacked excessive on top of weird, and felt behind her for the doorknob. *I could just slip back out.*

"Welcome to Ground Zero. What can I get for you?"

Or not. Bridgett lifted a shoulder and approached the counter and the smiling woman behind it. Hopefully the soup would be worth enduring the creepy décor. She placed her order and chose a table with a plain pumpkin next to the large front windows. Hoping to discourage the small town chitchat of friendly strangers while keeping the oddly disturbing room at bay, Bridgett sat with her back to the room and watched Garfield's sidewalks come to life with lunchtime traffic.

Her lunch disappeared with surprising enthusiasm and left Bridgett considering a second container of soup to take home. *I wonder if they'd share the recipe. Jeff...* The thought soured her stomach, and a single sob escaped before she had the chance to swallow it back. *Stupid man!* She blotted the sudden tears from her eyes, sniffed, wiped her nose, and prepared to scoot away from the table.

"Bridgett?"

She shoved the damp napkin into her lap and turned to stare at the man standing just inside the door. She tilted her head. Tall, lanky, redheaded. Familiarity stirred but eluded her grasp.

The smile he gave her lit his eyes behind the horned rimmed glasses. "You don't recognize me? That might be a blessing considering the last time we saw each other."

Bridgett searched her memory and came up empty. "I'm sorry..."

He set the two cups of coffee he carried on her table and took a step back. He laid a hand on his chest.

"Micha."

Her eyes rounded in surprise. "Micha Raynes? After all these years? You're kidding me, right?" Bridgett sat back and looked at him through narrowed eyes. "You grew up after you broke my heart."

Micha ran a hand through his hair. "Yeah." He cocked his head, his stare intense. "If you're still mad at me about that, I can give you the explanation you refused to listen to the Monday after prom."

Bridgett shook her head. "Oh, I think we can let that spilled milk flow under the bridge. After more than twenty-five years, the memory of me crying myself to sleep in my formal gown hardly stings at all."

"Ouch! Score one for the gorgeous woman of my youth."

Gorgeous? *Red eyes, mom jeans.* She continued to gather up her lunch trash, not in the mood for conversation. "What can I do for you, Micha?"

"Nothing. I thought I recognized you and..." He looked at the floor and scuffed a foot on the worn tile. "It looked like you were crying. I just wanted to make sure you were OK, old friend or not." He studied her. "Are you OK?"

Those eyes could always see clear through to my soul. She broke their stare and turned her head to look out the window. *Of all the people I never thought I'd see again...why today?* "That's not an easy question to answer." She stood and pulled her keys out of her pocket. "I need to get back to Mom's house."

Micha laid a hand on her arm. "I heard about your father. I'm sorry."

Bridgett looked at the ceiling as tears she couldn't stop stung her eyes. "Thanks." She stepped around him. "I have to go."

"No problem. I've always wondered if the beautiful girl I had such a crush on grew into a beautiful woman. It's nice to see that she did."

Is he flirting with me? Bridgett waved a hand, indicating her appearance from her jeans to her hair. "You need to have those glasses adjusted."

Micha straightened said glasses and flashed her a boyish grin. "Anyway, I'm glad I ran into you. If you're going to be in town for a few days, stop by the new bookstore. Maggie and I own it. I know Sis would love to see you."

Bridgett continued to the door. She stopped with her hand on the knob. Micha's words of flattery warmed a spot in her heart. Was it wrong to take comfort in what another man had to say? *Get over yourself, honey. Your husband dumped you, remember?* She squared her shoulders and turned to her old friend. She offered him her best smile. "I just might take you up on that."

~ * ~

Micha retrieved his coffee and watched Bridgett exit to the busy sidewalk. His eyes focused on her left hand as she pulled the door closed behind her. His brows rose. *No wedding ring?* Still single or single again? Either way, something to explore. There'd always been a spot of regret in his heart for the way their high school relationship ended.

"Bridgett, wait." Micha chased Bridgett down the hallway on Monday morning, scattering fellow classmates out of his way as he went. "Please, wait up."

Bridgett whirled, her blue eyes hard and cold and bright with tears. "Why should I? You stood me up for the senior prom, you jerk!"

"Look, I'm sorry. My uncle—"

"Is he dead?"

"What?"

"Is your uncle dead?"

Micha leaned away from the fury of her words. "No."

"Then you don't get to use him as an excuse." She ripped the class ring he'd given her three weeks ago off her finger and threw it at him. He flinched out of the way as it bounced off the metal lockers behind his head. "Don't ever speak to me again!"

The memory raised his eyebrows, and *what ifs* lined up in his mind like books on a shelf. What if his uncle Wyatt had wrecked his motorcycle on any day except the day of the prom? What if they'd had cell phones on the panicked six-hour drive twenty-five years ago? What if he could have made Bridgett listen once they got home? What if she hadn't thrown his class ring in his face and called him a jerk? What if college hadn't taken him out of state before she'd had a chance to cool down? Questions with no answers. Bridgett had been a closed chapter in his life for a long time.

Micah watched her cross the street and climb into a black SUV. *Maybe not so closed.* It wouldn't take a lot of skill to find her. He'd bet money her mom still lived in the big two-story house on Steeple Avenue. Maybe... *Don't go there, Raynes. She didn't even know who you were.* The thought brought him back to reality. He watched her back out of the parking space and remembered the tears in her eyes. Maybe she'd filed him away years ago, but she certainly looked as if she could use a friend. Romantic fantasies aside, friendship was something he could offer her if he got the opportunity.

Micha prepared to leave. Maggie would have a fit if her coffee arrived cold. With the door half open, he jostled the drinks when his phone rang. Speak of the devil. He backed up, put the drinks on the table, and pulled the phone from the clip on his belt.

"Hold your horses, Miss Impatient. I'm on my way."

"Is that so?"

It took a second for Micha to process the unexpected voice. "Sorry, Ian, I figured it was Maggie complaining because I'm sixty seconds late with her afternoon caffeine fix. What's up?"

"Do you still have a kitten looking for a home?"

Micha grinned. "I sure do. One little female, the calico one. I thought Polly was all you could handle."

"It isn't for me. I want to surprise a lonely friend."

The grin faded. "Ian, it's never a good idea to surprise someone with an animal. Caring for a pet takes time and dedication. And on top of that, I should warn you, I have a strict no return policy."

"Rest easy, son. I wouldn't dump one of your babies on an unwilling human, nor would I consider returning her if my surprise fizzles. If things don't work out, then Polly inherits a playmate."

Sounded perfect to him. "Can you stop by tonight?"

"Umm..."

"What?"

Ian cleared his throat. "Could we meet now? Do you think you could sweet talk Maggie into holding the fort on her own for thirty minutes or so?"

Micha looked at the cooling coffee.

Ian spoke again. "You could tell her it's a kitten emergency."

Micha snorted a laugh. "Yeah, that'll work." He glanced at the clock over the door. "I'll see you at the house in thirty minutes. Don't be late, or I'll let you tell Maggie why she's handling the lunch time shoppers by herself."

~ * ~

Ian loaded purchases in the back of his Mini. Cat litter, litter box, scoop, food, scratching post, and a couple of cat toys—everything his brief experience with Polly told him was necessary to keep a young cat happy. In the back of his mind a continuous prayer lifted that Karla would be pleased with his gift. Alongside the prayer was the memory of contentment on her face as she held Polly. He looked at his watch. It would be close, but he'd make it to Micha's house before Maggie was forced to strangle them both.

He stuffed the final bag into the car, just a few things that caught his eye for Polly. A bit of sparkle drew his attention, and he pulled two rhinestone studded collars out of the bag, a red one for Miss Polly and an orange one for the calico. The receipt for the trip fluttered to the ground. Ian rolled his eyes, snagged it, and stuffed it in his pocket. Fur babies were almost as expensive as the non-furry variety.

The Mini stopped in front of Micha's house with five minutes to spare. Anticipation lightened his heart as he hurried up the walk. The door opened before Ian had a chance to ring the bell. Micha stood in the entry holding a small bundle of multi colored fur.

"Right on time." Micha stepped aside so that Ian could enter.

"Wouldn't want to give that sister of yours an excuse to hurt either of us." He reached out and brushed the mottled fur with a finger. "Last one, huh?"

"Yep, I'd pretty much resigned myself to keeping her, but if you're sure she's going to a good home..."

Ian reached out and lifted the kitten out of Micha's hands. "You can bank on that. My house or Karla's." He held the kitten up and looked into the black, white, and orange face. *Jester* was the first word that popped into his head. Maybe he could suggest it to Karla as a name.

"A woman?" Micha leaned back against the wall in the small entry, crossed his arms, and studied his friend with a smile. "Wait till I tell Maggie. When she finds out you wanted the kitten as a gift for a woman, all will be forgiven as she plans your wedding. Anyone I know?"

Ian ducked his head and continued to stroke the kitten. He hadn't voiced his intentions aloud to anyone other than his girls. Karla didn't even know where his heart was headed. "Well, let's not be too hasty. I've only known Karla for a week or so. I certainly wouldn't want any premature rumors getting back to her." His eyes came up to meet the younger man's. "But you might know her. She's lived here most of her life and you grew up in Garfield. Karla Black?"

Micha straightened, and Ian watched his expression change from curiosity to surprise.

"Karla Black... over on Steeple Avenue...huge two-story house?"

Ian nodded. "You do know her, then."

Micha laughed, "Oh, I know her. I haven't seen her in a while, but I've known her for almost thirty years."

He shook his head. "So she's the object of your affections. That's almost funny."

Ian raised his eyebrows. "Funny?"

"Well, yeah. I grew up with a serious crush on her daughter. I saw Bridgett earlier today, and after a discreet examination of her bare left hand, I was thinking about going over there later."

Ian sucked in a deep breath. "Tread lightly there, Micha."

Micha rocked back on his heels. "Why do you say that?"

Ian drew a hand down his face before meeting the younger man's stare. "Have you ever known me to gossip?"

"Women gossip, men share facts. If you have facts to share, spit it out."

"Bridgett is home because she is having some problems in her marriage."

He puffed out some pent up frustration. "Played that tune."

"Exactly. I don't know her whole story, but I do know yours. She could probably use a friend, and I can't think of a better one than you in any circumstance, but I'd keep my heart on a short leash until I had the whole story."

CHAPTER FIFTEEN

*Meow....meow...meow...*The plaintive kitty cries had started the second he put the car in gear. It continued for the entire trip across town. Ian parked his Mini in Karla's drive and looked at the tiny ball of fur huddled in his lap. He stroked a finger over the small head. "Poor baby, you didn't like your first car ride very much, did you? That's OK, we're here."

Either the lack of movement or the soothing voice managed to penetrate the frightened feline's defenses. The mewing stopped. She raised her head and blinked in the light.

"That's a girl." Ian picked her up and cradled her to his chest. "Now we need to have a talk while you finish calming down." He shifted her so that she could see the house. "This is your new home. There's a woman in there who is going to take great care of you, but we have to make a good impression on her so she doesn't toss us both out." Ian fumbled in his pocket for the orange collar, set the animal in his lap, and fastened it around her neck. He slipped a finger beneath it to make sure of the fit. "There you go, not too tight." The kitten shook her head and raised a paw to scratch at the bit of plastic encircling her neck. She rolled over and squirmed, doing her best to dislodge it.

169

Ian scooped her up. "That's enough of that. I bought that for you because I raised girls, and I know how much they like shiny things. You'll look pretty, and I'll bet Karla won't be able to resist you." Ian smoothed the ruffled fur under the collar and studied his handiwork. "Are you ready to meet your new human?" The cat regarded him with a curious stare. *Get on with it, you've stalled long enough.*

Ian climbed out of the car with both hands folded around his gift, bumped the door closed with his knee, and hurried up the walk. The door swung open as he climbed onto the porch. Karla stepped out to meet him.

"I heard you pull up and wondered what was keeping you. I..." Her voice trailed off and her eyes shifted to his cupped hands where tufts of fur were visible between his fingers. "What have you got there?"

OK, kitty, do your stuff. He held up his offering. "This is Polly's sister."

"Oh." Karla reached out and took the fur ball into her hands. She raised the baby to her face and ran her chin through the silky fur. When she moved back through the door, Ian trailed close behind. "I'm ready to go, just let me grab my jacket. Are we dropping the kitten off someplace before we eat?"

"Well...I...umm...I hope not."

Karla turned to face him, brows raised.

"The truth is, Karla, I picked her up for you."

Karla's gaze dropped to the kitten.

Ian hurried on. "I know I should have asked first. Alicia always did say I'm too impulsive, but you looked so content with Polly yesterday that I just thought...I mean...Polly is such a good companion for me, and I have everything this one needs out in the car." He stopped and tried to gauge Karla's expression. "If you don't want her, she can come live with me."

Karla bowed her head and scratched between the kitten's eyes. Purring filled the entry hall.

"Karla, will you say something? I'm sorry if I overstepped—"

"What's her name?"

Ian pulled in a hopeful breath. "If you plan to keep her, that's up to you. I was thinking she looked a bit like a court jester."

Karla held the kitten up and studied the tri-toned face. The corners of her mouth ticked up when a tiny paw reached out and batted at her chin.

"You've got a playful streak, don't you, little one? Do you like the name Jester?" The two females continued to stare at each other. Karla's smile became a laugh. She looked up at Ian. "I think she agrees with you on her name."

Ian stood a little straighter as some of the tension rolled off his shoulders. "How can you tell?"

"She winked at me."

"OK. So does that mean you'll keep her?" He raised a hand when Karla bit her lip. "Maybe just for a week or so...see how you get on together. She can always come to stay with Polly and me if it doesn't work out."

Karla lifted her chin. "You think I'm a quitter?"

"Of course not."

"Well, good." She snuggled the kitten closer. "This is a lovely gift." Karla took a couple of steps closer, raised up on her toes, and brushed Ian's cheek with a quick kiss. "Thank you."

Her quiet words tickled his neck while the warmth

of the simple kiss cut straight to his gut. Something internal clicked into place. *Can a heart be lost in just a week?* He wrapped her in his arms before she could step away, angled her chin up, and pressed his lips to hers. The fog around his question cleared a bit when Karla wrapped her free arm around him and answered his kiss with softened lips and a body that seemed to melt into his embrace. A current of something unexpected charged the air.

Meow!

Karla jerked away. "I think we squished her."

"Or electrocuted her." Ian drew in a deep breath. "Did you feel—?"

"Did you say you had some things for her in your car?" Karla fanned her face. "Because I think going to get them right now would be a very good thing."

~ * ~

Bridgett pulled into her mother's driveway and parked next to the Mini. Her expression rolled into a sneer of disgust. Why couldn't this man go away and leave them alone? *What more do I have to do to get my point across?* She reached for the door handle, prepared to do battle. *Nicolas won't be happy.* "Nicolas can go jump off a cliff." Her phone chimed with an incoming text. She looked at the screen. *Buffy.* She'd left Dallas a week before with no warning and no explanation. Buffy probably wasn't the only concerned or confused friend. She slid the message open.

What's up?

Bridgett tapped in a reply. *Visiting Mom.*

No, I mean, what's up?

172

Bridgett studied the text on the screen. She wasn't quite ready to share Jeff's betrayal with her friends. *What do you mean?*

The response was immediate. *Sorry, hope U R sitting down.*

There was a video attached to the message. She could see Jeff's face beneath the play button. Her finger shook as she stabbed the little arrow to start the clip.

Jeff sat in a booth at a restaurant she couldn't identify. A blonde woman she didn't recognize sat beside him. There was no sound other than the clink of dishes and the background roar of multiple voices. Bridgett's eyes went round as Jeff leaned in to whisper something into the woman's ear. The bottom fell out of what remained of Bridgett's world when the two people in the video leaned close to share a passionate kiss. Jeff pulled back and tucked the slut's blonde curls behind an ear then slid his hand down to cup her cheek. The video zoomed closer. The expression of tenderness she saw on her soon-to-be-ex-husband's face was one she could barely remember. The thirty-second video came to an abrupt stop.

Bridgett looked at the time stamp. An hour ago. While she'd been sitting in a coffee shop, alone and desolate, crying tears of sorrow over her pond-scum husband, he'd been enjoying a comfy meal with the answer to all of her questions of why.

"Oh, he's gonna pay for this. If he thinks he can just brush me aside with a nice settlement and a pat on the head, he can think again." She scowled at the screen. *Thank you, Buffy, for all the ammunition I need to blow that plan to smithereens!* She'd be taking more than tears and confusion to her appointment with Harrison Lake.

Bridgett slammed out of the car, thoughts of confrontation with Mom and Ian replaced by a boiling rage that had her shaking and talking to herself. "That sleazy, low-down snake! He was just waiting for David to be out of the house. Twenty-three years of being the faithful wife, raising his children, putting up with his workaholic life style." *Is the blonde the first?* The thought stopped her in her tracks. *Has he been cheating on me all this time?* Could she be that stupid?

The front door banged against the door stop with the force of her entry. Bridgett sent a single glare toward her Mom and Ian. *Dear heaven, is that a cat?*

"Bridgett?"

She ignored the question in her mom's voice and headed for the stairs. "Two can play at this game!" Bridgett climbed to the second floor, then stabbed at her phone as she entered her room. "I need the number for M & M's Books and Gifts." The number appeared on the screen along with a handy dial-it-now link. She touched the numbers and waited for the call to connect.

"M & M's Books and Gifts."

The sound of Micha's voice replaced some of the ache in her soul with the comforting thought that someone still found her attractive. Jeff might not want her anymore, but Micha had made his thoughts on the matter pretty clear.

"Micha, it's Bridgett."

"Hey. I didn't expect to hear from you so soon."

Bridgett swallowed. "I wanted to apologize for being so weepy earlier. This week has been hard with the anniversary of Dad's death. I was just a little nostalgic when you saw me, remembering Garfield through

Daddy's eyes."

"You don't need to apologize to me. We were friends once. If there is anything I can do to help, I hope you'll let me know."

Bridgett licked her lips. "That's exactly why I called. Mom has her weekly ladies group meeting tonight. I'm at loose ends and feeling lonely. I was wondering if you'd like to have dinner with me."

"Dinner? Well..."

She held her breath when he hesitated. *Please say yes, please say yes, please say yes.*

"Sure. I guess we can do that. The store closes at six. I can pick you up at seven."

Her breath of relief flooded the room. "Perfect! I'll see you then." Bridgett disconnected the call before he had a chance to change his mind. She crossed to her closet and began sifting through her clothes. She hadn't packed with dating in mind. *Dating?* The word had her breath shuddering in her lungs.

She pulled out a black T-shirt with long lace sleeves and a lace insert in the back. Add this to her black skinny jeans and heels, and she'd look fine. The *other* woman in the video floated through her mind. Bridgett held the lacy shirt in front of herself, shook out her hair, and pouted her lips. *Honey, you may be ten years my junior, but you don't have a thing on me!*

~ * ~

Pam's dining room was a beehive of activity as the last of Valley View's women departed the weekly Bible study. Karla's heart overflowed with feelings both new and old—emotions she'd never thought she'd feel again, some she'd never wanted to feel again...until the day Ian intruded on her grief and helped her see that she wasn't alone. Helped her see a different future than the one she'd settled for.

Across the table Terri and Samantha were both showing their appreciation for the sugar-free version of tonight's dessert. Pam's pumpkin pie cheesecake had been a big hit with the ladies. Both of the mommies in waiting were indulging in a second slice.

Callie sat at the end of the table with Kate on one side and Pam's empty chair on the other. She kept looking at Karla from beneath her lashes, and Karla wondered if the kiss she could still taste on her lips was visible to her oldest friend. The very idea had her grabbing for a napkin and rubbing her lips. Part of her longed to share what she was beginning to feel for Ian with her friends, part of her wanted to hold them close and secret for just a while longer.

Pam hurried back into the room and swung into her seat. "Wow, that was a great study on friendship. I just love the verses that speak of David's relationship with Jonathan." She looked at each of her friends in turn. "It makes me feel so very blessed to have you all in my life. There have been times when I don't know what I would have done without you."

"Let's not get mushy," Callie said. She nodded toward Sam and Terri. "You'll have the hormones at the other end of the table gushing."

Terri wrinkled her nose at Callie and forked up another bite.

Sam pushed her plate aside. "Ha ha. But speaking of friends, I got a nice long email from Iris today. She wanted me to tell you guys hello."

Kate leaned forward and smiled at her daughter-in-law. "That's wonderful. I know how much you miss her."

Samantha nodded. "It's hard for her to be so far away. Well, Alabama isn't all that far, I guess." Despite her steady voice, her eyes brightened with moisture. "Who knew she'd grow up to be a volleyball jock at Auburn?"

Terri passed her a napkin. "She always did love the game, and with those long legs..." Her voice bled off in a sniff.

Callie shook her head. "Don't start, you'll have us all in tears. What did she have to say?"

Sam wiped her nose. "She said that Alabama is beautiful this time of the year. And she's enjoying her classes. She checked out the church Sisko recommended, and she's already made a few new friends." She dug her phone out of her pocket. "Let's see, Antonia and Beverly. They're talking about getting an apartment off campus next semester."

Terri finger combed her hair away from her forehead. "And Steve's about to have a cow. He says she's too young to live unsupervised in a strange place."

Sam's laugh was a snort. "I did not remind Dad about our living arrangement six years ago, but I did remind him that Iris is the most level headed eighteen-year-old either of us knows." She lifted her shoulders. "Daddy will get over it. This is good for Iris. These are the kinds of friendships you carry with you your whole life. Like the one between David and Jonathan."

Conversation around the table lagged for a few minutes. Karla picked at her dessert,

Half of a regular slice that she still hadn't finished.

She started to bring up the subject of Ian several times, but something stopped her. *Last week my life was over, seven days later I'm standing on the edge of a whole new life. There's no way to explain that to them.*

Callie finally laid her fork aside and pinned Karla with a look. "You haven't had much to say this evening. What gives?"

Karla shook her head and tried for a casual answer. "Nothing." *Liar!* She gulped a breath at the self-recrimination and let it out in a long, slow exhale. "I mean...a lot...maybe..." She threaded her fingers through her hair. "It's all too much to process."

Kate frowned across the table. "Is Bridgett still giving you grief? Nicolas will have her hide."

"Bridgett? No. I haven't talked to her since this morning." She remembered the early morning delivery. "I know you guys are already praying for Bridgett's situation, but she got divorce papers today—"

"Oh no," Terri said. "Bless her heart."

Karla nodded. "She was expecting them, but it pulled the rug right out from under her. I've seen her upset a lot lately, but this was on a whole new level. She was gone most of the day. Ian was at the house when she came home, and she didn't speak to either of us, just stormed up the stairs and closed herself in her room."

"Maybe I should call her," Pam said. "We were pretty close, once-upon-a-time. I've been through the whole divorce mess. It might do her good to talk to someone who can identify with what she's going through."

"It couldn't hurt," Karla agreed. "I tried to get her to talk to me before I came over here. She wouldn't even acknowledge that I was at the door."

Callie reached across the table and laid a hand on Karla's arm. "We'll ramp up the prayer coverage, for both of you. Nothing breaks a mama's heart quicker than when her baby's hurting and she can't fix it."

Karla's gaze tracked around the table, lingering on each face. "Thanks guys, you're the best friends in the world."

Kate leaned forward. "Now that we have Bridgett taken care of, can we get back to the thing you said about Ian being at the house this afternoon?" She held up a hand and lifted a finger with each of her next points. "You had coffee with him on Wednesday, dinner on Saturday, lunch on Sunday, and"—she titled her head—"lunch?"

Karla nodded.

"And lunch today. That's four meals in less than a week. I don't see Nicolas that much, and we're married. So I'll repeat Callie's question...just to get us back on track. What gives?"

Did I really think I could avoid this conversation? Her mouth opened, but nothing came out. She clasped her hands in her lap and lowered her eyes. "It's crazy."

"Tell us anyway," Pam urged.

Karla looked up, her bottom lip caught between her teeth. "You guys really think it's OK that I'm spending time with Ian?"

Callie propped her elbow on the table and her chin on her fist. "We've had this conversation...like yesterday. We all think it's great, but it's what you think that matters."

Kate nodded. "We're thrilled, Nicolas is thrilled. We all think it's wonderful that you've found someone to help you transition into this new phase of your life."

"Especially a handsome someone." Terri added. "I can't wait until we have a chance to get to know him better. I bet you two make a striking couple."

The support flowing around the table fortified Karla's nerves. She swallowed and accepted her fate, because once the words were spoken, there would be no pulling them back. Karla leaned forward and gave voice to her feelings for the first time. "I think we're...um. Is there a more mature word than dating? That sounds so high-schoolish."

The room fell silent. Sam was the first to move. She jumped to her feet, circled the table, and clasped Karla in an enthusiastic hug. "As the most recent member of the high school crowd, just allow me to say...you go, Grams!"

"Thanks, sweetheart."

Sam pulled back. "When can I met him?"

Kate motioned her daughter-in-law back to her side of the table. "Have a seat, girlfriend. We all have questions, but that's a good place to start."

Once again Karla looked around the table. She knew her grin was smug and didn't care. "He's escorting me to the Fall Festival Wednesday night."

With that info delivered, she pushed away from the table. "I need to head home."

Callie held up a hand. "Hold up. You're leaving, just like that?"

"Yep, it's late and I'm tired. Ian brought me a kitten today—"

"Oh, that's sweet," Kate said.

Callie continued to study Karla with a frown etched between her brows.

"I thought so," Karla continued. "I don't want to leave her alone for too long on her first day in the house." She gathered her stuff and headed for the door. Unable to resist a parting shot, she stopped just across the threshold and glanced at her friends over her shoulder. "You guys were right. I like it."

"You like what?" Callie asked.

Karla grinned. She was being an unmerciful tease. *It's so good to laugh again!* "Ian kissed me twice, and I like it...a lot." She bolted for the door, leaving shocked looks on five faces and just as many questions hanging in the air behind her.

CHAPTER SIXTEEN

Micha pulled into the drive in front of the big two story house on Steeple Avenue. He hadn't been here in almost thirty years, but the house hadn't changed all that much. The shutters and trim glowed white in his headlights. Last he remembered, they were black. Today, the trees were taller, the lawn fuller, and the bikes were missing from the front yard. *We all grew up.*

The front door of the house opened while his car still idled. The woman he saw outlined in the light spilling from the house sucked the breath from his lungs. *Oh yeah, she grew up.* Micha pulled air into his chest. *Careful, Raynes, remember what Ian said.*

The older man's words of caution had circled in Micha's brain all afternoon. After she'd called to invite him to dinner, he'd taken some time to pray about the situation and his renewed attraction for Bridgett Black.

Not Black.

The fact that he didn't even know her last name layered a bit of reservation over his interest. Bridgett was in trouble and likely needed a friend. He was happy to fulfill that role, but despite any problems, she was a married woman, end of story.

Micha had been a Christian since he was old enough to walk down to the altar in children's church. He valued his relationship with Christ and didn't intend to compromise it by blindly chasing after a twenty-five-year-old what if.

But.

Micha conceded the *but* with a painful sigh. He'd also been the Christian spouse, cheated on, dumped, and left with soul-deep questions and no ready answers. If he could use his experiences to encourage an old friend without putting his heart back on the chopping block, where was the harm in that?

The figure in the doorway cocked her head and crossed her arms.

Oops...enough daydreaming. He opened the door and climbed out of the car. "Sorry." He hurried up the walk. "I took one look at the house, and I was a teenager again." He motioned to the yard. "Looks like the lawn recovered from all the baseball and football games."

"And soccer, and volleyball, and whatever other sport my Neanderthal brothers and their friends were into."

"So says the only girl in the family."

"Yeah well..." Bridgett turned a brilliant smile in Micha's direction. "Enough about what was. Tell me about what is." She gave a quick spin, stopped with her lace covered back to him, and glanced at him over her shoulder. "How do I look?"

Good enough to eat. Micha cleared his throat. *Get a grip.* "Amazing. You were beautiful this afternoon, but tonight?" *All Black lace and heels...*he swallowed hard. "Stunning."

Bridgett, pulled the door closed, clutched his arm, and led the way down the steps. "You always were a sweet talker." She snuggled up to his side. "So, handsome, where are we headed?"

Handsome...sweet talker...Lord have mercy. What have I jumped into? Afraid the upscale steak house he'd originally intended would send the wrong message to the woman hanging on his arm, Micha rewrote his plans on the fly. He dislodged his arm with as much grace as he could and put some distance between them. "Do you like Chinese? There's a nice little place in town."

"I'm good with that." She winked at him. "Dinner tonight is more about us than food anyway." She paused while he opened the passenger side door, turned to him before she slipped inside, and laid a hand along his jaw. She rubbed a thumb along his chin. "I'm just so glad you found your way back into my life. I've missed you."

Missed me? Micha's quick step back had him stumbling over his own shoes. She didn't know who he was a few hours ago. *What is she up to?* He grabbed the doorframe in one hand, Bridgett's hand in the other. "Hop in and buckle up."

He closed the door, grateful for the console between the seats and more than a little anxious to put a table between them once they reached the restaurant. He was flattered, any man with a pulse would be, but he had to find a subtle way to ask about her marital situation and make his intentions clear.

Micha rounded the hood of his car and glanced at Bridgett through the windshield. She blew him a kiss. His eyes rounded behind his glasses. How had this evening, and his innocent intentions, gone so far south in less than ten minutes?

He took his seat behind the wheel, startled when

Bridgett leaned into his space and took a deep breath.

"I love the cologne you're wearing. It's so sexy and manly."

He stared out the window and pushed his glasses up with a finger. "Um...thanks. Better sit back now and buckle up. The cops in this town are seat belt crazy."

She rubbed her nose across his earlobe.

Something in his gut tightened. "Bridgett."

She plopped back into her seat. "OK. But I have friends in the department if you change your mind about getting cozy."

Micha backed the car out of the drive and pointed it toward town. *I can handle this...I can...I will.* "Yes, the Garfield police. I've seen Nicolas a few times. It's nice to see him finally settled down with a good woman."

"You know Kate?"

Micha nodded, eyes on the road. "She's a regular at the bookstore."

"That's sweet, but I'd rather talk about us, not my family."

"OK, tell me what you've been doing for the last twenty-five years or so." He glanced her direction and saw her mouth tighten."

"Raising my family."

"You have kids? That's awesome."

A genuine smile lit her face. "Two great kids. Edie just went back to school for her junior year of college. She's studying architecture."

Micha stopped at Garfield's only light and looked at Bridgett. "That's an interesting career choice for a woman."

Bridgett's chuckle filled the car. "She was never a girly girl, despite my best efforts. I'd buy her dolls, and she'd stuff them in the closet and steal David's Lego and erector sets. No pop star posters on her walls. She favored skyscrapers and bridges."

The light turned, and Micah continued down Main Street. "David is your son?"

"Yeah."

"Older or younger?"

"He's the baby."

Micha caught the tension in her voice and waited to see if she continued.

"I always thought he'd study veterinary medicine."

"I take it he chose another path?"

This time an unpleasant snort echoed through the car. "That's putting it mildly. He enlisted in the Marines. He's in San Diego right now learning how to get shot at and survive...I hope."

Micha pulled into the lot in front of the Chinese restaurant and turned off the ignition. "I can tell you have issues with his choice, but you must be proud that he isn't afraid to follow his dreams."

Bridgett shook her head. "I really don't want to talk about David." She reached for the door handle. "This looks like a nice romantic little place."

Micha groaned as he climbed out of the car.

~ * ~

Bridgett fastened herself to Micha's side as they walked into the restaurant. It felt good to be with a man interested in her company. She just needed to loosen him up a bit.

The small dining area was decorated in aqua and orange. Decorative Oriental plaques hung on the walls.

They looked like jade, but Bridgett was pretty sure they were plastic. The lights were soft, the booths had nice high backs, and the place wasn't crowded. It was the ideal place for the two of them to get reacquainted.

The petite Asian hostess led them to a corner booth. Bridgett took a seat and scooted over, leaving plenty of room for Micha to sit beside her. She patted the space in invitation, pouting a little when he slid in across from her instead.

He's so shy. Bridgett found that more than a little attractive. It was certainly a fresh experience. Jeff was the epitome of self-confidence. *And look where that got me.*

The hostess lingered next to their table long enough to take their drink orders before giving them the privacy Bridgett wanted. Once she scurried away, Bridgett smiled across the table, eager to pick up where they'd left off. "You're all caught up on me. What have you been up to since you broke my heart?"

"Bridgett..."

"Take a joke, sugar. I wouldn't be sitting here if I was still mad at you." She propped her elbow on the table and put her chin in her hand. "I don't see a ring on your finger. Is Micha Raynes a confirmed bachelor?"

Micha frowned down at his left hand. "Not by choice."

Bridgett raised her eyebrows. "Divorced, widowed?" She licked her lips. "Never got over me?"

He rubbed his brow. "Divorced."

She leaned in closer. Maybe his heart was as wounded and empty as hers. "Share?"

The small Asian woman reappeared with their sodas.

Bridgett rolled her eyes at the interruption and tapped impatient fingernails on the tabletop.

Once the drinks were positioned, the old woman folded winkled hands at her waist. "You make choice?"

"Thanks, May." He laid his menu on the table and addressed a question to Bridgett. "Do you know what you want?"

"Oh, I'm not picky. I'll have what you're having." *Whatever gets this little prune of a woman on her way the quickest.*

"Great. We'll each have the sesame chicken with rice and an eggroll."

The older woman inclined her head. "As you wish."

Bridgett watched her shuffle away and then turned back to Micha. "Where were we?"

Micha took a sip of his Sprite.

"Oh yeah, you were about to tell me about your failed marriage."

Micha's shoulder lifted in a gesture of dismissal. "Not much to tell. She ran off with one of the trainers from our gym. I haven't seen her in six years."

The words sounded dry and rehearsed to Bridgett's ears. She shook her head. "Oh come on. There's bound to be more to the story than that. How long were you married?"

"Eight years."

"Kids?"

"No."

"Were you happy?"

"Why do people always ask that question?" Micha studied her from across the table. "We obviously weren't as happy as I thought, or we'd still be married."

The similarities to her situation slammed Bridgett

with unexpected emotion. Her throat ached with unbidden tears, but she swallowed them back. "So she cheated. Do you hate her?"

His eyes widened. "I...umm..."

She leaned forward, her voice hoarse and urgent. "Tell me the truth."

"I think I did for a while."

"Now?"

"I like to think I've forgiven her, even if I haven't had the chance to tell her that face-to-face." He shook his head. "It didn't happen right away. There was a lot of bitterness and a lot of questions." His eyes met hers. "I'd tried to be the best husband I knew how to be...a Christian husband. I believe in the sanctity of marriage. The idea of one man and one woman, a lifelong commitment."

He twisted his fork in his fingers. "I didn't know what to do once she left. I had a lot of conversations with my pastor back in Michigan before I could accept the fact that the divorce wasn't my choice. He showed me that God made provision in his word for a spouse betrayed by unfaithfulness. I'm not bound by that commitment any longer."

"I—"

The food arrived at their table, and Bridgett was thankful for this interruption. She took the time to collect herself. She wasn't all that interested in what the Bible had to say about her situation, but if he could shed some light on how to deal with the hopelessness and her battered self esteem, she'd keep him talking all night.

Bridgett picked up her eggroll, turning it in her fingers to dissipate some of the heat. She dipped in it the bowl of orange sweet and sour sauce. "So"—she looked up at Micha—"how long did it take you?"

"To what?"

She nibbled the roll, giving herself the time to frame the question and ask it without blubbering. "How long did it take you to get over feeling unloved? It's a...I mean...it must be tough to come to grips with being an undesirable failure." Her free hand came over her mouth. "I mean, not that you were." She dropped her gaze to her lap. "But I can see where it might feel that way."

"Bridgett, look at me."

She hesitated for a few seconds. When she finally raised her eyes, she found his expression intent on her and full of sympathy.

"Are we still talking about me?"

She shrugged, rolled her eyes, and bit her lip. *I won't cry, I won't cry, I won't cry.* "Maybe."

Micha shifted their plates, reached across the table, and waited until she laid her hand in his. "Sweetheart, you've done a great job at keeping the conversation on me, so we'll just keep it that way."

She was forced to look away again. Didn't he realize that the sympathy on his face was killing her?

He rubbed her knuckles with his thumb. "I was hurt, but I was never unloved. At the risk of sounding like a weenie I'll admit there were nights when I cried myself to sleep. Those were the nights God held me the closest. Satan makes it easy to blame yourself. To hold the hurt close and nurture that seed into a crap load of bitterness." He tugged her hand until she raised her head. "He's a liar, Bridgett. You have to let go of that. God will always love you. His is the only love you can always depend on."

Bridgett pulled her hand away. Why did everyone keep trying to cram God down her throat? She'd leaned on Him for years, and she'd still been betrayed. Tossed aside for some blonde bimbo.

She straightened, picked up her fork, and forced a smile to her face. "This looks really good." She speared a piece of the chicken and held it across the table. "Here, try a bite of mine."

He sent a frown across the table. "We have the same thing."

"Oh yeah." She pulled the fork back with a giggle. "Silly me."

"Can I just say one more thing before we drop this?"

"I'm listening." Bridgett stuffed the chicken in her mouth.

"When you decide you're ready to talk this out, I'm here for you."

She sent him a wink. "Thanks, sugar."

Their meal passed in a strained silence. The food was probably very good, but it tasted like straw in Bridgett's mouth. She glanced at Micha from under her lashes a few times, but she was unable to interpret the emotions on his face.

~ * ~

Micha paid the check and loaded Bridgett into his car. He still didn't know her story, but he could guess at most of it. She spent the first few minutes of the drive back to her mom's staring out the side window.

Father, show me how to help her. She's wounded, and I know that feeling well. Show me how to gain her trust and get her to open up.

Bridgett shifted in the seat and held out her hand. Micha took it in his and squeezed. *Poor kid.*

He stopped in front of the house and walked her to the door. He turned to face her, planning to re-enforce his offer to help, and stumbled back when he found his arms full of a passionate woman. Her hands pulled his face to hers, her lips clamped to his with an intensity that sorely strained his resolve.

It took him a second, but he managed to get his hands around her wrists and force her down and away. "Have you lost your mind?"

She grinned up at him under the glare of the porch light. "No, I know exactly what I want...*who* I want." She sidled a little closer. "Why don't we get back in your car? I can come to your place..." She trailed a finger down his chest. "Fix you a nice breakfast in the morning."

"You didn't hear a word I said over dinner, did you?" He dropped her wrists, stepped to the edge of the porch. "I've gotta go."

"You'll regret that decision when you wake up alone."

"Oh, I don't doubt that for a second, but I'm man enough...moral enough...to walk away anyway." He ran a hand through his hair. "Ian said you had some issues, but—"

"Excuse me. Ian...Ian McAlister?

He nodded.

Bridgett's face went red. She pointed to the driveway. "Get out."

Micha blinked at her. "What?"

"I don't need you two gossiping about my problems

behind my back."

"We weren't. We—"

"Leave."

He took the steps down to the sidewalk. He turned to look at her. "I meant what I said. I'm here for you if you need to talk."

She lifted her chin, pointed her nose to the sky, and slammed into the house.

CHAPTER SEVENTEEN

Bridgett leaned against the closed door, grateful for the physical barrier between herself and the man who'd just humiliated her. *Honey, you humiliated yourself. What would your father think of your behavior?* She bent to remove the spikey-heeled shoes that had pinched her toes for the last couple of hours. *My feet don't hurt half as bad as my pride!* Micha's rejection replayed in a continuous loop in her head. Each time she circled back to the moment he broke off their kiss. The anger in her stomach twisted with shame and coiled just a little tighter.

Have you lost your mind?

She straightened and threw one of the shoes against the opposite wall. The reckless action released some of the unbearable pressure in her chest. The resulting black scuff on the white paint drew her eye. "Daddy will kill—"

A sob clutched her throat. She wrapped her arms around herself as reminders of loss and failure overwhelmed her. *Nope, Daddy won't do anything. Daddy isn't here. David's off doing his own thing, Jeff finds me utterly replaceable, and Micha?* Well, he didn't want her either. *Four for four with the men in my life.*

"When did I become unlovable?" she whispered to the walls.

Tears clouded her eyes. She'd spent hours this afternoon on hair, makeup, and clothes. Then she'd offered herself to Micha in the most blatant way she could think of. Her desired outcome was still a bit cloudy, but after his flirty remarks earlier in the day, was a little affection too much to ask for? What had she received instead? He'd preached at her. In place of the reassurance she craved, he'd given her a sermon. She needed to feel attractive and wanted. *I need to know that I still matter to someone.*

God will always love you.

"Yeah, right!" Bridgett looked toward the ceiling, her eyes overflowed, and her chin quivered. If God loved her she wouldn't be standing here in the first place. *Guess we'll make that five for five.* The second shoe crashed against the wall and landed next to the first. She drew in a couple of deep breaths and fought the urge to collapse where she stood.

"What on earth is going on down here?"

Bridgett spun and there was Mom, standing at the top of the stairs, holding that stupid cat that Ian McAlister...

Ian said you had some issues.

Ian. Six for six then. But why should he care what she did or with who? He didn't even know her. The pressure in her chest became a living beast scratching for release. *How dare he?* "Why is everyone out to ruin my life?"

"What are you talking about?"

"I did not stutter." Bridgett's voice was harsh and loud. She climbed the steps, stopping once she stood eye-to-eye with her five-foot-nothing parent, and leaned into her mother's space.

"Choose!"

"Excuse me?"

Bridgett motioned to the cat. "Choose, right here, right now. Me or Ian."

"Bridgett, what's gotten into you?"

She stared at her mom. *Maybe if I showed her the video, she'd pick me.* A shiver of rage washed over her. Bridgett needed to be loved on her own merits, not pitied. She gathered what little pride she had left. "No! No more nonsense. I'm sick to death of being the last choice in everyone's life. I'm your daughter, for mercy sake. I've expressed my opinion about your relationship with this man, and you've brushed it off as useless. I've offered my company if you're lonely, and you've passed over me for some man you hardly know. I'm done." She straightened and crossed her arms. "Make a choice."

Mom lifted her chin and met Bridgett's stare head on. "You've been trying to bully me ever since you got home. You need to remember that this is my house. You don't make the rules, and you don't get to tell me how to live." She nodded to the bottom of the stairs. "Now I don't know what happened to bring you home in such a foul mood, but if you want to talk about it, woman to woman, we can go sit in the kitchen. I'll make us both some hot chocolate. If you want to continue to act like a spoiled five-year-old, you can go to your room. You choose."

The words bounced of Bridgett like phaser fire on a force field. "I'm not doing anything until you can look me in the eye and tell me that you don't plan to speak to Ian McAlister, ever again." She glared at the ball of fluff in her mother's arm. "And that includes getting rid of that...that thing. We never had a cat while Daddy was alive, we don't need one now."

Karla looked from Bridget to the cat. When she finally met Bridgett's gaze, the expression on her mother's face took her down a step.

"That's not going to happen."

Bridgett's eyes narrowed.

Mom shook her head. "I've watched you grow up into a beautiful, independent woman. You're smart and capable, and I value your opinion, but I think you're wrong where Ian is concerned. You're letting your grief and your marital problems get in the way of your good judgment." Mom sat on the step and settled the cat in her lap. When she continued, her voice was calm and reasonable "My relationship with you and my relationship with Ian are two different things and not mutually exclusive." She patted the empty space beside her. "Come sit down. Talk to me about what's got you so upset."

"I'm done talking."

"And I'm done arguing. I've never tried to live your life in place of my own. By the same token, I refuse to allow you to live mine. That has nothing to do with choosing one person over another, it's just giving myself the same respect I've always given you and your brothers."

Bridgett crossed her arms. "So you're going to continue seeing Ian McAlister?"

"I am."

"If you do that..." Bridgett stared down at her mother. *How can Mom not want me either?* She swallowed, making a physical effort to unclench her jaw. "If you do that, I'm not your daughter anymore."

Mom jerked back as if the words had delivered a

tangible slap. Tears filled her mom's eyes.

Bridgett enjoyed a moment of relief. *There's no way she'll choose that man over me.*

Her relief turned to uncertainty when Mom's face went hard with determination.

Can she?

"Bridgett, I carried you under my heart for nine months. I loved you before you were ever born. It will take more than a fit of jealousy from you to change that."

"You think this is jealously?"

"I think Jeff delivered an enormous blow to your heart. You're reeling from that. Trust me, no one understands that feeling of loss better than me." Her mom's green eyes heated with an emerald fire. "But trying to dictate my life will not cure the ills in yours. Sweetheart, the best thing you can do right now is wrap yourself in God's love and seek His plan for your future. I know you think He's turned His back on you, but if there is space between you, He didn't put it there."

Mom's words scored a bullseye in Bridgett's heart. She ignored it. "I'll pack my stuff and leave."

Mom stood, one hand on the bannister, one hand holding the kitten, a single tear gleaming on her cheek. "That's certainly your choice."

The simple answer called Bridgett's bluff and stole her breath. She stared at the woman she'd always depended on. The one who'd always loved her...until now. She swallowed bitterness. *I guess I've lost her too.* She clomped up the remaining stairs and brushed passed her mother.

"Get some rest, baby, talk to God. It'll all look

better in the morning."

"It certainly will, because I won't be here." Bridgett slammed into her room. She wouldn't spend another night where she wasn't wanted.

~ * ~

Karla's hands shook as she lifted the coffee cup to her mouth. Her first sip of the decaffeinated brew stung her upper lip and scalded her tongue. She pulled it back with a jerk, grateful for the extra room in the oversize mug that kept the steaming liquid from sloshing over the rim and adding her fingers to the casualty list. A glance at the clock on the stove showed the time as twelve-thirty in the morning.

Her daughter was up there packing her bags. How had it come to this? Karla's fingers drummed a restless tattoo on the sides of the mug. Bridgett had always been a daddy's girl, with a small portion of drama queen added to the mix. *She'd outgrown that, I thought. I know she's hurting over Mitch and Jeff, but her behavior has not been that of a rational adult.* Karla closed her eyes and imagined her hands around Jeff's neck. She held that picture for the space of a breath and then released it. *Sorry, Father.*

Did her daughter really think she could come home and bully Karla into bending to her demands?

Karla looked up at the ceiling as a particularly loud thud reverberated from the room above her. She was putting on a grand show. At least there was no one else in the house to be disturbed. She covered her mouth as a yawn made her eyes water. *I should be sleeping, not sitting here in the wee hours while my forty-three-year-old daughter throws a temper tantrum.*

Karla closed her eyes and tried to pray for the twentieth time in the last hour. *Father...* That's where her thoughts dwindled. She wasn't sure who to pray for, Bridgett or herself. And if she could nail down the correct recipient, she didn't know what to ask for. The perfect world solution of Bridgett renewing her faith and Jeff coming to his senses while she enjoyed the freedom to pursue her own chance at happiness sounded good, but God wasn't a genie in a lamp. He wasn't likely to wave His hand over the situation and tie up all the messy ends of her life in a neat bow. Sometimes you had to walk through the mess.

Her shoulders slumped and her head bowed. "Father, You've always been in this place. Before we moved into this house, Mitch and I walked through and dedicated each room to You. We stood in the rooms that would belong to our children, and we brought their names and lives to You and renewed our intent to nurture them according to Your word. You've seen messes, and hurts, and anger, but at the end of the day, You've always been our source of joy and peace. Your presence has always made our house a home. Father, I'm not asking you to calm the storm we're living in, but can you please bring peace to my heart and restoration to Bridgett's?"

Karla raised her head. The storm still raged in the room above, but the deep breath she pulled into her lungs carried calm to her heart as surely as it carried oxygen to her blood. Verbalizing her request aloud didn't help God hear it any better, but the act always settled things more firmly in her spirit.

Trust Me.

The soft words finished what the deep breath started. Karla relaxed into the arms that had never failed her.

"Thank You, Father." Karla looked up as a door slammed over her head. Thumping and creaking came from the direction of the stairs. Her heart fluttered in her chest. Never in her wildest dreams would Karla have imagined the scenario playing out in her house.

Trust me.

"I do trust You, but it's hard to separate worry from trust where your child is involved." Karla folded her hands around the mug of coffee and waited. She didn't quite know how to address Bridgett's current mood, but standing in the doorway wringing her hands while her daughter vacated the house didn't feel like the right move. She looked up when Bridgett appeared in the doorway.

"I'm out of here."

Karla refused to give into the tears that stung the back of her eyes. Instead she nodded. "OK. I'd appreciate a phone call to let me know where you are."

"OK?" Bridgett's brows rose. "You don't care that I'm leaving?"

Karla looked down at her hands. "You know better than that." She took a deep breath. "I really don't understand what's gotten into you. For the first time in a year, I have a chance to be happy. It saddens me that you don't want that for me...that you would rather keep me locked in my grief."

"That's ridiculous. I don't want you locked in grief. I just want you to be the mother I've always depended on." She hefted the strap of her bag. "Why don't you call me when she comes back?"

Karla cringed from the sting of the harsh words. *Jesus, please help me make her understand.* She raised her head and stared at her daughter. "Leaving is your choice, but I want you to think about something."

Bridgett crossed her arms and waited.

"You're forty-three. Even though you think that the last couple of weeks have ruined your future, God willing, you still have a long productive life ahead of you. Once you're free of Jeff, there will plenty of time for you to find love with another man. To build a life that makes you happy. When that time comes, if he's a good man, one who loves you and treats you well, you'll have my blessing."

Karla shrugged before she continued. "I'm not forty-three, sweetheart. I'm sixty-five, and life is so very short. I'll always want the life I might have had with your father. But that wasn't God's plan, and it's taken me every day of the last year to come to grips with that. And do you know what I've decided?"

Bridgett stared past her mother, eyes bright, lips pressed into a thin line, and refused to answer.

"I've decided that if there's a chance for me to find happiness, to overcome this suffocating loneliness...I'm going to grab it with both hands, and thank God for it."

Bridgett snorted. "That's a pretty speech. Did your friends write it for you?"

She shook her head and ignored her daughter's sarcasm. "No, not really." She paused, working it out for herself as she explained it to Bridgett. "I've been dragging my feet on this. Trying to talk God into leaving me alone with my misery. He won't. He keeps whispering to my heart, telling me that He isn't done with me, that He has better things for me than I could ever imagine for myself." Karla ran her finger around the lip of the mug. "I don't know that those better things include Ian McAlister. But I do know that I enjoy his company, and I've decided that, for now, that's enough."

"Regardless of what I think." It was a statement, not a question.

Karla nodded. "That upsets you, and I'm sorry."

"Then we're done."

Bridgett left the kitchen, and Karla remained at the kitchen table. She sipped her coffee and flinched when the front door slammed. This was certainly the toughest love she'd ever dished out, but underneath the hurt and stubbornness, Bridgett was a reasonable woman and there was a forty-three-year-old core of love. Karla didn't think it would take much solitude for her daughter to realize she was wrong.

~ * ~

Bridgett wheeled her luggage out to the porch and slammed the door as hard as she could. The noise, like a gunshot echoing on the midnight air, satisfied her.

Everyone she knew had rejected her. The thought stung. *Well fine. I'm a big girl, and I know how to take care of myself.* She loaded her things in the back of her car and tried to decide where to go from here.

Home was less than three hours away, but she wasn't ready to face what waited for her in Dallas. Nicolas and Kate would probably welcome her in their home, but the thought of her big brother's reaction to this latest argument with Mom had her crossing that off her list of options almost as quickly as the thought materialized.

A plan might have been a good idea before she delivered any ultimatums, but sometimes you had to take life on the fly. Bridgett sat in the car while it heated and chewed her bottom lip. Bad news...Garfield didn't have many choices when it came to long-term lodging. Good news...larger towns could be found in any direction she drove. *So pick a direction already.* Bridgett backed out of the drive and headed north. Ten minutes of driving would have her in a comfortable rent-by-the-week micro apartment. *I probably won't even need it that long. I've been here for over a week, Mom's gotten used to my company. It won't take long for her to get tired of puttering around in that house, alone. She'll be begging me to come home before the first week's rent runs out.*

CHAPTER EIGHTEEN

Karla scurried around her kitchen Wednesday morning putting the finishing touches on her dessert for the evening's festivities at Valley View. She dabbed a bit of butter onto her hands and spread it across her palms. The butter would keep the gummy concoction she was about to delve into from sticking to her hands. She scooped up a small amount of the orange colored rice cereal mixture, rolled it into a ball, and placed it in an aluminum cake pan lined with wax paper. She looked at her creation and then studied the picture on the recipe card with a tiny feeling of accomplishment. Once she added a little piece of tootsie roll to the top for a stem and piped on a single green frosting leaf they really would look like tasty little pumpkins.

She bent to the task and, within the hour, she had four dozen little pumpkins finished and ready for tonight's celebration. She crossed to the sink and ran her hands under the warm water to remove the remnants of the butter, frosting, and marshmallow. The kids would get a real kick out of these, and she might have a chance at the spooky dessert award.

The members of Valley View Church loved to eat when they fellowshipped, and they took pride in doing it well. Tonight's spooky dessert award would take second place to the chili cook off, though. The bid to win the golden ladle always generated its fair share of good natured competition. *I know exactly what Benton is doing today.* She smiled at the thought of her friend's husband bent over the stove trying to recreate the chili that had won him first place four out of the last six years. She didn't envy Callie the mess in her kitchen.

Her ringtone filtered in from the living room just as she snapped the last lid in to place. *Bridgett?* A day and a half, and she still hadn't heard from her daughter. It was clear that Karla had under estimated the depth of Bridgett's anger. Karla shook her head and reminded herself that Bridgett wasn't a child anymore. They'd been butting heads for over a week, and frankly, the restored peace in her home was a blessing. The girl needed to accept that she didn't run Karla's life. *But I still worry.*

Karla reached the phone just as the call went to voice mail. She touched the screen. It wasn't her daughter, and that broke her mother's heart. But it was Ian, and the sight of his name brought a smile to her woman's heart. A smile she thought she'd lost for good.

She didn't take the time to listen to his voice mail. Instead, she touched the icon that would return his call. *I hope he's not cancelling out on our evening.* The thought sped through her mind before she could put a handle on it. *Oh, stop being a nervous Nellie!*

"That was fast. I haven't even had time to put down the phone."

His voice did pleasant things to her insides. *Be honest, at least with yourself. You like everything about the man.* Her response came out saucy and more than a little flirty. "Well, I could hang up and wait a couple of hours to call you back if that suits you better."

"You wouldn't break my heart so early in the day, would you?"

Karla enjoyed his teasing and decided to give him the same in return. "I doubt your heart is as fragile as that." She took the phone to the couch and sat while his laughter filled her ear. "But you should know up front, if you've changed you mind about meeting my friends tonight, I'll supply every trick-or-treater that comes to my house this weekend with toilet paper and your address."

"You do that, and when they're done here, I'll give them shaving cream and a ride back to your place."

Karla's shoulders shook with laughter of her own. "I say we call it a draw before it ever starts."

"Done." There was a hesitation before he continued. "I called to get some details about the chili contest for tonight. Are visitors allowed to participate?"

"I can't imagine anyone sending you or your crockpot packing, but you don't have to—"

"*Have to* has nothing to do with it, my dear woman. I'm more competitive than I like to admit. I thought it might be fun to give some of your friends a run for their money, unless you think that would be the wrong track to take for this first outing."

"The more the merrier as far as I'm concerned. No one is going to be the least put off either way."

"If you're sure. I make a pretty mean pot of chili."

"Then I say give it your best shot. Even if you walk away with the prize, the only one you'll annoy will be Callie's husband, Benton. And the most he'll do is corner you to pick your brain for the secret ingredients in your recipe."

"That's what I needed to hear. I'm going to let you go, I have cooking to do."

"OK, I'll see you in a bit. Oh..."

"Yes?"

"Chili has to be there early so they can get it judged. You'll need to pick me up thirty minutes earlier than we planned."

"Just a little more time in the company of a beautiful woman." Ian's voice embraced her. "I'm already counting the minutes."

Goose bumps stood to attention on Karla's arms as the phone went dead in her hand. She shivered. Two weeks ago she hadn't known Ian McAlister's name. Now, the thought of spending the evening with him...

Karla chewed her lip as several realities struck home at once.

The overwhelming grief of the last year was ebbing. The loss of the continuous sorrow didn't dampen her love for Mitchell one little bit. The good memories of their life together were still there for any time she needed the comfort of them. Around that core of memories, her feelings for Ian bloomed like a flower in the spring sunshine. Each moment she spent with Ian nurtured a hope for a shared future.

She turned that over in her mind. "Is it possible to...?" She hesitated over the word that danced on the tip of her tongue but decided that honesty with herself was the first step on this fresh new path. "Love...in such a short time?"

Her hand flew up to cover her pounding heart, and she looked around the room guiltily.

Did I really... Karla swallowed. *Did I really say* love?

She stared at the far wall and tried to calm her racing

pulse with deep breaths. A furry body landed in her lap with a soft plop. Karla ran her hand over the kitten's back and waited for Jester to lift her eyes. "I love Ian McAlister," she whispered. The cat blinked while Karla licked her lips as if trying to taste the words. Her eyes closed as Jester circled in her lap and settled into a rumbling nap. The words snuck passed her lips a second time, louder and firmer. "I love Ian McAlister."

Karla leaned back into the cushions, her head resting on the back of the couch, her emotions mixed. What was good news for her would not be accepted by her daughter. Bridgett would surely disown her.

~ * ~

Bridgett paced the boring little room she currently called home. Her path took her from the microwave sitting on a mini fridge to the wall on the other side of the full-sized bed. Twenty steps one way, twenty back. She could have added three steps to the trip if she'd included a detour to the tiny bathroom, but it hardly seemed worth the effort. Around and around, back and forth. If the carpet hadn't been the industrial variety, there'd be a path worn down to the cement beneath it by now.

She twisted her fingers together as she walked. Her meeting with Harrison Lake was later this afternoon. The divorce papers on the nightstand drew her attention. Her lips crept up in a wicked smile. "Not so cut and dry now, you slimeball."

The video of Jeff's little tete-a-tete with the blonde strumpet had already been emailed to the lawyer. *Strumpet.* Bridgett rolled the word around in her mouth.

She'd read it in a novel somewhere years ago, and it stuck in the back of her brain with no real excuse to use it until now. It was an ugly word, but then so was *divorce.*

So...at two p.m. she would begin her counter offensive on the man she'd sworn to love forever. If nothing else, she hoped to come away from this meeting with a plan. Her restless breath shuddered into the room. *Maybe I'll sleep tonight if I know where my life is going.* In the meantime, the four walls of her self-made prison were driving her crazy. She stopped in the middle of the circuit and threaded the fingers of both hands through her hair, thoughts of Jeff replaced by a far deeper betrayal.

Why hadn't Mom called to apologize and invite her back home? She had to be sorry about her harsh words. And lonely. It had been two days. "Not if she's hanging around with Ian." The whispered words held a sneer.

She turned back to the bed and sank down on the edge of the mattress. "Oh, Daddy, I'm so sorry. I've done everything I can do to get Mom to come to her senses. She's determined to ruin everything you guys built. Just like Jeff is throwing away everything we have." She blinked back tears, but one managed to escape, trail down her cheek, and drip from her chin. Something in her heart struggled for recognition. A still small voice she longed to smother.

Let Me help you. Let Me guide your steps. Let Me love you.

Bridgett shored up her defenses against the God who'd destroyed her life, but the truth remained the truth.

She spoke to her father. "My relationship with God might be in serious trouble right now, but I still know

where you are. I know you can't"—she bit her lip—
"wouldn't come back, even if you could. I get it that
you can't hear me, and I know you don't care about
what happens down here, but it matters to me." She
leaned back on the mattress, rolled over onto her side,
and wrapped her arms around a pillow. "It matters to
me."

~ * ~

Ian dug a fresh spoon out of the drawer, dipped it
into the chili, and tasted it cautiously. He tossed the
dirty spoon into the sink with twelve others and
allowed the flavors of his concoction to settle on his
tongue for a few seconds.

"Hmm..." He reached for the salt grinder and gave it
half a twist, dispensing about four granules over the top
of the meaty red mixture. He stirred, grabbed another
spoon, and tested again.

"Ahh" He nodded in satisfaction. "Perfect and
unbeatable." In his humble opinion, of course. He
turned the flame down to the smallest flicker. The chili
could simmer while he dressed for the evening.

"And this time, I'll be dressing myself, thank you
very much." He wandered into his bedroom and
considered the clothes in his closet. Karla had assured
him that the evening was casual. He leaned towards
jeans and a polo shirt. But, he was escorting his
woman... He straightened and pulled the words back
for further examination.

His woman?

Ian twisted the words, and the implication, in every
direction. He'd already acknowledged, to himself, that

his heart belonged to Karla Black if she wanted it. The physical attraction coming to life between them was a pleasant surprise. The kiss they'd shared on Monday had contained enough electricity to power Garfield for a week. But a relationship, even between established senior citizens, had to have a stronger foundation than physical attraction to survive. And they'd known each other exactly ten days.

Is it too early? Ian's answer was immediate. "Not for me." But did Karla feel the same? Did he even have the nerve to broach the subject so soon?

He bowed his head in the doorway of his closet. "Father, if I heard you correctly a few days ago, I know that you have plans for Karla and me, plans that link our futures. I don't mean to rush her or You, but if You could give me some direction...some clue about how and when to make that happen, it would be much appreciated." Ian paused and looked into his heart. "Alicia made me promise to have a life without her. Don't let me mistake a pledge to her for Your will. I don't ever want to get ahead of You and what You want for my life."

Ian straightened and perused his clothes. He didn't want to be overdressed, but he didn't want to look careless either. Maybe his new black jeans instead of the faded blue, and a button down shirt in place of the pullover. He glanced at the clock and kicked his preparations up a notch. His woman was waiting.

~ * ~

In the two story house across town, a similar clothing issue was being addressed, with far less aplomb. Five outfits lay on the bed, discarded for one reason or another. Karla looked at the mess, shook her head, and returned to the closet. The soft green sweater beckoned. She pulled it out and held it up in front of the mirror. She'd bought it to go with the black skirt, but that wasn't exactly written in granite. Black slacks would look nice as well.

Karla let a breath out into the room. A sweater and black slacks, how complicated was that? *A whole bunch when your insides were tied in knots.* When you felt love stirring for a man you'd known for ten days, a man who made you feel things you never dreamed you'd feel again.

She closed her eyes. "Oh, Father, I need wisdom. Who knew I could feel like this? Please help me sort this out. You have a plan for my life. Help me find it."

Karla stepped out of the jeans and sweatshirt she'd worn all day. She pulled the black slacks up, smoothed them over her hips, and slipped the sweater over her head. The reflection in the mirror didn't really look like her. The look of contentment on her face. The fire in the green eyes that stared back at her had been missing for too long. Her step was springy as she went into the bathroom to work on her hair and makeup.

CHAPTER NINETEEN

Bridgett left her late afternoon appointment with Harrison Lake, eyes red from the emotional visit, heart filled with a new determination. The conversation with the lawyer had provided the balm her troubled thoughts needed. He'd assured her that Jeff would not be allowed to simply walk away from their marriage. She would get the chance for a face-to-face meeting if that was what she really wanted, and a chance to voice her side of this to a judge.

"Not that I have a side," she muttered. "But that face-to-face? Oh yeah." One chance to tell Jeff...*What exactly?* "I don't really know." But she did know this. If skating out of their marriage with the baby blonde stuck to his side, without a single word of explanation, was his intention...she'd be more than happy to throw a wrench into his plans. Bridgett chewed her lip and accepted reality. In the long run, he'd get his way, but she planned to make his journey as complicated as possible. *A point scored for discarded wives everywhere.*

She dug in her pocket for her keys. They came free tangled with a crinkled piece of paper. She separated metal from paper with a frown and unfolded the note. *Oh yeah.* It was Tara's phone number from her visit to the police department a few days ago.

I should call her. Maybe they could arrange dinner or something for Friday night. "If I have to spend too much more time in that tiny apartment, I'll go crazy." *If Mom would just*...Bridgett buried that thought under a sharp exhale, slid into the car, and thumbed her phone to life. She tapped numbers onto the screen and waited for the call to connect.

"Hello."

"Hey, Tara, it's Bridgett."

"Hey back. I was beginning to think you weren't going to call me."

"Yeah, sorry about that. I misplaced your number and didn't see your note again until just now. A long story. Anyway, I thought I'd see if you wanted to do dinner or something Friday night. I need to get out, and a girl's night sounds just about perfect."

Bridgett's heart sank at the silence that filled her ear. "Problem?"

"Not...really," Tara said. "I sort of have plans for Friday night. You're welcome to come along if you want, but..."

Bridgett perked up. "What did you have in mind?"

"I'm shooting pool in a tournament at The Black Hole."

"The Black Hole?"

"It's a bar out on highway nine. It'll be loud and rowdy, not really a...Christian thing, I guess. But it's ladies' night and drinks, even sodas, are two for one."

Bridgett did not miss her friend's hesitation over the word Christian. *Honey, if you only knew.* "A bar?" The thought intrigued her.

"Yeah...I completely understand if that isn't something you want to do."

"I'd love to."

"Really? Because we can do something next week instead."

The thought of another week of solitude, self-imposed or not, made Bridgett's stomach ache. "Absolutely not. I'd love to hang with you this weekend. I don't know where it is though. Could you pick me up?"

"Sure thing."

Arrangements were made, and Bridgett disconnected the call. A bar? *I've never been in a bar.* The thought of bright lights, loud music, and the company of single, attentive cowboys—*it's Oklahoma, there will be cowboys*—appealed to her. Jeff might have tossed her aside, David may have ignored her, Micha may have rejected her advances, and Mom? *Well, Mom is obviously not the person I thought she was.* There were bound to be unattached men at The Black Hole who could make her forget the hurt for a little while.

"Not that I intend to bring one home with me. I'm not a"—*the blonde smiled from her memory*—"slut out to get my claws into anything wearing jeans and cowboy boots. But a little flirting, maybe a dance or two... Boosting my ego can't be a bad thing."

What did one wear to a bar? Bridgett's finger's tapped the steering wheel while she considered the limited selection of clothes hanging in the apartment's tiny closet and remembered the challenge of dressing for her evening with Micha. *Major fail.*

Bridgett shook her head, started the car, and headed toward the mall. This called for some retail therapy. "Maybe I should call Tara back and ask her what she's wearing," she mused aloud. "Oh yeah, and sound like the good little church girl she already thinks I am? No way." *I'm sure I can figure it out.*

~ * ~

"Wow, you said busy, but I didn't expect anything like this."

Karla chuckled at Ian's observation. They'd given up on the idea of finding a parking spot anywhere close to Valley View's gym and had retreated to the far corner of the lot across the street. "It's a big night for everyone, especially the kids." She motioned to a space between the buildings. They had a clear view of a throng of costumed kids milling around several large inflatable slides and bouncers. "You're lucky this year."

Ian turned off the ignition and looked in the indicated direction. "That's a lot of children." He turned in the seat, eyes crinkled at the corners. "Other than having you by my side all evening, how am I lucky?"

Karla shook her head and ignored the compliment. *I could get used to it though.* "The weather is mild enough for the inflatables to be outside, so we might actually be able to have a conversation without screaming at each other.

He patted her hand. "I'd be content to stare at you from across the table."

She looked past him as heat worked its way up her neck to her cheeks. This man knew just how to tangle her up on the inside. *Aren't I too old for that?*

Ian laughed. "Now that I have you sufficiently flustered, let's get our food into the building." His expression turned just a bit sly. "I don't want to miss the judging. I have a winner in my crockpot."

"Confident much?"

"You only have to taste to believe."

"I can't wait." She let herself out of the car, bent into the back seat to retrieve her cereal pumpkins, and waited for Ian and his chili to join her. "Follow me," she said.

Karla walked up the lengthy sidewalk. Questions and doubts assaulted her and churned up her emotions. *What will people think when they see me with a man? Everyone in that gym loved Mitch almost as much as I did. Will they make Ian feel welcomed or uncomfortable?* Nervous sweat filmed her forehead. *What was I thinking? Maybe I really am the silly old woman Bridgett claims I am.*

"Karla, did you forget something?"

Karla started out of her reverie. "I'm sorry?"

"I asked if you'd forgotten something. You stopped on the walk without a word. I said your name twice before I got your attention. Is something wrong?"

Karla looked at him, undone by the sweet look of concern on his face. She shook her head. "Just a moment of nerves. I hope you won't take this the wrong way, but this is harder than I imagined it would be."

Ian cocked his head. "May I share something with you?"

Her brows crept up in question.

"I've thought about this moment a lot today. Meeting your friends, circulating among people who knew and loved Mitch and might see me as an unwelcomed replacement. It's been a bit daunting. Know what I decided?"

"What?" Her voice was a rough whisper.

"That none of these people walk in our shoes every day. That if they loved Mitch, then they want you to be happy. I also prayed about it."

"You did?"

"I asked God for some direction, and He clamped a lid on the worry. We aren't doing anything wrong, sweetheart. We loved our spouses until they were taken from us. If God has chosen to give us a second chance, who are we, or they, to argue?"

Karla felt her shoulders relax. "That's the perfect answer." *And exactly what I've been telling Bridgett. Maybe I should listen to my own advice.* She motioned to the double doors of the gymnasium, still several yards away. "Then why are we standing here? Let's get that chili inside. You've got a contest to win."

~ * ~

The cavernous building was packed with people and echoed with bits and pieces of conversation. Ian looked around and, as huge as the space was, could not imagine sharing it with the inflatable slides and swarm of children he'd seen outside. He followed close behind Karla. She stopped and handed her dessert to a dark-headed woman, large with child, stationed behind a long counter.

"Hey, Karla, these look awesome. I saw the recipe on Pinterest. Looks like you did an amazing job."

"Let's hope they taste as good as they look." Karla took a step back and crossed her arms. "They have you working the desserts? That's torture with a capital T."

The woman laid a hand on her belly. "We have a deal. I'm here to check everything in. I don't have to cut, serve, touch, or smell them." She faced Ian, and familiarity tugged at the corners of his mind. Her smile of welcome reached all the way to her blue eyes. "Ian, I'm so glad you could make it."

Ian's lips ticked up in an answering smile. "I...umm...I'm happy to be included."

The dark haired woman laughed. "I've caught you off guard. I'm Terri Evans. I don't think we've ever been introduced, but I run Tiny Tikes. I've seen you a few times when you've picked Millicent up for Rachel."

The pieces snapped together in Ian's mind. "Of course. I have seen you zipping around over there. It's nice to have a name to go with the face."

Terri patted her belly. "Well, I don't do a lot of 'zipping' these days."

"This is her third baby in five years," Karla supplied. "I'm surprised she has the energy to crawl."

"Trust me, there are days..." Terri turned back to Ian. "You guys go mingle and have a good time. We'll get better acquainted later. I want to make sure that you meet my husband, Steve."

"Come along, Ian, we've been dismissed."

"It was nice to meet you, Terri."

"Same here." She pointed to the other side of the room. "Chili drop off is over there. Better hurry. Judging starts in five minutes."

Karla led the way through the maze of people to another row of tables.

Ian bit his lip when he recognized the blonde checking in the entries. Memories of doctor's appointments with Alicia and this woman's unfailing kindness to the both of them flooded his heart. He pushed the sadness away. "Callie, so nice to see you again."

"Hi, Ian. Here." Callie cleared a spot for the heavy crockpot. "Put that down before you drop it."

Ian set the chili down with a grateful sigh, circled the table, and drew Callie into a huge hug. "I never got the chance to thank you."

Callie hugged him back. "It was always my pleasure. Alicia was a beautiful woman. I wish I could have done more."

Ian added a squeeze to the hug. "God had a plan."

"Dropping off or picking up?"

Ian took a step back at the masculine voice, and Callie pulled a tall bearded man to her side. "Ian, this is my husband, Benton. Benton, Ian McAlister."

Ian took the hand Benton offered. "Good to meet you. Your wife helped me through some rocky times a couple of years ago. I was just thanking her."

Benton put his hands on his hips and scowled. "I hear that's not all you're out to do."

Ian glanced at Callie before looking back at the man. "Uh..."

"I've heard all about your plot to dethrone my chili."

"How—?"

Benton gave a bark of laughter. He placed an arm across Ian's shoulders and turned him to face Callie and Karla. "You have much to learn, my young initiate, if you plan to hang with this group. Allow me to provide your first lesson." He motioned to Karla and Callie. "These two..." His eyes roamed the gym, and he finally pointed to a dark haired woman deep in conversation with Terri Evans. "And those two? Closer than paint on toenails. They have a code. They share *everything*. You tell one, you've told all four."

"Benton—" Callie began.

"Shush woman. He's better off learning this now. It's his only defense." Benton turned back to Ian. "The only way to get around the code is to swear one of them to secrecy before you speak. And even then—"

"Are you done?" Karla asked, her words buried under a layer of laughter.

Benton lowered his voice. "There are a couple more you need to watch out for. I'll point them out later."

"Thanks?"

"You should thank me, and you should be very afraid." He clapped Ian on the back, snitched a chip from a nearby bag, and brushed a kiss across Callie's forehead before ambling away.

Ian watched him go. "That was...interesting."

Karla shook her head. "He's a goofball."

"But we love him," Callie finished.

A young man in a ball cap mounted the stage, microphone in hand. "Hello out there. Anyone hungry?"

A rowdy "Yes!" echoed from the rafters.

Karla took Ian's arm. "Let's find a seat. Things are about to get started."

An hour later. Ian carried his third place ribbon back to the table and laid it next to his bowl. *Third place?* He watched with amused frustration as the golden ladle was awarded to Benton Stillman.

Karla rubbed his arm. "Sorry, you can always try again next year."

"Count on it." He pursed his lips. Everyone had eaten well over the last hour. Now a new line formed to sample the remains of the first place offering. *Maybe I...*

Benton slid into the seat beside him. "Hey, Karla. Callie and the girls are looking for you."

"Oh?"

"Yes, they're back in the kitchen, something about your recipe."

"OK." Karla stood and laid a hand on Ian's shoulder. "Do you mind if I...?"

Ian waved her away. "You go right ahead. I'll visit with the chili master here."

Karla headed for the kitchen, and Benton dropped a bowl of chili on the table in front of Ian.

"Better luck next time, old man."

"What's this?"

Benton sat back in his seat and crossed his arms. "Some more of tonight's education. A sample of the best chili you'll ever wrap your lips around."

Ian stared down at the rich meaty mixture. He nodded and removed a clean white handkerchief from his pocket, shook it open, and wrapped it carefully around the paper bowl.

Benton watched the exercise with a frown. "Saving it for later?"

"Not exactly," Ian answered. "I'm taking it to a lab tomorrow to have it analyzed. Then I'm going to share your secret with each of the women you warned me about. Your reign is over as of tonight."

Benton's whole body shook with laughter. "That's extreme."

Ian removed the handkerchief and spooned up a bite. He chewed it slowly, evaluating the flavors. *Garlic, chili powder...and pepper sauce?* He'd never admit it to the man sitting next to him, but it was the best he'd ever tasted. He proceeded to scrape the bowl clean. "That wasn't half bad."

"Whatever." Benton stood. "You got a few minutes? I have a couple guys I want you to meet."

Ian wiped his mouth and fingers and pushed his chair back. "Lead on." He followed Benton across the room and out the big double glass doors into the parking lot. His new friend continued around to the street side of the building and stopped under the metal stairs leading down from the second floor. Noise filtered out of the building, and childish squeals echoed from the play area where kids bounced, climbed, and otherwise ran themselves ragged. Parents would sleep well tonight.

Ian stopped short when he recognized a couple of the other men he'd met this evening waiting beneath the stairs. He struggled to recall the names, but even without the names, he knew they were the husbands of Karla's friends.

The younger of the men stepped into the light. His dark hair brushed his collar, his blue eyes almost black in the shadows.

"Having a good time?"

Ian frowned and finally placed him as the writer, Steve Evans. Ian looked left and saw the curly headed lawyer, *Harold...Harry...Harrison. Yes that's it, Harrison Lake.*

Ian allowed his gaze to move from face to face. Reality smacked him between the eyes. *I've been neatly separated from the herd.* He leaned against the building and crossed his arms. He could tell by their expressions that it was time for the third degree. The fact that none of them knew where to start was evident in the way the three men shuffled their feet and looked at each other.

"Questions, gentlemen?"

Benton cleared his throat. "I...uh..." He kicked at a rock on the sidewalk.

Discomfort rolled off of him in waves that Ian could almost see.

"Nuts! Look, we got you out here so we could have a talk without the women interfering."

The muscles around Benton's mouth tightened, and Ian heard him swallow before the bearded man's eyes pinned him with a steely glower. "We need to talk about Karla. Mitchell Black was the best friend I ever had." Benton straightened. "It's my job to look after Karla just like he'd look out for Callie if the situation were reversed." He stepped closer and Ian would have taken a step back if it hadn't been for the wall behind him.

"She's happier tonight than I've seen her since Mitch died. For that, I'll say thanks, but..."

Ian's brows rose when Benton's expression went ridged with purpose.

"I..." He motioned to the two other men. "We wanted to let you know that if you do anything to hurt Karla, the three of us will see to it that your life isn't worth living. You need to be straight with us. Where are you going with all of this?"

Ian tilted his head. "Going? I've known her for ten days."

Harrison spoke for the first time. "But you have a very determined look on your face."

"And a very possessive manner," the writer added. "Our question stands. What are you determined to do?"

Ian studied each of the men in turn. There was no

intimidation in their expressions, just loving concern for the woman who'd found a home in his heart. He could appreciate that. He took a deep breath and uttered the first words that formed in his mind. "I plan to marry the woman just as soon as she'll have me."

CHAPTER TWENTY

Ian stared at the ceiling from the comfort of his bed on Thursday morning. He laced his fingers together and rested his hands between his head and the pillow. His lips twitched as he replayed last night's events in his head.

The men had been so embarrassed at the *necessity* of challenging his intentions, so judicious in their care of Karla. They'd won his respect in that short confrontation. His final response, though, gave him pause.

I plan to marry the woman just as soon as she'll have me.

He wasn't sure when that had become his plan, but it certainly was. But *as soon as?* His heart was in the white flag lap running hard for the checkered, now his head had the pedal to metal, racing to catch up, needing to take the air off his reckless heart's bumper. *Not,* Ian assured his heart, to red flag the race, but there were caution flags whipping in the breeze, and they should be heeded to insure a safe finish for all.

He chuckled at his analogy. One too many Sunday afternoon races, but the comparison stood. The left side of his brain ticked of the reasons for restraint. He'd known Karla for days not months. Even if he could talk her into marriage, where would they live?

Where would they worship? Karla's daughter couldn't stand the sight of him. And last but hardly least, he needed to speak to her eldest son about his intentions. It sounded old fashioned, but it was a courtesy he owed Nicolas Black as man of his family.

Ian's heart countered each ugly objection. Love didn't exist on a timeline. When it was right, it was right. End of discussion. It didn't matter where they lived as long as they were together. One house or the other, or sell both and move to the beach. Problem solved, next question. They would worship at Valley View, of course. Ian had a comfortable eight-year-old relationship with the members of Grace Community Church. Last night only reinforced that Karla's attachment to Valley View went decades deep. He wouldn't think of asking her to change it. The daughter? Well, you couldn't please everyone, and hadn't he just told Karla last night not to try? And speaking to Nicolas Black? Ian could do that today if he decided to get his lazy butt out of bed.

The arguments for caution didn't make sense when faced with the facts. Ian eased his mind off the accelerator and allowed his heart to rush headlong to the finish line. He tossed the blankets aside, rolled out of bed, and straightened slowly, allowing sleep dormant joints and muscles a chance to pop and stretch. Getting old wasn't for the faint of heart, but the happiness beckoning on the horizon infused him with renewed energy.

A bite of breakfast, a run by the coffee shop, and then he'd swing by the Garfield police station. The chances of catching Nicolas Black in the office were slim, but he could leave his name and number. Ian remembered the speculative look on Kate Black's face when Karla introduced them. He'd bet money that he'd hear from the detective before the day was over.

Ninety minutes later, a tall cup of takeout coffee in his hand, Ian stood at the thick window that served as the gateway between the tiny reception area and the back rooms of the police department. He pressed the buzzer and waited.

A smiling brunette answered the bell. "Good morning. May I help you?"

Ian returned her smile and glanced down to her name tag. "Tara, I was hoping to talk with Detective Black. If he isn't in, could I leave him a note?"

Tara glanced behind her, tilting her head this way and that. "I think he's still back here." Her gaze roamed for several seconds. "There he is. Nicolas," she called. "Someone's here to see you." She turned back to Ian. "Wait right here, he'll be with you in a sec."

"I appreciate your help, Tara." Ian watched her walk away while his heart kicked into overdrive. *I wanted to speak to him, but I wasn't expecting—*

"I'm Detective Black. What can I do for you?"

Ian swallowed back nerves. "Detective, my name is Ian McAlister. I was hoping to have a word with you if you aren't too busy."

The cop's sandy eyebrows rose over blue eyes. "Ian... Wait right there, I'll come out."

Nicolas moved from the window and left Ian to pace the small lobby. He berated himself while he waited. He'd pulled himself out of bed and raced over here on a whim. Karla's son was going to come through that door any second. Just what did he plan to say to him? *You don't know me, but I want to marry your mother. Hi, I just met your mother eleven days ago and I'm in love with her. I was wondering if you'd...* His imagined conversation died as the officer came through the access door with his hand outstretched in greeting.

Ian wiped his damp palm on his pants' leg before accepting the handshake.

"Nicolas Black."

"Ian McAlister." An uncomfortable silence stretched on the heels of the introductions.

Nicolas hooked his thumbs in his belt as he studied him.

Ian tried to read the detective's expression and failed.

"You said you wanted to talk to me?"

Ian exhaled. "Yes, I..." He looked around the impersonal space. A half dozen folding chairs circled a beat up table on one side of the door. A dented vending machine occupied the space on the other side. The room offered no real privacy. His gaze came back to the rapidly cooling coffee in his hand. *Ah yes.* He raised the cup, "This has gone cold. If you have time to join me, I'll buy us both a fresh cup."

Ian stood under Nicolas's scrutiny while the detective tapped his fingers on the shiny leather of his belt. The hard cop eyes seemed a bit out of place in the boyish face of Karla's son. *I'm glad I haven't committed a crime. I'd admit to just about anything right now.*

"I can do that." Nicolas said. "I'll meet you at Ground Zero in thirty minutes or so. I just need to finish up the report I was working on."

Ian nodded. "That's perfect. Thanks for making the time."

"No problem. Something tells me we both have

things to say."

The two men stood where they were for a few seconds, each obviously waiting for the other to move or speak.

Ian cleared his throat. "I'll head that way now, get us a table."

Nicolas nodded. "Good idea, I'll see you shortly.

Ian turned and made his way to the door. He didn't need to look back to know that the cop's eyes followed him out and onto the sidewalk. The hair on the back of his neck stood to attention where he imagined Nicolas's eyes rested.

Once Ian was on the sidewalk, he tossed his barely touched coffee in a waste can. Despite what he'd told Nicolas, it was still hot enough to sting his fingers through the paper, but he'd have a fresh cup soon enough. His nerves were already bouncing like ping pong balls under the surface of his skin. He didn't need caffeine stacked on top of caffeine.

What I need are words.

Maybe he should have thought this through a bit before showing up on Nicolas's doorstep. *Alicia always did say I was too impulsive for my own good.*

His path to Ground Zero took him by Bings Jeweler. Something in the window flashed as he strolled by. Ian stopped and returned to the display. There were a multitude of shiny things to explore, but the light and his gaze lingered on one ring. A square cut diamond almost half the size of his pinky nail. The large stone, surrounded with smaller ones, seemed to pulse with an internal fire brighter than the sun hanging over his head. Ian whistled his admiration. He could almost hear it shouting *pick me, I've been waiting just for you!*

"Wouldn't that look lovely on Karla's left hand?" He closed his eyes. *Talk about impulsive*. He glanced at his watch. He still had fifteen minutes before he met with Nicolas. Looking wasn't buying, it was just being prepared when the time came.

Ian took a deep breath and wondered who he was trying to convince, because, deep in his heart, the decision had already been made. *I should wait...for a multitude of reasons*. He turned from the window, intending to take a step away, and found his feet weighted with lead.

He rolled his eyes. *Foolish...rash...impulsive*. The litany echoed over and over in his head as he pulled the door open and walked inside.

Ian left Bing's twenty minutes later with his stoic brain waging a fresh war on his reckless heart. He hurried to his destination, concerned that Nicolas would get there ahead of him and think he'd changed his mind. He entered the coffee shop and scanned the occupants, relieved not to see the cop. He opted for a table in the far corner.

The officer followed a few minutes later, crossed the room, and offered Ian a harried smile. "Sorry I'm late."

Ian shook his head. "Not a problem." He stood. "Have a seat. I'll get us something to drink. What's your pleasure?"

"Just hot and black."

Ian's response was a nervous snort of laughter. "A man after my own heart. I don't understand half the stuff they try to put into my cup these days. Just the way God made it has always been good enough for me." He returned to the table with two steaming cups and found Karla's son watching him intently. Ian handed one of the cups across and took his seat while the cop sampled the brew.

"Now that's a good cup of coffee. I know it's cliché to admit it, but what we have at the station most days resembles coffee in name only." Nicolas wrapped both hands around his cup, settled back in his chair, and focused on Ian. "Can I be honest with you?"

Nerves lodged Ian's heart in his throat. This man's sister hates me. Could that be a shared sentiment? *Why didn't I consider that before now?* He swallowed past the obstruction. "Of course."

"I get paid to observe things. What I saw a few minutes ago was a very nervous man. The way I see it, there are only two reasons for you to be uneasy around me. You've either committed some heinous crime, or we're here to talk about my mother."

Ian raised his right hand and laid his left over his heart. "No crime here, Detective."

"I figured as much, so let me take some of the nerves out of the situation." He leaned forward. "I've watched my mother grieve herself down to nothing over the last few months. She's lost weight, she's lost her confidence, and she'd deny it, but I'm pretty sure she lost a bit of the faith she and Dad hammered into me while I was growing up."

Ian knew his sadness was evident on his face when he nodded. "She lost half of who she was. That's difficult to understand until you've experienced it."

It was Nicolas's turn to nod. "I get that." He sipped his drink. "I know my sister has been more than a little rough on you. But you've put a smile back on my mom's face. As far as I'm concerned, that makes you sent straight from heaven."

Ian felt some of the tension slip from between his shoulder blades. "I'm grateful you're willing to give me a chance."

Nicolas twisted his cup in hands and shook his head. "Bridgett has issues right now. I'd apologize for her, but it'd be pointless. I will ask you to reserve judgment on her for a while. She was the only girl, and really spoiled. I think her attitude has more to do with Jeff's dumping her than with the relationship building between you and Mom. Once Bridgett gets some of this resolved, I think she'll snap out of it."

Ian met Nicolas's eyes. "I'm hardly in a position to judge your sister or anyone else. I do know that Karla has been very hurt by her actions, though. I hope for your mother's sake she finds some of those answers soon."

Nicolas shrugged. "It's not the first time they've butted heads. Bridgett was a drama queen when she was a teenager and always a daddy's girl. She needs to grow up, but that's just a big brother's opinion."

The sound of hissing filled the room. Ian glanced at the mug shaped clock that hung over the door and marked the top of each hour with coffee scented steam.

"I've gotta get back soon." Nicolas told him. "If we aren't here to discuss Bridgett's behavior, and you don't have a crime to confess, we need to get to the point, and that leaves Mom." He sat back, and crossed his arms. "What's up with you and my mom, Ian?"

The direct question dried up Ian's throat like a desert. He lifted his cup and took a cautious sip of the steaming hot coffee. *Truth and directness. This is a man who values both.* "I've become very fond of your mother in a very short time. It's taken me by surprise."

"How so?"

Ian met the steady stare of the detective. "I was married to my Alicia for almost fifty years. Before that we dated almost all through school. In all that time, I never looked at another woman." He tapped his fingers against his cup. "I believe in the long term, and I don't mind taking my time to get there. I've known your mother less than two weeks, and she already has my heart. My brain is having a hard time catching up. It's...disconcerting."

Nicolas laughed. "You don't have to tell me about uncooperative hearts. When I met Kate, I fell hard and fast. I knew what I wanted less than a month in." He shook his head, "Sometimes it's just the right thing, and you have to move forward or lose the best thing that ever happened to you."

"Exactly. That's what I wanted to talk to you about. You're the man of the house in your father's absence. I'm just old fashioned enough to feel like I should speak to you about my intentions before this goes any further. I'll be honest, I'm relieved to know that you don't object to a relationship between your mother and me. I wanted your blessing, but not having it probably wouldn't have stopped me."

"And that cements what I just said," Nicolas told him. "You care enough to break down or ignore the obstacles. That doesn't offend me." He leaned forward. "Let me ask you a question. Have you prayed about the situation?"

Ah, Karla, you did a good job here. Ian nodded. "Every day since our paths crossed."

"And you don't feel God telling you to pull back?"

"Just the opposite." Ian sighed. "Nicolas, I am

hopelessly, completely, no-going-back, in love with your mother."

Nicolas searched Ian's face, the blue eyes steady and intense. "Go on."

Ian held the stare and pulled a black box from his pocket. He set it on the table and flipped it open. The diamond seemed to collect all the light from the room as it glowed. Ian let the stone do the talking.

Nicolas glanced down.

Ian heard a quick cough as if something threatened to strangle the younger man.

Nicolas looked back up with raised brows. "Good enough."

CHAPTER TWENTY-ONE

Ian jumped when the phone rang Friday afternoon. The motion sent a thorn deep into the pad of his thumb. "Ouch!" He yanked the stem free and watched the tiny drop of blood that followed. "Why didn't I have these confounded things stripped?" Because even at the bargain price of fifteen dollars a dozen, twenty-four dozen red roses had cost him a pretty penny. Tacking on another five dollars a dozen to have them stripped of the thorns hadn't made sense, especially since he was ripping the petals of all but twenty-four flowers. The phone summoned his attention once again.

Anxiety pooled in his gut when he saw Nicolas's number on the screen. Ian glanced at the ceiling and muttered a quick prayer. "I don't need any complications this late in the day." He connected the call.

"Hello, Nicolas."

"Are you about ready over there? Kate just called, and Mom is making noises about needing to get home so she can get ready for her evening with you. I don't know how much longer my wife can keep her occupied without making Mom suspicious."

"I need another hour or so. I've been over to her

241

house, so things are set there. Thanks again for arranging for someone to unlock her car for me."

Laughter filtered through the phone. "Not a problem. I'm just sorry I got hung up and couldn't get by there. Once I told Tyler what you were up to, it didn't take a lot of persuasion to have my partner go over and pop the locks. I just wish I could be there when she sees what you did."

"You and me both, but I'm not going to risk being seen before I spring the surprise. Anyway, I've got about four dozen more of these blood letters to tear apart, then I need to clean up and get the lasagna in the oven. I made it last night, so it just has to heat. Thanks for the tip there."

"Mom does love Italian. The pasta by itself would likely get you your way. Nervous?"

Ian chuckled at the question "Like a spider in a room full of arachnophobes, but I'll get over it."

"OK, I'll let Kate know she needs to keep Mom occupied for at least another hour before she takes her home. Add an hour for her to primp for your evening, and you should have plenty of time."

"That works. Thanks, again, for your help today, and Kate's. I couldn't have done all of this on my own."

"Hey, whatever makes Mom happy. I'm glad Kate was able to connect you with a florist who didn't mind having her entire stock of red roses wiped out in one purchase. There's only one flaw in your plan."

Ian's heart jumped to his throat. *Flaw?* "What?"

Nicolas gave an amused snort. "Calm down, what you're doing for Mom is perfect, but after tonight, Kate's going to think I'm a serious underachiever in the romance department. I'm going to have to work hard to top this."

Ian took a breath and forced the tension from his shoulders. "I'll help you think of something, but right now, I've got to get back to work." He disconnected the call and went back to tearing roses apart.

~ * ~

Karla hurried up the porch steps, turning at her front door to wave goodbye to her daughter-in-law. She still didn't know what had provoked today's invitation for lunch, which extended to a *quick trip* to the mall, and ended with a touch up to their manicures. Karla didn't mind the time spent with Kate, but if she didn't hurry, she'd be late for dinner tonight. Ian was cooking—*he's such a sweetheart*—and had declined to share the menu with her. But, if their dinner a week ago was any indication of his culinary ability, she didn't want to keep him, or the food, waiting.

Once in the house, she looked around for Jester and found the kitten asleep in a puddle of late afternoon sunlight spilling through the west window of the kitchen. She stooped and brushed a finger across the party-colored fur. *Finish your nap, little one.* She crossed back to the stairs, taking a quick look to see if there were messages on the home phone.

Nothing.

Her hand hovered over the receiver for a second. Five days and counting since her daughter had stormed from the house. She wanted to talk to Bridgett. If nothing else, to find out where she was staying. But Karla withdrew her hand. Her daughter's stubbornness was legendary. It was time she grew up. Karla knew from Kate, who'd heard from Nicolas, who'd gotten word from the dispatcher at the station, that Bridgett was going out with friends tonight.

It hurt Karla to rely on such convoluted channels for news, but at least she knew her daughter was still close by. The stalemate between them couldn't last much longer. Karla climbed the stairs. "Father, please let it be over soon. I care for Ian, but Bridgett is my daughter, and I love her. I shouldn't have to choose between the two of them. You've opened my eyes to the possibility of a future beyond the loss of Mitch. I'm so grateful. Please help her see that I deserve a life."

She paused on the landing to catch her breath. Why was it that young people buying a house never gave a thought to the inconvenience of growing old in that house? She'd been climbing these stairs every day for better than thirty years. There were days when she just knew they'd be the death of her.

Breath restored, she continued with her prayer. "Above everything, help her see how much she needs to restore her relationship with You. I know once that happens, the rest will work itself out."

Karla entered her room, tossed the single shopping bag on the bed, and withdrew her one purchase for the day. She held the bright purple sweater up and faced the mirror. Kate was right, the color looked fabulous against her skin. She couldn't wait to see how it looked paired with her black slacks and pumps. She shook her head. *I've gone from shopping denial to shopaholic in the last couple of weeks.* Karla smoothed her hand over the soft knit, enjoying the indulgent texture of the sweater's weave.

She stripped out of her jeans and pullover shirt and

slipped on the slacks and sweater. A bit of makeup, a hair touch-up, and a spritz of her favorite scent, and she was ready to go fifteen minutes ahead of schedule. She'd worried about being late, but if traffic worked with her, she'd be a bit early. *Maybe I can help. I did enjoy working in the kitchen with Ian last week.*

With that thought in mind Karla hurried down the stairs, grabbed her jacket, purse, and keys. Her heels clicked on the pavement of the sidewalk. She aimed her keys at the car and clicked the remote, confused when nothing happened. She hit the button again and received the same silence. "That's odd. Maybe I should have the battery checked in this thing." She hit the lock button instead and the horn sounded in response. Puzzled, she hit the unlock button and got the unmistakable click of locks disengaging.

Karla shook her head. *I must have forgotten to lock it last night.* She reached for the door and pulled it open. A flood of red fell at her feet, and a heavy floral scent filled her nose. She stepped back. "What in the...?" She stooped down for a closer inspection. "Rose petals?"

Karla peered into her car. Everything was awash in a sea of silky red. The seats, front and back, the floorboards, the dash. "There must be thousands of those in here." Her eyes went to the steering wheel and the envelope taped to the vinyl center. She pulled it loose, broke the seal, and leaned into the fading light.

My heart is laid at your feet just like these rose petals. I eagerly await your arrival. Ian.

Her hand dropped to her side as her heart fluttered beneath her ribs. "Oh, that sweet man!" Now the shopping trip made sense. He must have enlisted Kate's help. Brushing petals from the driver's seat, she slid behind the wheel. The scent of roses became stronger as her feet ground some of them to pulp. The man was just full of surprises. She couldn't wait to see what else he had up his sleeve for the evening.

Twenty minutes later she stopped at the curb in front of Ian's house and stared. Even in the waning October light she could see more rose petals. They formed a trail from the curb, up the walk, and right to the front door. She sat there, immobilized by delight. Mitch had been her first and only love, but she had never used the word romantic to describe him. Tender, gentle when the situation called for it, always a kind and thoughtful husband, friend, and lover, but romantic? She shook her head. They'd never shared candlelit dinners. He'd never been one to leave mushy notes in unexpected places. And flowers? A time or two, but nothing on this scale. She'd never really missed those things. There was too much good to lament over the one thing he didn't do well.

Karla climbed out of the car. "But, wow."

She followed the path. When she stepped onto the porch she found the heavy wooden door open, and through the decorative glass of the storm door, she could see the trail continue. She knocked, waited, and knocked again. She opened the door just a crack. "Ian?" *Where could he be?*

She opened the door and followed the petals. They led her to the kitchen. The table was set with china, crystal, and candles. The floor was littered with petals, and a vase sat in the center of the table loaded with the brilliant red flowers. The air in the room was pleasantly heavy with the scent of so many roses. *He must have just stepped out. I'll light the candles for him.*

Karla moved forward in a daze, picked up the lighter from the counter, and crossed to the table. She ignited a tiny flame and stretched to reach the farthest candle. She froze when she spotted the small black velvet jeweler's box sitting beside the plate that would be hers.

Her free hand flew to her mouth and smothered her gasp of surprise. "Oh, Ian. What have you done?" Karla sat, because her knees wouldn't support her any longer. She picked up the box with hands that trembled. She didn't open it, couldn't have opened it if she'd wanted to. Breath short, body quaking, she simply held it to her heart and cried.

~ * ~

Ian rushed into the kitchen and skidded to a stop. He dropped the container of Parmesan cheese he'd run next door to borrow on the counter and hurried across the room.

"Karla?" When she didn't answer he knelt by her knees. He saw the box in her hand and knew his surprise had taken an unexpected turn. Ian closed his hands around hers and lowered them, box and all, into her lap.

"Karla, sweetheart, look at me."

With a final shuttering sob, Karla met gaze.

"I didn't mean to make you cry." He took a cloth napkin from the table and dabbed at her cheeks. "I wanted this to be a happy evening."

Karla bowed her head and stared at their hands clasped in her lap. "I can't believe you did all of this for me." Her voice was a whisper, full of emotion and confusion. "When you weren't here, I just..." her breath hitched, "followed the roses. I think I ruined your surprise. I didn't mean to."

Ian laid the napkin aside. "The evening isn't over." He squeezed her hands before slipping the box free. He stayed on his knees, placed a finger under her chin, and raised her eyes to his.

"Karla, I know we haven't known each other for very long, but my heart tells me that this is the right move. We've both learned how very short and unexpected life can be. I've known for a year that I didn't want to spend the rest of my life alone. I'll be honest, I was willing to settle for companionship if that's all I could find." He stared at her through the flickering light of the candles. "I never dreamed that I'd stumble headfirst into so much more."

He flipped open the box and turned it so Karla could see the ring nestled inside. The diamond picked up the candlelight and sent it bouncing around the room. Her gasp of surprise and the fact that she didn't pull away gave him the courage to continue. He slipped the ring free of the velvet.

"Karla, I love you. I want to spend the rest of my life, long or short, with you. Will you marry me?"

"Oh, Ian."

He held his breath until she lifted her head.

"I didn't know I could ever feel this way again. I don't have the words to tell you what's in my heart." She stared into his eyes. "I love you, too."

"Is that a yes?"

Karla nodded.

Ian took her left hand and slid the ring home. He clasped her hand in his, pulled her down, and sealed their engagement with a kiss.

CHAPTER TWENTY-TWO

Bridgett turned left then right in front of the mirror. The dark denim of her new skinny jeans hugged her curves and looked great tucked into new suede cowboy boots. She smoothed the bright red shirt that stopped at the waist of her jeans with nothing to spare and studied the row of snaps that secured it. She undid an extra snap and allowed the lace of her new lingerie to peek out above the opening. Bridgett studied the effect and snapped it back.

Prude.

The little voice made her frown, and she yanked the snap apart. *There!* She shoved her breasts higher in the bra. "Come on girls, don't let me down now."

Hair fluffed, lips glossed, she pouted into the glass. *Forty-three never looked so good.*

Bridgett turned from the mirror when rapping sounded at the door of the tiny apartment. She cleared the distance in ten steps and looked out the grimy peephole. Tara waited on the other side, and Bridgett swallowed a laugh. *This is going to be so much fun.* Tonight was the beginning of a new chapter in her life.

She threw the door open. "Hey, girlfriend."

"Hey back." Tara looked Bridgett up and down. "That's a...nice outfit."

Bridgett took in Tara's jeans and sweatshirt and compared her friend's simple clothes to what she wore. "Too much?"

Tara shook her head. "Nah...just not what I expected. You'll see all sorts at the Black Hole. This is what I wear when I'm shooting pool. It's comfortable and it moves with me. You ready to go?"

"Absolutely. Just let me get my bag and lock up." She did, then pulled the door closed and jiggled the knob to make sure it was secure. She followed Tara out to a tall yellow pickup truck.

"Climb in," Tara instructed.

Bridgett went around to the passenger side, opened the door, and used the running board to hoist herself into the seat. "Climb in is right. You've got the whole country girl package right here."

Tara turned the key in the ignition. "BB gets me where I need to go, and I never lose her in a parking lot, as long as the sun is up."

"BB?"

Tara grinned. "Big Bird. Buckle up."

Bridgett stretched the seatbelt across her lap as Tara pulled out of the parking lot. The truck rumbled around her, and she laughed out loud, bounced in the seat, and raised her voice to make herself heard over the powerful engine. "I feel a little bit like a teenager sneaking out on an illicit date." She looked behind her and noticed a gun rack in the back window. Three rifle cases hung in horizontal brackets. "You hunt, too?"

Tara shook her head. "Nope, I love Bambi from a discreet distance. They don't have guns inside. I use them to hold my pool cues. It's handy, and if anybody gets it in their head to mess with me, it's a good deterrent. They think I'm armed."

"That's pretty smart." Bridgett settled back in her seat. "Pool sounds like an interesting hobby. Who taught you how to play?"

"Old boyfriend. He split, but the lessons stuck."

"And you win money?"

Tara nodded, her face going from defined to shadowed and back again as they drove beneath streetlights. "Sometimes. There's twenty-five hundred dollars up for grabs tonight. BB needs new tires, and I need a vacation. I intend to walk out of the Black Hole with that check in my pocket."

"I'll keep my fingers crossed for you."

"You do that." Tara glanced at Bridgett. "Speaking of old boyfriends. Have you been to the bookstore yet?"

Bridgett crossed her arms. "No, but I did run in to Micha."

Tara nodded. "I figured you would if you stayed in town very long." She chuckled. "Amid all the drama of high school, the day you threw his ring in his face is an unforgettable moment. He sure did grow up nice, though. Did you guys kiss and make up?"

The memory of their dinner and his rebuff at the end of the evening still stung Bridgett's pride. "Hardly. He was a jerk then and, as far as I can tell, he's just a bigger jerk now."

"Uh oh. Share?"

Share how she threw herself at his feet and he kicked her to the curb? *Not likely.* "Let's just say he's not someone I need in my life and leave it at that."

Tara shrugged. "Your story, your rules." She maneuvered the truck into a parking lot, dodged a few potholes, and picked a space some distance from the door. Here we are."

Bridgett trailed behind her friend, out of her element and a little nervous but anxious to see what lay behind the door. *Mom would have a cow if she knew I was spending the evening in a bar.* Yeah, well, Mom didn't know, and even if she did... Bridgett pushed the thought aside. *I'm a grown woman.* She's made it clear to me that what I think of her actions is irrelevant. Why should I care what she thinks of mine?

Tara pushed the door open, and Bridgett followed her through to a world she'd seen only on a TV screen.

Smoke hung heavy in the air, swirling in thick clouds around the low lights suspended above the four pool tables. And Tara had been right about the variety of dress. All the extremes were present. From the girl seated at the bar in a skirt so short it resembled a belt to a grizzle faced, over-all clad farmer nursing a beer in a dark corner. Bridgett relaxed. She fit nicely in the middle.

"Would you stop gawking?" Tara hissed.

Bridgett yanked her attention back to her friend. "What?"

"You're standing there, staring around with your mouth half open. People are going to think you've never been in a bar before."

Bridgett lifted a shoulder. "I haven't."

Tara closed her eyes and pinched the bridge of her nose. She looked up. "Are you serious?"

Bridgett nodded.

"Right, I forgot...church girl. Just stop staring, OK? They're just people, nice enough for the most part." She put her hand on Bridgett's arm and steered her toward the bar. "It's ladies' night. Let's get something to drink and find a seat. We've got about thirty minutes before the tournament starts."

They waded through the crowd at the bar. The room, as a whole, was a single step above shabby. The well-lit shelves behind the bar were stocked with an abundance of bottles. Blenders whirred, ice clinked, and trays came and went loaded with drinks of all colors and sizes.

Bridgett stuck close to Tara as her friend elbowed through the noisy crowd. "What do you want to drink? You order one, you get two."

She chewed her lip. "What are you getting?"

"Rum and Coke."

"You're driving later."

Tara narrowed her eyes. "Yes, Mommy, I know. I'll have my two drinks to limber me up for the tournament, then I'll stick with soda."

"What can I get you ladies?"

Tara's smile returned, and she faced the bartender. "Hi, Jimmy. Give us a second?" When the man nodded and moved away, Tara turned back to Bridgett, eyebrows raised in question.

Bridgett looked up and down the bar. She nodded to a tall, pink, icy looking thing in a stemmed glass. "What's that?"

Tara glanced around her. "It's a strawberry daiquiri."

"Looks like a slush."

"Pretty much, with rum."

Bridgett bit her lip. "Yum...I'm not a drinker. Can you get it without the rum?"

Tara rolled her eyes, turned back to the bar, and motioned the bartender back over. "Rum and Coke for me, virgin strawberry daiquiri for my friend."

While they waited for their drinks, Tara turned away from the bar and leaned back on her elbows. Bridgett mirrored her pose and looked around. "There aren't any tables empty."

"Busy night with the tournament and all," Tara agreed. "Hope you're ready to break in those boots." She kicked one of her feet up and wiggled her tennis shoe. "I'm comfy."

"Ladies."

They turned, dug money from bags and pockets, and accepted their drinks, two each.

"So we're just gonna stand here and drink these?" Bridgett asked.

Tara sipped. "Looks like it."

Bridgett nodded, picked up one of the glasses, and took a deep pull on her straw. The brain freeze was immediate, followed by warmth that spread from her throat to her stomach. She held the drink up with a frown. *How can it be cold and warm at the same time?* She took a more cautious sip. This time it was all warmth. The sensation tingled through her extremities. Her eyebrows came up. "This is really good."

Her friend grinned. "Sissy drink."

"Whatever." Bridgett said and continued to slurp it down. The dregs rattled in her straw, and she reached for the second one.

Tara raised her eyebrows.

"I don't want it to melt."

While she drank, the room came alive with music, and couples moved onto the tiny dance floor in the center. Bridgett watched them with envy. Handsome men smiled down into the faces of adoring women while they held them close and moved to the music. Each of those women looked loved and appreciated. *I need someone to hold onto me like that.*

She leaned over to whisper into Tara's ear and stumbled, sloshing her friend's drink onto the floor.

"Watch it, will ya?"

"Sorry, it's the boots, I'm not used to them yet. Anyway, do you ever dance when you're here?"

Tara studied the swirling mass of people. "Sometimes, if there's a guy here who appeals to me. But I'm not looking for a guy tonight. I'm more interested in the prize money."

Bridgett pouted. "That's fine for you, but I want to dance."

Tara studied her with a frown. "Bridgett, I don't think that's a good idea. You've never been in a bar before. Everyone in here is sucking down booze and you're drinking a pink Slurpee, for heaven's sake." She took out her phone and checked the time. "The tournament starts in ten minutes. Why don't you stay close to me for now? When I'm done, if you still want to dance, we'll go someplace a little less...rowdy."

A slow song came on, and Bridgett swayed to the music. "This place isn't so bad."

"Hey, beautiful, I've never seen you in here before."

Bridget turned toward the deep voice and met a denim clad chest. She let her gaze travel up and up until they met the most gorgeous green eyes she'd ever seen on a man. The brim of his cowboy hat shaded his face, adding planes and contour to the day-old stubble along his jaw. *Hello, handsome!* She twisted a strand of hair around her fingers. "That's because I've never been here before."

Tara stepped between them. "Go away, Dirk. She's with me."

"I want to dance," Bridgett whined.

Dirk nodded, reached around Tara, and pulled Bridgett to his side. "The pretty lady wants to dance."

Tara raised her hands and moved back to the bar. "Far be it from me to interfere. One word of warning, though."

Dirk waited expectantly.

"She's Detective Black's baby sister."

"Tarnation!" He ran a finger along Bridgett's jaw before backing away. "Sorry, beautiful. I'm not going there."

Bridgett moved closer to the retreating cowboy. She rested her hand on his chest. "I really want to dance. Just one dance. Tara won't tell." Her hand moved around his neck. "Pretty please."

Dirk looked from Bridgett to Tara. He lifted a shoulder in a what-can-I-do motion and pulled Bridgett close. He tightened his grip as they moved to the middle of the crowded dance floor.

Bridgett lost herself in his arms as they swayed to the music. Her head felt a little out of sync with the rest of her body, but snuggled in his arms, her heart ceased its incessant aching. *See, Jeff, He thinks I'm beautiful.* She sighed in delight when his hand brushed across her hair. *I just need a little tenderness. I need to feel like a desirable woman, not someone's cast away.* She nestled into his arms. It felt so good to be held.

He led her into a brisk turn, and her head swam. He held her close with one arm while his free hand trailed down her back. When she felt that hand slip lower, the fog in her brain dissipated. She pushed him away.

"What are you doing?"

"Just checking out the merchandise, sweetheart." Dirk grinned. "I like what I found." He opened his arms. "Come on now, don't be a tease. Let's finish our dance, then we'll go someplace quiet and make some music of our own." He pulled her back into his arms and lowered his head. She saw his lips headed toward hers, and she shoved him away with both hands. The unexpected motion carried his descending head on a collision course with hers. Dirk's forehead met the bridge of her nose with enough force to send her reeling.

"Oww!" Bridgett stumbled to a dazed stop. The pain in her face was unbearable. She brought her hand to the source of the ache, and it came away covered in red.

Before she had a chance to register the blood on her hand, Tara yanked her off the dance floor, shoved her into a chair, and pressed a wad of napkins into her hand.

"What...?"

Tara leaned down, hands fisted on her hips. "Your drinks weren't virgin, Dirk's an idiot, and you...I have no idea what you are."

"I think my nose might be broken."

Tara peered at her in the dim light. "I don't know about your nose, but you're going to have a heck of a shiner in the morning." She threaded her fingers through her hair. "As far as I'm concerned, you got what you were asking for. How am I supposed to look your brother in the eye on Monday morning?"

Bridgett shrugged.

"Yeah well, you sit here and think about that. The

tournament starts now, and I'm not taking you home 'til after." Tara gave her a final reproachful look and stomped away, leaving Bridgett to nurse her wounds.

The cold unconcern of her *friend*, the throbbing pain in her nose, the stares of the people passing by, brought Bridgett a single-minded moment of clarity. *I've got no business in a place like this.* No business and no transportation. She reached for her phone.

But who am I gonna call?

Nicolas would kill her, Mom would be horrified.

Then who?

I'm here for you if you need to talk.

Bridgett fumbled the phone as she remembered Micha's words after her blatant effort to seduce him. He'd tried to be her friend, and she'd tried to compromise his beliefs. She laid the phone on the table and touched numbers with one hand while holding the napkins to her nose with the other. Serves me right if he doesn't answer. *Please let him answer.*

It rang.

Heat suffused her.

And rang.

Daughter, this is not the place for you.

Her chest felt the weight of the words. A boulder crushing the breath from her lungs. *Pick up, pick up, pick up.*

It rang for so long she was afraid he was ignoring her.

"Hello."

"Micha!"

CHAPTER TWENTY-THREE

Micha glanced at Bridgett. She hadn't said a word since he'd picked her up. She kept her head tilted back and a fistful of napkins pressed to her nose. He hadn't missed the blood or the tears.

He turned back to the road, his lips pressed into a tight line. "Do you need to see a doctor?"

"No."

Micha couldn't help the sigh of frustration that followed her single word answer. "Fine, I'll just take you home."

Bridgett raised her head. "No...I mean yes." Her head sank against the back of the seat. "I mean, I do need to go home, just...not where you think. Do you know where the Budget Extended Stay is?"

His gaze flicked back to her. He knew where it was, he knew it was just two steps above a dive. *What's she...?* Micha shook the question from his head and turned left at the next set of stop signs. The car remained silent except for an occasional sniff from his passenger. Ten minutes later he pulled into the poorly lit parking lot.

"Which one?"

"Last one on the right." The answer was muffled, finding its way free of the napkins and the hand that

259

held them.

He pulled into an empty space and cut the engine.

Bridgett sat up and reached for the door handle. "Thanks."

Micha felt unaccustomed irritation boiling to the surface. "That's it?"

Bridgett stared at him, her huge eyes welling with fresh tears in the bad light. She pulled the wad of paper from her face. Micha assumed the dark smears around her nose and on her cheeks were blood. He looked away, his jaw so tense his teeth ached with the pressure.

"I just want to go in, clean up, and go to bed."

Micha forced his mouth to move. "If you think you can call me out in the middle of the night, climb into my car bleeding and tearful, then dismiss me once you're done...you need to think that through again." He heard the anger in his voice and tried to gentle his tone. "Tell me what happened."

When Bridgett bowed her head and refused to speak, he turned for his door. "Fine, keep the details to yourself. But, I'm not leaving until I'm satisfied you're OK."

"I don't need—"

He barreled out of the car, circled the hood, and yanked the passenger door open. *Stubborn, hardheaded woman.* Micha held out his hand. "Let me have your keys."

"But—"

"Keys."

When she laid them in his hand, his fingers closed around them in a white-knuckled grip. He held the other out to help her from the car.

Bridgett stood and stumbled against him.

He grabbed her and held her at arm's length. "Oh yeah, you don't need anything."

"I think I might be just a little tipsy."

He frowned at her.

Heat stung her face. *This is not the way I saw the evening going.* "I ordered a couple of non-alcoholic drinks. Tara said they weren't virgin after all."

Micha shook his head, took her by the arm, and steered her toward the door. "Well, it is a bar." He opened the door and led her through. He heard her hand patting the wall, presumably searching for the light switch. When the room flooded with light, he took an involuntary step back.

"Whoa!"

Bridgett bit her lip, and her eyes brightened with fresh tears. "What?"

Micha reached up and tucked her hair behind her ears. Bridgett's cheeks were smeared with red, and an ugly purple bruise radiated from the swollen bridge of her nose and stained the skin under both eyes. He cupped her chin and turned her face into the light. "We need to get some ice on that." He looked around and pulled her to the compact table and chairs in the kitchen portion of the small room.

"Sit. Are there wash cloths in the bathroom?"

Bridgett sat, nodded, and lowered her head into her hands. "I'm dizzy."

Micha pushed a hand through his hair. She was a three dimensional wreck. Physically, emotionally, spiritually. *First things first.* He entered the small bathroom and prowled until he found a handful of threadbare washcloths. He wet two with cold water and brought them back to the table.

"Here. Hold these on your nose while I go get the first aid kit out of my trunk." Micha handed her the wet compress and raised her hand into place. "I'll be right back." He stepped out, popped the truck lock, and grabbed a small black box. The boy's group he led on Wednesday night was a rowdy bunch of tweens. Always into something that ended in scrapes and bruises. He'd learned to go prepared.

He came back to the kitchen and filled a glass with water before crouching in front of Bridgett. He eased the damp rags away from her face. The water had done its job. The dried blood had moistened and should clean away without much pressure.

Bridgett inhaled a sharp breath when he began dabbing at the smears.

"I'm being as easy as I can, but I need to clean you up so I can get a good look at the damage."

She flinched from his touch. "Is it broken?"

Micha tossed the soiled cloth onto the table. He ran a finger along the gentle slope of her nose. There were no lumps or bumps that shouldn't be there. He rummaged in the box for a small bottle and shook two aspirin into her hand and scooted the water closer. "Take these." Next he pulled out a small white bag, twisted it, shook it, and laid it across her nose. "It's pretty swollen, but I don't think it's broken. The best way to tell for sure is a trip to the ER."

"I'll trust your opinion."

He straightened. "Your call." He pulled the extra chair away from the table and sat.

Bridgett stared at him over the ice pack.

Micha leaned forward, elbows braced on his knees, eyes steady on hers. "What is not your call is withholding the name of a man who blackens a woman's eye. You need to tell me who hit you. We'll send your brother out there to deal with it."

~ * ~

Bridgett studied him from across the table. *How can he be so sweet to me when I was so rotten the other night?* "There's nothing to deal with. It was an accident, just as much my fault as anyone's."

Micha didn't look convinced. "You blacked your own eyes?"

She didn't know whether to laugh or cry at the tone of disbelief in his voice. "Not really." Her eyes fluttered shut, every bone in her body weary. "Why do you even care? I mean, thanks for coming to get me and all. Thanks twice for looking after me. But, really?" She sat up forced to close her eyes against a fresh wave of dizziness before she met his gaze. "After the way I treated you the other night..."

Micha sat back, and crossed his arms. "I'm your friend. I'd have to be blind not to see how hurt you are, now and last week." His eyes filled with concern. "The vixen who offered to make breakfast for me was tempting, but it wasn't you, not really. You need to drag whatever has you so twisted up out into the open and deal with it before it gets you into some real trouble."

Bridgett studied him, remembering his story. Maybe, if she left the seductress behind, he could understand. She fumbled, one handed, for her phone, found the video, and scooted it across the table. She closed her eyes while he watched. When it ended she filled in the blanks, starting with Jeff's departure and finishing with Dirk's head crashing into her face.

His eyes never left hers while she talked. He never interrupted. His strong, steady presence gave her the courage to spill her heart.

She laid the ice pack aside and took a drink. "Things are really messed up. Not just now, but for a while...ever since Dad died, I guess." Bridgett fiddled with the glass. "The only explanation he'd give me...before I saw the video...was that Dad's death showed him that life was short. He wanted more than our marriage. More than..."—she motioned to the phone—"me. So now I've lost Dad and Jeff too. David and Mom are doing their own thing, and I'm the one left out in the cold." She bowed her head, her voice a weary whisper. "I know tonight was stupid, just like the other night when I was so awful to you." She twisted her fingers in her lap. "I'm more sorry about that than I can say. I saw that video and just...I needed to matter to someone."

"Sweetheart, a one night stand with me or some guy you meet in a bar isn't what you're looking for."

Bridgett touched her nose gingerly. "Kinda figured that out on my own."

"How about God?"

"What?"

"You matter to God."

Bridgett shoved up from her seat. The room tilted uncomfortably. She steadied herself with a hand on the back of the chair. "He doesn't..." The memory of softly spoken words in the bad light of the bar pricked her conscience. She faced Micha and looked at him through a haze of fresh tears. "Why should I?"

Micha frowned at the question. "Why should you what?"

She sniffed and raked her hair back from her face. "I came home looking for help, and all I've done is push people away when they tried to give it. You, Nicolas." Bridgett sniffed and wiped her streaming eyes. "Mom." She swallowed. "Ugly, selfish, and mean, straight down the line." She put her hands on her hips. "And God? I've been the ugliest of all to Him. I haven't talked to God since Daddy died. Why should I matter to Him now?" She turned to pace away.

Micha stood and intercepted her. He brought his hands to her shoulders and held her in place until she looked at him. "You matter," he repeated. "Psalms 139 verses seventeen and eighteen. 'How precious also are thy thoughts unto me, O God! How great is the sum of them! If I should count them, they are more in number than the sand: when I awake, I am still with thee.'"

When she ducked her head, Micha put a finger under her chin and raised her face back to his. "I memorized that when my wife left, because I needed to know that I mattered. You matter, Bridgett. God thinks about you a million times a day. He wants to love you. He wants to help you. But He's not going to force Himself on you. You have to meet him halfway."

"Do you really think...?"

"I know."

Bridgett closed her eyes. *I'm so tired of being alone.* She allowed her heart to reach out.

Father, are you still there?

I never left.

Her defenses crumpled, and she sagged into Micha's arms.

"He's still there," she whispered, afraid to break the moment.

"I told you so."

"Will you pray with me?"

"Absolutely." Micha gathered her close. "Father we need you..."

~ * ~

Karla and Ian snuggled on the sofa in her living room. She still couldn't quite wrap her mind around everything that had happened in the last few hours, but two things were certain. She was in love with Ian McAlister, and she planned to marry him just as soon as they could get the details worked out. They'd discussed some of those plans over dinner. Then he'd followed her home for a final cup of decaf and a little more time together.

Karla couldn't keep her eyes off of the ring on her left hand. Each time she looked at it, joy infused every cell of her body.

She frowned when a key rattled in the front door. Karla looked up as Bridgett came through, with Micha Raynes close behind, lugging her suitcases. Her eyes went round when she saw the bruises under her daughter's eyes. She yanked her hand free from Ian's grasp, leapt from her place on the couch, and met Bridgett in the middle of the room. Her hands cupped her daughter's chin and turned her head into the light. "Oh, baby. What happened?"

"I'm fine." Bridgett took her mother's hands and rested her forehead in the silver hair that only came to her chin. "Could I come home?"

"Baby, I never wanted you to leave in the first place."

"I know." Bridgett pulled Karla into a hug. "I'm so sorry for the way I've acted. Forgive me?"

Karla tightened her arms. "You know I do. But—"

"I'll tell you all about it," Bridgett whispered. "I promise."

She stepped away, and Karla saw Bridgett's gaze land on Ian. Her heartbeat accelerated when her daughter took a step forward. Karla stopped her with a hand on her arm. "Bridgett."

Bridgett patted her mother's hand and stepped away from the restraint. "You must be Ian." She sniffed. "I've heard a lot of good things about you. I think you may have met my evil twin a time or two over the last few days. I'm sorry if she gave you a hard time. We've locked her away in the psycho ward where she belongs, and I promise she won't be back." She held out her hand with a smile. "I'm the sane daughter, and I'm looking forward to getting to know you better."

Karla watched as Ian's brows rose over his blue eyes. She relaxed when Ian took Bridgett's hand in his with an answering smile. "Nice to finally meet you."

Micha cleared his throat. "If someone will point me in the right direction, I'll take these up."

"Oh, sorry." Bridgett pointed up the stairs. "Second door on the left."

Ian held out a hand. "Let me help you with those."

Micha nodded and shifted some of the load. "Thanks."

Karla watched the men climb the stairs. "Smart guys."

"What do you mean?"

267

Karla put an arm around her daughter. "They are giving us some space, let's not waste it. Come into the kitchen with me. I'll fix up an ice pack, and you can tell me what happened."

Bridgett laced her fingers with Karla's. "That's..." She pulled Karla's hand into the light and stared at the ring. When she looked up, there were tears in her daughter's eyes.

"Bridgett, I..."

"They're happy tears." She pulled in a deep breath. "I've been pretty ugly since I came home. I had a good talk with God earlier—"

"Oh, sweetheart..."

"Yeah. I think I'm on the road to being OK." She tapped Karla's ring. "Mom, I want you to be happy." She stopped when her voice broke. "This is going to take some getting used to." She looked up and Karla stared into her daughter's eyes. "Are you sure this is what you want?"

Karla nodded.

"Then that's all I need to know."

CHAPTER TWENTY-FOUR

Seven months later.

Female laughter rang from the line of pedicure chairs in the spa area of Garfield's newly opened, for women only, gym and spa, Soeurs Body Renaissance. The women's excited chatter mingled with the noise of bubbling water and the nature sounds coming through the speakers in the corners of the room. Karla sat in the middle of the row with Bridgett on one side and Callie on the other. Pam, Terri, Kate, and Samantha were all present and accounted for as well.

"This is such an amazing treat," Karla said. "A girl day at the spa. I feel so pampered."

"You're the bride. You deserve to be pampered," Callie answered. "Have you got everything packed?"

Karla nodded "More clothes than I'll probably need."

"That's silly," Terri said. "You can't take too many clothes on a vacation like this."

"I agree," Kate chimed in. "Fourteen days on a Caribbean cruise. I'm so stinking jealous."

Bridgett reached across and took Karla's hand. "By this time tomorrow, you'll be Mrs. Ian McAlister. I have to admit that it took some time, but I like it."

Karla squeezed her daughter's hand and mouthed a

thank you. "Are you guys sure you aren't upset?" she asked aloud.

Pam leaned forward. "Karla, we've had this conversation. We couldn't be happier for you if we tried."

"But—"

Samantha cut her off. "Grams, this is going to be the dreamiest wedding ever. You're getting married, by the captain of a cruise ship, followed by a two-week honeymoon. Would we like to be there...? Yes—"

"But really?" Callie interrupted. "Even though Kate offered to fly us all out there, that's just not practical. Take great pictures and get ready for the party of all parties once you two get home."

Karla leaned forward and looked at each of her friends. How could any one woman be so blessed? She leaned back and closed her eyes as the technician dug her lotion and oil drenched fingers into the arches of Karla's feet.

God hasn't just blessed me. He's blessed all of us. God has been beyond faithful.

Yes, He had and she didn't have to look very far into their collective past to find the evidence. Callie had her self-confidence restored. Iris, Samantha, and Steve were a family again. Terri's dreams surrounded her in the form of a husband and three beautiful kids. The dark places of Pam's past had been purged, the ashes of her pain traded in for joy. Samantha and Patrick were making a family for themselves, and the singular ghost that had haunted both Kate and Nicolas had been laid to rest in their happiness with each other.

Sudden tears overflowed her eyes. "You guys are just the best," Karla whispered.

"Uh oh, leaking bride." Terri held up her hands. "And not a dry nail in the bunch."

Karla swiped at her eyes with her shoulders. "Not a problem. You're all coming to the airport in the morning, right?"

Callie patted her arm. "You know we wouldn't miss it."

~ * ~

Spring twilight lit the cemetery that evening as Karla and Ian paused by Alicia's grave marker. Karla squeezed his hand, let go, and took a step forward.

"Alicia, I know you don't know me, but I wanted to say thank you. You had the foresight to know that this day would come and the wisdom to encourage Ian to look for it. I owe you such a debt. I've found my happiness because of your unselfish love. I promise to take good care of him." She laid a single white rose on top of the stone and reached back to reclaim the hand of her groom. "Thank you."

Hand in hand they crossed to Mitch's resting place. Karla lagged a step behind as Ian moved forward. "Mitch, I wish I'd had the chance to know you. I think we could have been friends. It's been a difficult season, but I think together, Karla and I have a handle on things now." He reached back and pulled Karla to his side. "I promise you that I am going to do everything in my power to make Karla feel loved and cherished for the rest of her life."

~ * ~

Karla came out of her bathroom with a few last minute items for her suitcase. Bridgett stood in her doorway of the bedroom, hands behind her back.

"Can I come in?"

"Of course." Karla motioned to the bag open on the bed. "I thought I was done, but I keep thinking of things. Then Hillie just called to make sure I packed an extension cord." She shook her head. "I feel like I'm taking the whole house."

Bridgett pulled two pints of ice cream from behind her back. "I brought us a snack if you have time to take a break."

Just what she needed. "I'll make time." Karla snapped the bag closed and shifted it to the floor with the two other pieces. "I'm glad the airline we're using lets the luggage fly for free." She sat on the bed, propped herself against the headboard, and held out her hand. Bridgett handed her a carton and scooted in next to her.

"Banana Split. My favorite." She accepted a spoon and scooped out a bite. "I don't think we can do this without something serious to discuss and tears."

Bridgett grinned. "No tears, but I do have news."

Karla savored her treat and waited.

"I've decided to put the house in Dallas on the market and come home to Garfield. If the offer still stands to move in here, I'd like to accept."

Karla stuck her spoon in the carton and wrapped an arm around Bridgett's shoulders. "Of course the offer stands. I couldn't bear to sell it, and maintaining two homes in the same town just made no sense."

"I still don't know why you guys just don't live here. This house is bigger than his."

"Yes, but his is newer, and it's just one story. I will not miss climbing those stairs a dozen times a day." Karla shrugged. "The rest is a marital compromise."

Bridgett raised her eyebrows.

"His house, my church."

"Ah."

Mother and daughter sat in silence for a few minutes. "What does Micha have to say about your decision to move home?" Karla asked.

"I haven't told him. He made it plain six months ago that all we could be was friends for now. He didn't want either of us thinking about a future together while my life was in such turmoil. He's been so very careful the few times we've seen each other. We're never alone. He told me that he never wants anyone to have the opportunity to point a finger and say that I didn't try to save my marriage because of him."

"I always did think that boy had a good head on his shoulders."

Bridgett snorted. "That isn't what you said on the night of my senior prom."

Karla held up her spoon and Bridgett tapped hers against it.

"So, now that the divorce is final?"

Bridgett swallowed another bite. "Who knows? I know God has a plan for the both of us. If I said that being close to Micha wasn't part of my decision to move home, that would be a lie, but mostly, now that I have a choice, I just want to come home. Dallas is too busy for me, it always was."

Karla put her ice cream aside and turned to her daughter. "I'm proud of you, sweetheart, Dad would be too. I know this last year and a half has been rough on you, but you've managed to land on your feet."

Bridgett wiggled her toes at the foot of the bed. "Well, one foot anyway, but I think I'm finally headed in the right direction." She nodded at the half melted ice cream. "You done? I'll take it down stairs. You need to get your beauty sleep. Tomorrows a big day, and there's a handsome man in your future."

~ * ~

When eight a.m. Saturday morning rolled around, Karla found herself standing in the middle of an already crowded airport. Bags were checked and boarding passes secured. All that stood between Karla and her new life was a trip through the security screeners and a three-hour flight to Florida.

Karla faced the small army of friends and family gathered to send her and Ian on their way. Love mushroomed from this group like steam from a pot. She waded into the crowd to say her goodbyes.

Benton kept an arm around Callie's shoulders as Karla folded her best and oldest friend into her arms. Callie hugged her back and sniffed into a tissue. "Don't do anything I wouldn't do."

Karla grinned. "No promises." Someone tapped her on the back, and she turned to find Pam and Harrison standing behind her.

Pam held out a box. "I made you guys some cookies for the trip."

"Chocolate chip," Harrison said. "Guaranteed to be better than the stale peanuts you'll get on the flight."

Karla hugged the box to her chest. "Chocolate on my wedding day? I knew I could count on you."

Terri and Steve rushed through the sliding glass doors, their three little ones in tow. Terri skidded to a stop at Karla's side. "I was so afraid we'd miss you. Seth couldn't find his shoes, Lilly spilled juice on her shirt, and Marcus ...well, you don't need to know about his diaper." She threw her arms around Karla's neck. "I'm so excited for you!"

Karla squeezed her back. "That makes two of us."

"Have fun on your big boat, Grams."

Karla stooped down to Bobbie's level. "I will. I'll bring you and brother a present when I come home."

The little girl's blue eyes sparkled. She grinned at Samantha and Patrick. "Gram's is bringing me and Chad a present, and I didn't even ask her to."

Ian threaded his way through the group and laid a hand on Karla's shoulder. He waved at the line of people waiting to go through security. "We need to get in line."

"I know, let's tell the kids goodbye."

Kate, Nicolas, Bridgett, Hillie, and Rachel stood in a clump just outside the entrance to Security. Karla dispensed hugs to all. "I'm going to miss you guys so much. I can't wait until the reception. It's going to be like *The Brady Bunch* once the other boys get here, three girls and three boys." She took Ian's hand. "I'm the most blessed woman in the world."

Ian pulled her into his arms, tilted her head up, and placed a kiss on her waiting lips.

Friends and family applauded the move.

He tugged her toward the entrance to the security area.

"Wait!"

Karla turned at the voice and found herself folded

into Iris's arms.

"What are you...?"

The youngster grinned. "School's out for the summer. My plane from Alabama landed thirty minutes ago. I was so afraid I'd miss you."

Karla cupped Iris's chin in her hand and took in the new maturity on her face and the new shorter haircut. "Look at you. This new phase of your life agrees with you."

Iris nodded. "I think that makes two of us." She pulled Karla close a second time. "Happy wedding day!"

Ian took her hand. "We need to go."

Karla smiled at her groom, turned for a final wave, and found herself in a shower of red rose petals. She looked up as they rained down around her. *Thanks, Father.*

~ * ~

Three days later, Mr. and Mrs. Ian McAlister stood on a wooden platform, high in a tree in the middle of a tropical rainforest. Karla watched as harnesses were attached to the line and listened to the tour guide give instructions on where to put their hands and feet. The guide clipped them to the line.

"Nervous?" Ian asked.

Karla looked at the floor of the forest, a long way down. Her eyes traveled the length of the zip line. She couldn't see the end of it. She swallowed. "Nope, I'm good."

She stepped to the end of the platform, gulped a deep breath, and took the leap into the unknown. It was OK, because Ian was with her, and she knew that's where he'd be for the rest of her life.

ABOUT THE AUTHOR

Sharon Srock went from science fiction to Christian fiction at slightly less than warp speed. Twenty five years ago, she cut her writer's teeth on Star Trek fiction. Today, she writes inspirational stories that focus on ordinary women and their extraordinary faith. Sharon lives in the middle of nowhere Oklahoma with her husband and three very large dogs. When she isn't writing you can find her cuddled up with a good book, baking something interesting in the kitchen, or exploring a beach on vacation. She hasn't quite figured out how to do all three at the same time.

Connect with her here:

Blog: http://www.sharonsrock.com

Facebook: http://www.facebook.com/SharonSrock#!/Sharon Srock

Goodreads: http://www.goodreads.com/author/show/64487 89.Sharon_Srock

Sign up for her quarterly newsletter from the blog or Facebook page.

Made in the USA
San Bernardino, CA
02 April 2018